I've travelled the world twice over,
Met the famous: saints and sinners,
Poets and artists, kings and queens,
Old stars and hopeful beginners,
I've been where no-one's been before,
Learned secrets from writers and cooks
All with one library ticket
To the wonderful world of books.

THE BLUE-EYED BOY

Blue-eyed boy Joel Sefton, handsome and attractive, was mugged and dumped behind supermarket trash bins. Yet there were less admirable traits underlying his charisma, and many had good cause to hate him. It was a secret in the past of a WPC that proved vital in penetrating the blue-eyed boy's activities, and their labyrinthine effects.

Books by Clare Curzon
in the Ulverscroft Large Print Series:

THE FACE IN THE STONE

CLARE CURZON

THE BLUE-EYED BOY

Complete and Unabridged

ULVERSCROFT
Leicester

First published in Great Britain in 1990 by
William Collins Sons & Co. Limited
London

First Large Print Edition
published February 1992
by arrangement with
Harper Collins Publishers Limited
London

British Library CIP Data

Curzon, Clare
 The blue-eyed boy. — Large print ed. —
 Ulverscroft large print series: mystery
 I. Title
 823.914 [F]

ISBN 0–7089–2585–5

Published by
F. A. Thorpe (Publishing) Ltd.
Anstey, Leicestershire
Set by Words & Graphics Ltd.
Anstey, Leicestershire
Printed and bound in Great Britain by
T. J. Press (Padstow) Ltd., Padstow, Cornwall

1

11.17 of a Friday night in early October. DI Angus Mott, returning to base to tackle paperwork, encountered Mike Yeadings looming in his office doorway. "Angus, I thought it was your car I spotted parking. Spare me a minute, will you?"

Mott joined the Detective-Superintendent and closed the door behind him. "I'm knee-high in alligators over these muggings, Mike. We've had too many. People are jittery, want to know what progress there is."

"So do I, lad."

Angus looked glum. "Well, for your ears only, sweet nothing. When they ask upstairs, you could say we're busy looking for a pattern."

Yeadings grunted, slumping in the swivel chair. "No brownie points for Laura Norder, then." His eyes took in the younger man's weariness. "Pity that's not equally true for the muggers. It seems

1

they've marked up another. This time a death."

Angus ran a hand through his crisp, fair hair. "Sooner or later it had to happen. When and where?"

"I've just had it from Control. Central Reading. An anonymous 999 call. A dead youngster, male. Could be just another Friday night fracas which went too far. Get down there straight away, will you? Goldbasket Superstore. The body's tucked away at the back of the trash containers in the rear car park. Know the place? Medic and Forensic notified. You should be there before them with any luck."

Mott picked up his sergeant from the queue at the canteen hatch. Beaumont's language was explicit. "Look!" he protested, and hung out a white-coated tongue. "Know what that is? A long-felt want. The longest, feltiest in Thames Valley. We just get in, and me only an arm's length from life-support."

"Save your breath and run," Angus said tersely. "We have a body."

Two patrol cars were already on the scene and a van with the SOCO's team who were already at work measuring

2

and photographing. Mott and Beaumont made it with four minutes to spare ahead of the local police surgeon, a burly, bushy-browed man built on the lines of a country vet exercised in heaving up fallen Shire horses. For all that, his big hands were gentle as he inserted his fingers inside the neck of the dead man's sweatshirt. "No vital signs. I suppose you want photographs before I move him?"

"That's done: scene, body *in situ* and close-ups of injuries. Any more you fancy, just ask. Screens are on their way, so you'll get an early temperature reading."

They stood a little apart, while uniform men moved in with the canvases to block off any public view. Mott was on the verge of remembering the other's name. Something unlikely, like Lightbody or — "Dr Littlejohn, we met once before. The Fredericks girl; heroin OD last winter."

"Aye. Detective-Inspector Mott, is it not? How's your Super these days? And his wee girl?"

"They're well. There's a little brother now. He's fine too."

The doctor darted him a swift glance.

"No sign of Downs' Syndrome this time?"

"As healthy as they come."

"Good. I'm a little behind with the news. Been on sabbatical abroad."

"Enjoying the sun?"

"You could say so, I suppose. Ethiopia for six months. The tail-end of the last famine. I left just in time to miss the next one. Never want to see anything like that again. This sort of thing — " and he nodded towards the construction being erected — "will be a garden-party by comparison."

It was a strange way to describe what they went back to inspect. The latest victim was possibly still in his teens. Had been. The slender wrists and fingers were witness to the soft life, but his end had been a cruel one, the face savagely slashed by some jagged instrument.

"Frenzied attack," Littlejohn wondered, "or a deliberate attempt to hide the lad's identity? Well, that's your worry. Mine is to say how and when."

"We've no ID for him yet. He hadn't any papers; no notecase or credit cards. We may have to wait until someone reports him missing."

4

Mott hunkered alongside, nauseated by the stench of the rubbish containers, six monster cylinders on metal wheels, crammed to the top with refuse, much of it organic and decaying. Underfoot his shoes crunched on broken glass. Alongside, within the bay of shoulder-high walls, there were wads of cardboard taped together, the flattened remains of huge cartons. Their soaked loose ends flapped soggily in the rising wind, stinking of urine. Across all the other stomach-turning smells came evidence of cabbage leaves and carrots, softly rotting.

He knew it would all have to be gone through minutely. You'd think the killer had chosen the site deliberately, meant it to be as demeaning for the victim and as disgusting for any investigators as could be managed.

Dammit, Angus thought, I'm overtired and letting my work get to me. Too many innocent lives wasted, too many debased villains getting away with unprovoked violence; and all we ever have to go on is a report of running footsteps, sometimes a clatter or a startled cry, just once the glimpse of a face between cap and

5

upturned collar as three indeterminate figures fled the scene.

"Any guesses on the number of attackers, or the weapons?" he asked.

Littlejohn grimaced. "Your boss wouldn't thank me for guesses, but I'll tell you one thing. Look, here and here. There again. The selfsame shape of tear. One weapon mainly, I'd say. Let's turn the laddie and have a look on his flip side."

He folded the arms as gently as if the boy were on a hospital cot, then rolled him on his face. "M'm. That's what killed him, I'd say — if I wasn't too discreet to blab before the path lab's had him. One great whack behind and below the right ear. Nasty. Limbs in early stages of stiffening, you'll notice."

Mott looked down at the exposed upper legs as the designer jeans were rolled back to expose the buttocks. He waited while Littlejohn inserted the thermometer, then reached over to remove it and scowled at reading it under the light. "Right. So your SOC lads'll need to give me regular ground temperature readings now. It's freshened quite a bit since sundown, but it's a bit more protected from wind just here inside these low walls. No hints on time of death yet awhile. It's going to be a calculator job."

"Is that the lot?"

"Aye. You can bring on the bag, zip him up cosy. I'll leave you to it, then."

The big man rose stiffly to his feet, stared down once more and growled, "Happens all the time. It's a damn shame. Somebody's son."

Mott walked down with him to the white tape which now marked off the area, and one of the uniform men called across, "Got the supermarket manager here, Inspector. He wants to bring his car through."

"Leave it in the street. Mr Markham — that's right? Come through, sir. Maybe you can tell us who this is."

But the manager didn't recall ever seeing the dead young man before, and Mott couldn't blame him for not looking all that searchingly. He could always have a second chance when they'd tidied the body at the morgue.

"Not one of your assistants, then?"

"Definitely not, dressed like that. Could have been a casual customer, I suppose.

You'll have a photograph, I hope, to show my cash-desk girls. Can't have them upset when it's not anything to do with us. Frighten some of our customers off too, I shouldn't wonder."

He was working himself out of shock by grumbling. Mott left him to DS Beaumont and went for a slow walk round the perimeter of the car park. When he arrived back Beaumont was closing his notebook, nodding like a toy dog in the back window of a car, letting the manager talk himself out while he blanked off, thoughts elsewhere.

"Any idea whose these cars are, Mr Markham?" Mott asked. "There seem rather a lot, considering the store's closed."

"There could be stackers still in," the man said doubtfully. "You know, they replenish the shelves, price the new stock. We still do a lot of that at night. Shan't change till the new system comes in and we go computerized. Then the restocking will be done by regular staff throughout the day. Just the shelves will show the price then, and it'll come up automatically on the customer's check list."

"How many in, tonight?"

"Three, plus one of my trainee managers. Friday's a busy day and we stay open till seven, then we have to replenish ready for a second rush on Saturday."

"There are considerably more than four cars here."

"They could be nothing to do with the store. We used to put a barrier across at the road end after we'd closed, but vandals kept breaking it down. Now anyone can come in and leave their car parked."

"There's a Tandoori restaurant a few doors down. They get a lot of supplies from us and we don't complain if their customers park off the street in our yard. So long as they don't leave vehicles overnight and obstruct access for deliveries next morning."

"DC Silver's listed the licence plates," Beaumont told Mott. "He's radioed them through for a computer check. I'll send him up to the Tandoori when you're through. Patel can go with him. Bit of local colour, make it more matey."

"Right. We'll need more uniform men. Get a list of everyone working late at the store. Find out who's responsible for dumping the rubbish and put a stop notice on it being removed or added to. They'll have to find other receptacles meanwhile. Mr Markham, it would save a lot of time if you'd open up and let my Scene of Crimes Officer have a desk and telephone. I'm afraid we need to keep you here a while, so you'll probably want to ring home yourself and explain you'll be some time yet."

The man bit at his lower lip. "You must realize this is extremely inconvenient for me. And what's happened has nothing whatever to do with my firm."

Mott let the silence build up before he nodded towards the burden that was being carried past. "Not too convenient for him, either. I don't suppose mugging was any concern of his before it just happened. Somewhere there's a family doesn't have any idea they've been involved either. Don't ask me to feel too sorry for you, sir."

Josie Sefton groped round her feet for the receiver, lifted it and pushed the LR button yet again. Busy. Well, so it could be for a long time yet. Everyone would be doing the same thing, hotly clutching their credit cards, still sickened by the sight of the sufferers on the Disaster Appeal programme.

For twenty-six minutes she'd been trying, all through the first part of the TV news and into the adverts between — the trivial tinsel she was supposed to be hooked on, while in Bangladesh men, women and tiny children waded waist-high in polluted floodwater or crouched hopeless on some slight elevation to dry out.

On the screen a sveltely tailored Adonis was now posing in heroic stance with one instep on the sill of the new super model saloon, cordless telephone in hand, while a seductive female arm stole under his arm and across his chest. "For the man who has everything . . . " the silky voice-over suggested.

The ad could be for any of the luxury props — car, suiting, after-shave, custom-made shoes, Telecom. Wrong again, Josie: it was for watches. The two arms entwined, her bare flesh jewel-braceleted, his virile wrist cuff-linked and extended to reveal the desirable wafer-flat dial. The times shown synchronized. Two achievers eminently rewarded: God's in his heaven, all's right with the world.

Meanwhile, Bangladesh.

Josie's wasn't a cordless phone, but it had been updated to a box with button selectors and a cooing tone. Comfortably duck-toed and dressing-gowned in the armchair, she reached down by her feet, lifted the receiver and pressed LR again. She supposed the letters stood for Last Repeat, but she could be wrong (remembering an older brother's long-ago scorn when she'd proudly read off the GB above a car licence plate as 'Gonna Broad'). She wasn't much better at guessing abbreviations even now, Civil Servant or not. Whitehall was full of the tricksy things, IQ-Test fodder.

Despite a reasonable Upper Second from London University in Geography, she hadn't distinguished herself in the CS Entrance Examination, but she knew she was a damn sight better at her job than a lot of those who had done. Some there were who sparkled and some who could cope with the task in hand. She'd met too many of the first kind (already on their way up past her) to admire them: the Delegators. For them the Yuppie ads on TV. As for herself, she actually enjoyed the tussle with people and things which filled her 9.30 to 5.30 day, provided she was left alone to get on with it.

She prodded LR once more, with the same result. She might as well give up — as countless thousands must simultaneously be doing all over the country — and go to bed. On Monday the bank would tell her what to put on a cheque.

Meanwhile she'd be left in a worry-cycle: how much she could honestly afford; was there still something left to economize on; would she actually get round to doing it or, too busy, let the Appeal eventually slide into oblivion?

Frankly, what she wanted was for the situation to disappear, her conscience slightly lightened. A single phone call, twenty pounds and her credit card number could clear it now. Instead, she'd lie awake remembering the hopeless faces, the vast horizon of polluted water, the problem's inevitable repetition into an endless future. Nothing she could do would solve the crisis; but quite simply she was ashamed of being in the lifeboat, cushioned.

She said something of the sort when her flatmate Gaynor came in bringing the brisk chill of the autumn night. "Don't be so wet," the Welsh girl countered, grimacing into the hanging mirror, running her hands through her blown hair, then with one finger tracing imagined lines under her eyes. "Ugh, there's a lived-in face for you, if ever one was. And this is an *early night*! Josie, you moon, you should have come along. More fun than miserable old TV. See a bit of real life for a change!"

So many simultaneous realities, Josie reflected, settling eventually against her pillow and staring up into the dark; some realities floating independently, some briefly colliding — to combine, or wetly burst like soap bubbles. She tried to home in on the image, using the bright, multicoloured bubbles in lieu of counted sheep, but they grew into sad, dark faces behind her eyelids and stared their accusation.

"Monday," she promised Bangladesh, then turned to arranging a personal programme for tomorrow, finally organizing herself into sleep.

Nan Yeadings heard her husband's car enter the drive, checked with a quick glance between the curtains and then went out to the front porch to greet him. "I wasn't really expecting you back this side of midnight. I heard the local late newsflash: there's been a body found."

Mike pecked her cheek and grunted. "No point in my hovering over it at this point. They work better for my not breathing down their necks. Angus has gone to take a look."

"What about next of kin?"

"Unknown. No identification on the body. Until there's something to work on I'm only in the way, but I guess our weekend's taken the chop again."

He bolted the front door and put up the chain. "Apparently Dr Littlejohn's back, been on sabbatical in Ethiopia; bit of a busman's holiday, I should think."

"Well, don't tell me anything about it. I don't want to know. We've trouble enough on our own doorstep."

Mike moved into the hall, gave her a sympathetic hug. "Had a bad day, love?"

"Not really. Long, though. I'm ready for bed. There's some goulash if you . . . "

"I had something anonymous and filling in the mess, thanks. You go on up. How about a hot toddy apiece? I'll just have a peek at the wee varmints and then bring a tray up with me."

Sally's bed was empty but it didn't alarm him. He went through into the next room and she was where he had suspected, curled up asleep in her polka-dot duvet underneath Luke's cot. He had to kneel to lift her out but she didn't wake, merely stirring in his arms as he carried her back to her bed. He didn't think she sleepwalked, but it wasn't total wakefulness either when she left the warmth of her own snug nest and went to check on her baby brother. More likely something confusedly akin to his own need to look at them both before he could take his rest. Sally might be short on articulate expression, but her instincts were normal enough.

He tucked her in gently, kissed the blunt little face and went down again to boil the kettle and slice a lemon.

It was not until just after eleven next morning that a call came through from divisional headquarters. There was still no positive identification for last night's dead man, but all the cars except two had been accounted for in the supermarket car park. This left a four-year-old Datsun on the stolen list and a TVR Sports with last year's registration. The police computer gave the owner of this last as a Joel Sefton of Marisbank, Callendar Lane. Yeadings came away from the phone muttering the address to himself in an effort to recall the locality.

"You know where it is," Nan said, having listened in the background. "On the Pangbourne side of Reading. That's where I ran over the hedgehog driving back on New Year's morning. There are seven or eight old houses strung along Callendar Lane, Edwardian, in their own grounds."

"Marisbank rings a bell," Yeadings

repeated. "I seem to remember going there when I first came to Thames Valley. The old chap was a JP. There was pressure on about a search warrant. Sefton might have been the name, but anyway he retired soon after and died a year or two later."

"Oh, *Sefton's*," Nan said knowledgeably. "Why didn't you say? I've been there, to a coffee morning for the Imperial Cancer Research Fund. Molly Cove took us. The house is up a curving drive, hidden by rhododendrons. Mrs S. is a rather formidable lady, middle sixties, used to be an actress or something. We didn't stay long, for fear Sally dropped crumbs on the priceless Aubusson."

"The JP's widow," Yeadings supposed. "Apparently there's a grown-up family, some of them still at home. Joel is the youngest."

"Not necessarily your dead young man, though. How will you find out?"

"Angus will ring up unofficially and ask for him. If he answers, it will be a query about the car. If young Sefton's not at home, a message will be left for him to ring back."

18

"If he fails to do that, it's still not conclusive."

"It would be close enough to risk asking someone in the family to look at the dead man's photograph."

"That sounds as if I'd better put the lunch forward or you'll miss out again."

Angus rang sooner than expected. "I spoke to an older sister," he said. "Joel was out. When I asked if they expected him back soon, she said he'd better turn up if he knew what was good for him. It seems today's the old mum's birthday and she's giving a family lunch. This evening they'll all be going into Windsor to the theatre and then a special late supper out. Miss Sefton sounded a bit peeved, though she attempted to laugh it off. I asked if Joel had been home last night and she dried up. It's my opinion he wasn't."

"Sounds like our young man."

"Afraid so."

"Right. I think this is one I'd better show my face at. If they sit down to lunch about one, they should be through by two-thirty. I'd rather not tackle the old lady, especially on her birthday. Is there an older brother?"

"Two. Five siblings in all: female, male, male, female, male. We got this background from PC Lavender on the desk. His mother goes in three days a week to cook and housekeep. The brother you want is Christopher, early thirties. He's divorced and gone home to mother. 'Something in the City', so the story goes."

"In that case he should be shock-proofed. I'll be in touch, if and when."

2

JOSIE'S taxi emerged from between
the walls of rhododendrons, rounded
the last curve and pulled up behind
a new BMW saloon which in Erica's
typical fashion had been abandoned centre
stage before the entrance steps. Before
Josie could pay her driver Christopher
appeared, money in hand, his good-
natured face puckered in concern that
she should have felt obliged to come
down by train. "Josie," he said, kissing
his sister warmly, "lovely to see you,
but why the deuce didn't you ask Erica
for a lift? Or I could have met your
train."

She smiled back. "I don't make plans
that far ahead." But he would have known
as well as she did that any favour asked of
Erica was an invitation to patronize her
younger sister.

"You're looking well, Chris. I guess
Mother's keeping you busy, running all
her necessary errands."

21

He looked apologetic. "You know how it is."

She did. Every aspect of life at Marisbank. The way her visit had started was so typical as almost to be cliché. The familiarity of the place and the inevitability of proceedings from now on were at the same time heart-warming and disturbing. There was this insistence on family, and the implication that in breaking away she had failed it. The silver cord loosed, but the golden bowl was constantly proffered to remind her what she was missing.

Thank God Mother wouldn't start laying it on too thick while feminist Erica was about. The sniping would be reserved for a more intimate occasion, with the implied reproach that older sister had used undue influence in showing younger sister how to rebel.

"I've put on half a stone," Chris confessed. "Does it show?"

"Not with such excellent tailoring. You look — prosperous. Do say the same of me. I'd like to think I spread my London weighting wisely."

"You're thinner again. Very smart too.

I like that brown thingummy you're wearing. Nice colour."

She did look elegant and she knew it. Anything less would have had the others picking on her for attempting to subsist on the salary of a junior Civil Servant.

"You know," said Christopher, humping her small suitcase up the circular stairway to her old room, "we really ought to meet up for lunch or something, both working in town as we do."

Her laugh was a derisive hoot. "Betwixt Whitehall and City there is a great gulf fixed. London they both may be, but as remote from each other as my tomato and cheese sandwich from your Mansion House turtle soup. And although I'm readily replaceable, yet for some reason at midday I daren't be more than five feet from my desk. Whereas you, Chris, are uniquely useful and can lunch until four."

"You exaggerate. How does your room strike you?"

The pretty new curtains and the bowl of mixed dahlias were predictable. As was his anxious need for approval of everything remotely connected with his personal life. In business, she'd heard, her brother was quite different, confident, detached, cool, single-minded. Even at times ruthless. "Perfect," she said. "And a damn sight tidier than I'm accustomed to."

"I was sent into Reading for a duck down double duvet this morning," her brother admitted. "Mother suddenly took against blankets. For you, I mean, not herself. I kept thinking of that awful comedy sketch years ago on the radio. You wouldn't remember it. A woman who got tied up asking for a dozen double damask dinner napkins. In the end I didn't dare attempt it, just circled the bedding department till I saw one and caught the girl's eye."

"It's lovely. So's the cover. I'll remember to compliment Mother on going so modern."

"You know why, of course. She does miss you a lot."

"That bait won't hook me. Anyway she doesn't miss me really. She just likes everyone in attendance as corps de ballet. *My five children. A wonderful, united family.* The matriarchal line. I don't know how you can go on letting her run your life."

Josie turned back from the window and saw his face crumpled with misery. "Oh, Chris, I'm sorry! That was stupid of me. I do know, of course I do! It's Kit, isn't it?"

He nodded, grimacing. "That's what swung the custody case my way, you see. I didn't tell you before, but you must have guessed. We had to convince the judge that Kit would be better off with us here. It was touch and go, even with Martine running after that racing driver, no set home or anything. They normally like the mother to keep the children, especially a girl. A caring, live-in grandmother was my trump card."

"And it is better for her here." Josie made a statement of it, but she really wanted to know.

"Yes, oh yes." He moved away, nervously jingling loose change in his trouser pocket. And they both knew that if that wasn't exactly a lie it was a refusal to face the question squarely.

"Look, Josie, I'll leave you to settle in. Come down when you're ready. You'll find Erica out in the conservatory with Mother. Lovely to have you home." Then Chris had slid out of the room, out of discussing his daughter.

Josie unstrapped her case and transferred its contents to the drawer left open for her, then carried her night things across to the bed. Her old slippers had been put out in a prominent place and she took the hint, then ran her fingers through her shoulder-length fair hair in front of the cheval-glass. There was no excuse left for not going down to join the family.

Her mother and sister were no longer in the conservatory. Through the glass she could see them strolling together in the garden, Erica gesticulating vigorously as she talked, Harriet, with her ballerina's self-consciously flat-footed walk, acting the listener. But not actually paying attention after the first sentence or two. She would have gathered the gist of her daughter's theme by then, *précis*ed the rest, and serenely turned her mind to subjects of greater interest. Erica, from the look of it, was pushing the subject of the Exhibition Garden.

Josie smiled to herself and went through

to the drawing-room, almost overlooking her brother Paul who was sunk in a wing chair. They hadn't met since Easter, but he didn't greet her, looking up with a swift smile as though she had been out of the room only a few minutes. "M'm. Very snazzy jerkin."

"I might have known you'd find the right word for it. Christopher referred to it as my thingummy."

"Suède hip-length jerkin, trimmed leather, chestnut and black, to catalogue it completely. I could even venture to price it."

"Well, you'd be wrong. It was Gaynor's, bought in a lavish phase and rapidly repented of, being too tight. She wore it once and passed it on to me at half price."

"Well done! Rather the way we stock up Wardrobe when we can. And it disappears in similar manner."

"How is the unit?"

"God, I thought for a moment you said 'eunuch', referring to me. Things go well workwise, thank you kindly."

"And personally?"

"Equally. I have a little friend staying

with me at present. Quite a sweetie."

"Girl?" Josie ventured.

"She is indeed. It's rather amusing, though. Nancy by name. Referred to by the irreverent as my live-in nancy."

Josie smiled, well knowing that the flip wit was necessary carapace. Paul lived for his filming, and beyond it ventured only occasionally into close relationships. Each romantic encounter to date had ended in disappointment. He seemed always to be looking for what wasn't there.

"How are things governmental?" he asked brightly.

"I've no idea, but things bureaucratic are much as they ever were, possibly a little worse."

"Sorry, I tend to confuse Whitehall with Westminster. Just a country boy, you know."

Josie had gone across to one of the long windows. "Aren't we all, at heart? I get quite nostalgic, feeling all this space about me. But it will take only a day or two and I'll be longing for London again."

"The ceaseless traffic, the carbon fumes, the buffetings and breakdowns of the transport system . . . "

"That's commuter pollution, brought in from outside. No, I mean the quiet of London backstreets at night. Strangers' voices passing under your window. Traffic sounds, yes; distant, and muffled by double glazing — a comfortable background murmur. It's reassuring, knowing you're among humanity and belong. Fields and trees have the opposite effect on me. They remind me I'm on my own."

"How metaphysical we are," he sparred, but his voice had softened. He came over and put an arm round her waist, squeezing gently. "It's good to see you, Josie. Brightens the day."

She turned her head to look at him levelly. "Mother's birthday."

"Quite so. To be endured with an appearance of seemly enjoyment."

"The main thing is that we're all here. It means a lot to her."

"And there's the rub. One of us isn't. The blue-eyed boy himself."

"Joel's away? I didn't know."

"Out on the tiles last night, it seems. Hasn't made it back yet. Probably getting unhungover."

"I hope nothing's happened. Does

Mother realize he's missing?"

"She doesn't appear to. But then she wouldn't admit it. We're all pretending like mad not to notice, so why shouldn't she? Let's hope he makes it in time for lunch, or our concerted effort's wasted: the defector revealed. He of all her precious chicks!"

Josie pulled a face, and slipping a little silver-wrapped package from her handbag, went across to leave it with the other gifts on a rosewood table.

Through the open door from the hall came Mrs Lavender carrying a tray with glasses. Behind her Christopher bore in the punch bowl. "Don't look so affronted, Paul," he said, grinning. "It's brandy punch, not the childhood version."

Mrs Lavender waited to slip in a word of greeting to Josie, then added, "Your mother and sister are just changing their shoes. They'll be along in a minute."

Christopher gazed rather wildly round the room. "Kit not down? I'd better warn her. Can't leave her to come in last." He went quickly out again in search of his daughter.

"Does that mean Joel is likely to beat

her to it?" Paul asked of Mrs Lavender.

"No, sir. I'm afraid he's not back yet. Mr Christopher says to carry on notwithstanding. I don't quite know what to do about the table, though."

"Wait until after the first course," Josie decided, "then clear away his setting along with our dishes. Paul will discreetly remove the chair, won't you? Then we can close ranks while Chris is carving. We can't go all through lunch with a yawning gap in our midst."

"It's too bad of him," Mrs Lavender pronounced, about to close the door on herself. "He must know how it's bound to upset his mother."

"She thinks it's deliberate," Josie said in a low voice. "But suppose it isn't. What could have happened to him?"

Yeadings drove himself out to Callendar Lane and cruised slowly under arches of autumn trees looking for the name Marisbank. Having spied it on one of a pair of pillars, he turned into the curving drive between walls of evergreens which abruptly ceased to reveal the house basking in bright October sunlight. It was

Edwardian italianate, even had a square campanile: gracious to live in, but must be exorbitant to heat in winter. The grounds fronting it were open landscape, the gravel drive sweeping up to the level of a central terrace behind a stone balustrade. Two cars already stood before the porticoed double doors.

He had preferred not to bring a WPC, since he had no intention of involving Mrs Sefton at this point. He had spoken by phone to the housekeeper, Mrs Lavender, and when she let him in at a few minutes past 2.30 he told her, "Don't mention my name. Just say someone to see Mr Christopher Sefton on unforeseen business. I don't want anyone alarmed."

The family were still at their coffee, keeping up the pretence that nothing was amiss. Harriet had performed in the best showbiz tradition, exclaiming over each of her presents as she opened them and betraying only by a slight tightening of her lips that the occasion fell short of perfection. Everyone present knew that the charade couldn't go on indefinitely. Erica, always restless under restrictions, would be the first to break out and raise a storm. Mrs Lavender's announcement of an unexpected visitor for the man of the house was a welcome diversion.

When Christopher had left them Josie moved across to her sister. "Erica, I saw you out in the garden before lunch. Have you any more plans to develop it?"

"Suggestions," their mother corrected her sharply. "Only suggestions, which I shall look into, of course. But do tell the others, Erica, about the ideas you had in mind. It will be interesting to hear their comments."

Face to face with Sefton in a room across the hall, Yeadings was instantly reminded of the man's father, the sometime JP. His large-boned frame was the same, the slight tilt of the square head as he listened, the colouring — pale blue eyes, pinky freckled skin, a touch of ginger in the fine, fair hair. But the son carried more weight. Perhaps there was also a difference in the essential man, a noticeable lack of verve; and a difference of texture, as between granite and sandstone. The other had looked fit

33

to weather anything; this one was clearly subject to erosion.

The policeman switched back his glance from the smooth, manicured hands to the slightly protuberant, pink-lidded eyes. "Mr Sefton? My name is Yeadings." He reached for his identification card, his gaze still on the man's face, uncertain how his news would be received.

The eyes of a disappointed man, he sensed; but not yet apprehensive. Don't I look like a copper, then?

"Thames Valley Police." He caught now the quick flash of recognition, perhaps alarm.

"I've heard of you, Chief Inspector."

"Detective-Superintendent, sir. Serious Crimes Squad."

"What can I do for you, Superintendent? Is something wrong?" Slowly, giving himself time to face up to bad news.

Yeadings halted. "Have you any cause to think that, sir?"

Sefton stood straighter, drawing audible breath, impatient. "Please tell me."

"It's not certain, but it could be bad news. You have a younger brother, I believe — "

"Oh my God. Then that's why — "

"Sir?"

"He failed to turn up for a family occasion. Mother's birthday. Bad news, you said. Does that mean he's — "

Yeadings waited and made the man say it. The word came out after a marked pause, flat and controlled. " — dead?"

"His car remained parked in Reading overnight, sir. And there has been a fatality. A young man we've not as yet been able to identify."

"Joel? God! I thought perhaps — some foolishness."

"More than that, I'm afraid. If this is in fact your brother."

"Can't you tell? I mean, he would have his driving licence on him, credit cards."

"Not even his car keys, sir. It would appear he was mugged, everything taken."

Yeadings stayed impassive, watching the colour drain from the other's face. He saw that the skin had suffered recent sunburn as if from unaccustomed exposure. The surface pinkness remained about the puckered eyes. "Are you all right, sir?"

"I — yes. Yes, Superintendent." He stood bowed a moment, then raised a troubled face to the policeman. "What do you want me to do? Break the news to the family?"

"If you would first take a look at the body — ? We haven't any suitable photographs yet."

"Of course. There's still a chance, I suppose, that it's someone else. I understand that my brother didn't return home last night. Not that that's conclusive. Where did it happen? Reading, you said. When?"

"Some time yesterday, sir. After dark, we think. In the car park of the Gold basket Superstore."

"Last night? So why the delay?" Initial shock was rapidly changing to outrage.

"Apart from there being no identification papers on him, the face was badly disfigured. Nevertheless, I think that it should be possible for someone as close to him as yourself . . . "

"Close?" There was something in the voice that Yeadings couldn't quite place. Bitterness, sarcasm? "We weren't all that close, Superintendent. Too many years

36

between. But I see what you mean — brothers, yes. I should probably recognize him as well as anyone. Certainly not Mother. You mustn't — I don't know how I'll ever be able to tell her. Joel, of all people!"

"He was special to her?"

Sefton stood stock still, his mind seeming elsewhere. "He was everything the rest of us failed to be." The words were so low that Yeadings barely caught them.

"So he would certainly have been here today, for the birthday celebrations?"

"Eh? Oh yes. Nothing would have kept him away. Unless he'd — "

Yeadings looked at him sharply. The last two words stood apart from the rest, but the man had stopped himself in time. What had he been on the point of revealing? 'Unless he'd — *had some better alternative? — wanted to upset her?*' Whatever had been in the man's mind, he wasn't going to share it. The involuntary words had been instantly regretted.

"So will you come with me now?"

"I'd better excuse myself to the others," Sefton said. "I'll say it's urgent business.

Would you perhaps wait in your car? I'll follow you in my own."

"Thank you, sir. It will be the hospital mortuary." He could have arranged for Angus or Beaumont to meet Sefton there, but he wanted to stay in touch, needed to watch the man's reactions. There was something mixed in with his anxiety that wasn't entirely shock or grief. Something for the moment inexplicable.

Yeadings moved his weight from one foot to the other, hinting at leaving. "If it is as we fear, I shall need to talk to the family later. We can arrange some suitable time, after you've spoken to them. But as soon as possible. It is vital that we know his likely movements for yesterday."

Sefton nodded. His eyes met the Superintendent's with a new defiance. "*Vital*. That's ironic. Joel's dead, and your job's vital. Well, I suppose this is all routine to you." His mouth set hard. "I shall do whatever's necessary to meet your requirements, Superintendent." Stiffly he distanced himself, holding the door open for Yeadings to precede him into the hall.

Passing him, the policeman was aware of a fluid movement at the edge of his vision. He turned towards the shadowed staircase and saw a woman in a purplish silky dress motionless halfway up, the fingers of one hand looped into a long string of pearls. Her face was turned back towards them but he couldn't read her expression.

"I'm just going out for a while, Mother. Something unexpected has come up. I shan't be more than an hour. Be sure you get some rest, ready for tonight." Sefton sounded hearty and totally unconvincing.

She made no answer, but Yeadings felt her staring intensely after them as they left by the front door. Nervy, he supposed. She was elderly, widowed, evidently cocooned by her grown-up family. There could be trouble when she learned what had happened to a specially precious youngest son: possibly a personal complaint to the Chief Constable, outrage that the police should be incapable of maintaining order in the streets, were so slow to follow crimes to their source and get convictions.

And she'd have a point there. Besides all the regular urban crime, seven muggings in twelve weeks, and progress practically nil. It wasn't a record to be proud of.

3

"ARE you all right, sir?"
The voice seemed to come from a long distance away and Christopher Sefton looked up slowly. The Superintendent's face was out of focus, peering into his own.

"Quite all right, now, thank you. It was just a momentary — "

"I think we could find you a cup of tea round at Outpatients. I could do with one myself."

They went out by one door, along a path and in by another, then there were corridors and people moving past, footfalls and voices. Then a space opening out with low tables and easy chairs. DS Beaumont saw them coming, nodded towards the table he had vacated and went to join the short queue for service. He came back carrying a tray with two black coffees, one tea, a small jug of milk and some wrapped sugar.

Yeadings nodded briefly to commend

40

the sergeant's covering of all preferences.

"Tea or coffee, sir?" Beaumont asked Sefton.

"Oh, tea, I suppose. Thank you."

Beaumont passed it across, handed Yeadings one coffee and took the remaining cup to a place across the table. "Mr Sefton has identified his brother's body," Yeadings said unnecessarily.

"I'm sorry to be so feeble," the man said. "It's one thing to accept the words, but face to face . . . and such injuries . . ."

Everything possible had been done in the short time available to tidy the body into a viewable state, but it was still horrific. And this was his younger brother. Possibly Sefton had never seen a corpse before, certainly not anyone done to death by violence. It was a long way from the civilized drawing-room he'd lately quitted.

Beaumont shifted his gaze from Sefton to the Superintendent, who had unexpectedly taken over the job from him. Without question this was due to the dead man's family connections. A DS would do for any old mug off the street, but if you lived out Callendar Lane way and your dad had once been a JP, only the top brass was good enough. Once they'd suspected who the dead man might be, Yeadings would have contacted Kidlington, buzzed the Chief Constable himself. Hence the personal attention. Now that the identity was confirmed, who was to carry on?

"Detective-Sergeant Beaumont will return with you, sir, and will ring me when you feel the family is ready for me to ask a few questions. I regret that this is necessary, but we must get as clear a picture as possible of your brother to help our investigations."

"But it was a mugging," Sefton said, bewildered. "He was a random victim. How can we be of any help? You must have information from the earlier cases. Isn't there anyone you already suspect, to be checked up on?"

"This is a fatality, sir, however it came about. We can't assume anything. We need, for example, to pin down the time of death precisely, because of possible alibi claims. So anything we can learn of your brother's movements for last night are of the greatest importance. And I should appreciate if you would look out a good likeness of him in case we require to circulate copies."

"Yes, yes, of course, Superintendent. But I can't see that the family can help much. I haven't the least idea what he was up to, and I hardly think he would have confided his plans to my mother. As for the others, they were nowhere near here yesterday."

"Yet they may have had knowledge of his intentions or habits. I am afraid I must insist on speaking to the whole family, Mr Sefton, and I'm sure they would prefer I do so at the house rather than ask them all to come to the divisional station."

The man looked flustered. "I had no intention of hindering your investigation, Superintendent. By all means, come. I just feel it will be useless, but please do whatever is normal and necessary. We shall all do everything we can to help."

Inspector Angus Mott looked up as Yeadings came in. "Well, lad?" the Superintendent demanded. "Anything come to light?"

"They axe trees, don't they, to produce

all this?" Angus waved a sheaf of papers at him.

"So what's written on 'em? Anything to any purpose?"

"I spent an hour or so with Cecil Markham, the supermarket manager. Much to his irritation, it being Saturday and the store seething with mums, dads, kids and shopping trolleys. There's something of interest about the car park. You recall he said it stays open day and night since the barrier was wrecked? Well, it seems they then tried another dodge: the pay-and-display system with a ticket dispenser permitting a two-hour stay. No charge, and no one on the staff deputed to go round checking windscreens; so guess what?"

"Useless idea. People just don't bother."

"*Most* people don't bother. That's the local ones who know the way it goes. But some meticulous citizens, and those coming in from areas where the rules are respected, actually press the machine's button and get a ticket stamped with the hour and the day."

"Go on."

"There was one on the floor of young

44

Sefton's car. Not stuck on the glass. Didn't even have the backing taken off the sticky side, but it was there, and it did indicate a time for the car having been left in the car park last night. 22.57."

"Or the time that a killer wants us to suppose it was left in the car park."

"It could be a deliberate con, yes."

"Any fingerprints?"

"Whoever took the ticket from the machine wore gloves. Forensic are working on that. The latents in the car are Sefton's own on the driving side, but also overlaid with smudges from gloves. Woven ones, further description to follow."

"No gloves on the body."

"They could have been in his pockets and taken with his valuables."

"Does a nineteen-year-old wear gloves to drive, then take them off when he gets out of the car on a fresh autumn evening?"

"Depends on who it is he gets out of the car to meet. We need to check his habits, find out if he's used that car park before, what he'd be likely to do about the ticket machine."

Yeadings grunted. "Meanwhile we wait to see if Forensic find any traces of blood or skin in the back of the car. If they do and it's from his group, we can assume he was killed elsewhere and brought in his own car to be dumped."

" — in one of the jumbo refuse containers," Mott offered. "But, because it was towards the end of the week, they were all filled to a maximum level. So he had to be tucked away behind them, the result of that being that he was spotted a day or two earlier than if he'd been covered over and eventually decanted at the rubbish tip."

"Allowing us to get nowhere faster," Yeadings appreciated with irony. "How is the Incident Room shaping up?"

"Chief Inspector Atkinson is seeing to things. All the mugging info has been passed through. We've got desks, and communications are about complete. The caravan is being sent to the Goldbasket car park. I'll be working from there myself."

"We'd better show our faces," Yeadings suggested. "The CC wants action reported daily. Put any car park data in the

46

computer, then stand ready to go with me and question the family. I'm handling this one personally."

Harriet Sefton had been in the garden when Christopher arrived back. It was unthinkable that he should break the news to her there. Suppose she collapsed?

"Mother," he said nervously, "could you come indoors a moment? I need to talk to you."

She seemed curiously obtuse. Perhaps it was because of all that nonsense with Erica over lunch. The girl should have known better than to try and force her mother's hand in front of the assembled family. Admittedly she had to make her plans quickly in view of the proposed merger, but their introduction was too sudden, too callous. This had been Mother's home since Grandfather bought it when she was a small girl. Over the years she had put so much of herself into both the house and the planning of the grounds. You couldn't without warning turn on her and imply she was too old to cope; that Florafaun Frames should buy her out and run the

47

place as a glorified wholesale Garden Centre.

And that hadn't been all. There was the question of access from the river. Clearly Erica had spent some time on researching the possibility, but she hadn't let on to anyone else about that aspect. So how had Mother beaten her to it? She must have had her suspicions all along, had Erica's development plans investigated. Even with his own contacts in the City, Chris hadn't heard any whisper about a mini marina.

Harriet went on walking towards the river bank now, heedless of his request. As she mostly was to him as a person, he admitted silently.

"'Iron bars'," she observed, "'do not a prison make.' Who said that, Christopher? How stupid, whoever it was. In this case steel tubes. Stove-enamelled; is that the correct description? Can't you see it? Like a cattle market, penning in the crowds who want to go rushing upstream in power boats, upsetting the fishing, and their wash eroding the banks. Then fruit cages and pergolas and lattices and rose arches springing up all over my lawns and flowerbeds. Animal cages too, I shouldn't wonder! You know how the girl gets carried away with her tasteless ideas. We should probably have wild creatures, like Longleat."

Briefly the humour of it struck him: the big cats on Florafaun display in the Seftons' modest three acres! "Mother, you weren't listening to me. Can't you leave all that now and come indoors? I do need to speak to you, to all the family. And it is urgent."

She glanced across at him with distaste, as if he had said something improper. "Is it about Kit? I'm not sure that I want to discuss her for the moment."

"No, it's not Kit, but it is very serious indeed."

Now her dark eyes swivelled to meet his. "Very well." Something in their depths seemed to shrivel. Surely she couldn't have guessed, but then Joel's absence . . .

"In the house."

"So you said," she fired at him with asperity. "There is no need to repeat yourself. I'm not wholly in my dotage."

Already knocked slightly off-balance,

he recognized. She wouldn't normally descend to snappishness. A look could be as effective.

In the conservatory she seated herself opposite him, ankles crossed, hands in lap, like a schoolgirl ready for a group photograph. "Now, Christopher."

"It's bad news, Mother. About Joel. You know he didn't come home last night — "

"It wasn't the first time."

"No, well . . . Oh God, Mother, can't you see? Something's happened to him. That was a policeman who came to see me after lunch."

Harriet looked wooden. "You mean an accident? He's been hurt and you went to see him. Why you?"

"I went to — identify him. Mother, I'm sorry. Joel's dead, dear. Somebody's killed him."

"The car?" It was like a rook's rough caw.

"Not an accident. He was set on in Reading last night, robbed and — "

"One of those awful muggings? Oh no! Not dead. They don't kill people, they just do it for the money, don't they?"

"This time they went too far. Maybe he fought back. I don't know."

"Where is he? I must go to him!"

"Mother, no! It won't do any good. The police are coming here in a few minutes and we all have to help them. They're going to need to know about Joel's movements yesterday. We must do everything we can to help them find who did this before it can happen to anyone else."

"I don't care about anyone else!" Her voice rose in a wail.

It brought the others from their council of war in the drawing-room. Christopher had to go through it all again while Harriet sat unmoving in a rigid, tight crouch, forward over her knees.

Paul whisked out and came back with a glass of brandy. When he held it out to her she looked up with a sort of loathing and dashed it to the tiles.

"Mother," Erica said severely, "this won't help."

"Leave — me — alone," Harriet demanded between clenched teeth. She stood up stiffly, without any of her customary balletic grace, and steadied

51

herself against the chair back. "I shall be in the garden. You can come for me when the police arrive, Christopher. I will see them on my own."

This time it was Josie who let them in. Beaumont, seated on the stone front steps, had called through to warn her, but from the hall window she had already observed the two men leaving the dark green Rover, and came out to receive them. Both tall, the younger was thirtyish, athletically built and handsome with curly fair hair cropped short. She sensed the sexual challenge in him, making her withdraw; but the other man was safer. In his forties, dark, rather heavy-featured, with a wide, humorous mouth and thick black eyebrows, he was more immediately approachable. I'm a sucker for the father-figure, Josie thought wryly. Mustn't let him get too close or I'll go soft.

"Superintendent, Inspector," she said, offering her hand. "I'm Josephine Sefton. My brother Paul is going to round up the family. I don't know whether you want us all together or one by one . . . "

Yeadings nodded. "As a group would

be quite suitable, but I think first I should appreciate a private word with your mother."

Her assessment had been right: the man was acceptable, even kindly. She saw Paul, hovering in the background, pick up the conversation and disappear. Then she led the two policemen across the hall and into the drawing-room.Cream-coloured holland blinds had been lowered over the west windows, softening the autumn sunlight.

"My brother gave me a photograph for you. You asked for it, I think." Josie handed the Superintendent an envelope. "I'm to look after you until everyone's ready," she said. "Do please sit down."

"Thank you, we'll just wait." Both men remained standing. Through the open window Josie could hear the crackle and amplified voice of their car radio, then some reply from the man who had come back with Chris.

Yeadings opened the envelope. The snapshot was taken in brilliant sunshine, a laughing face, a compact, slender body poised jokily on a stone mushroom, one ankle on the other knee. A gipsy face, with prominent, wide-slanting cheekbones, bold eyes and an expression of almost reckless taunting. One aspect of the dead young man, one instant fixed in time: Christopher's impression of his younger brother. Had he taken the snap, been the object of the mocking regard? From how many other different ones, Yeadings wondered, had he chosen this photograph?

Moving slowly about the room, he was aware of the girl observing him. When he looked across at her she met his gaze and smiled sadly. None of that over-awareness of his job that made people look away, or else glare their hostility. She saw him equally as a person, someone she was required to communicate with.

"We're rather a complicated family," she said. "Shall I give you a background?"

"Please do."

She began, as was proper, with her mother Harriet; sixty-six today and widowed for eight years. Her late husband had been one of the flour-mill Seftons but he'd opted out of the family business to study and practise Law. When they'd married, in their early thirties, he moved into Harriet's family home, her parents both having died within seven months of each other a year before. His name had been Eric, from which the eldest child Erica had taken hers. She was now thirty-four and a high-powered business lady, managing director of a firm manufacturing steel tubes.

"Locally?" Yeadings inquired.

Josie halted and turned her warm gaze on him. "You do like details, don't you? It's administered from Reading, which is a showroom and the sales centre, and some of the equipment is assembled there. The original privately-owned factory which started out with metal garden furniture is in Birmingham."

"How did your sister reach her present position?"

The girl gave a wry grimace. "Erica trained as an accountant and her first job was with the firm. I suppose you would find out anyway — and certainly Erica isn't embarrassed by the fact — but she, er, had an affair with the owner. It went on for years. In the end he — committed suicide, leaving the marital home and all his money to his wife, and to Erica the factory. We supposed she'd sell the business, but instead she took over the running of it, appointed a young designer with new ideas, borrowed from a bank and diversified the output. Expansion meant more factory floorspace, and to get more capital she has recently taken on a partner. That's how it is at present."

She ended abruptly, almost primly, leaving Yeadings to wonder at the new partner's standing. A sleeping partner perhaps, in both senses of the term? But that was surely peripheral to the inquiry, as must be the run-down on Erica Sefton's business successes. "Thank you," he said. "And your brother Christopher I have already met."

"Insurance, underwriting, all that sort of thing," Josie summarized offhandedly.

"He is unmarried?"

"Divorced. Christopher's really quite a detached person in his way. He only lives here with Mother because of Kit."

Yeadings waited.

"His daughter," Josie explained. "She's eleven and goes to a local day school. Christine in full, Kit for short. We tend to pass on paternal forenames. Chris won legal custody because we're a family and his ex is rather footloose."

Somewhere in all this, Yeadings realized, the girl had lost her warmth towards him. She was issuing facts because as an investigator he required it of her. Had she cooled because of his imagined attitude or because of the nature of the information? Too many skeletons — or at any rate poorly fleshed bodies — in the cupboards she was opening? The distance lengthening between them fixed him firmly outside the family circle as she withdrew.

"Paul comes next," she catalogued. "He's twenty-eight, lives in London, directs small-screen films, mostly drama series. You may have seen his name on TV when they roll the credits at the end. Then there's me, twenty-three and a Civil Servant."

Yeadings smiled. "That's all there is to you? Nine till five, then you cease to exist?"

"Nine-thirty to five-thirty, actually." The smile with her correction restored their earlier empathy. "I share a Kilburn

57

flat with a girl PRO. We get along pretty well, because of — or despite — being quite different. I come here sometimes for a few days when I take time off, as now, but the flat is my home, so I try not to make it an expected thing."

Holding Mother at bay lest she be swallowed in the family maw, Yeadings appreciated. He nodded. "Do you enjoy your work?"

The question surprised her. "I do, actually. I even see the point of it. I wouldn't stay on otherwise. One's work is very important, isn't it?"

"A large slice of life," he agreed.

She looked at him directly again, with some of the personal curiosity he'd recognized in her at first. "How about you? Do you like your work?" There was a challenge there too.

He hesitated, conscious that any apologia for 'the fuzz' and its function could go down badly with her generation. "It satisfies a personal need," he admitted, "most of the time. I like puzzles. I prefer an ordered climate to the chaos of crime. I'd be a hypocrite if I said I like people. Some of those I spend a lot of time with

58

I find pretty loathsome. But I do need to be involved with people."

"To employ your full potential," she suggested, as if it were learned from a textbook and given her own tick of approval.

"You could say that. A job should stretch you a bit or it can't give satisfaction. But I have to accept the limitations that mine imposes. I identify criminals, stack up a case against them. Beyond that I'm not responsible, can't trespass."

"That's where my father picked up the threads. He was a solicitor, you know. Sorted problems out, even took some criminal cases. But he retired early at fifty-five, and became a JP."

"Which is the next stage, the fourth."

"Third, surely?"

"The first being the MPs who create the legislation."

"Abetted by us Civil Servants who lick it into shape."

"The System," Yeadings summed up, smiling. "And any system is as good as the people in it."

She regarded him seriously. "I'm glad

you're — not cynical." He saw she was trying desperately to make him meet her on a sympathetic level. "My brother — Joel — you're going to find out things that . . . he wouldn't have wanted you to know."

Yeadings waited, but she found it too difficult to go on. "We all have secrets," he offered her.

"I didn't — I mean, he was rather a stinker in some ways, but in the end he would have been all right, I'm almost sure. If he'd lived. That's what's so awful: that he didn't have the chance. To get past the present phase."

"He was nineteen, I understand. It's a dangerous time."

Yeadings didn't elaborate, remembering a long list of suicides, accidents, desperate crimes and follies he'd witnessed for that age.

"That's what I mean. What happened is because of the stage he'd reached, not because Joel was who he was." She was pleading with him. "I know that can't make any difference to the case, but I want to be sure you at least understand."

There was no promise he could give her. He nodded gravely. "Thank you for talking to me."

"If there's anything more you want to know — about the family, I'll try to help. You won't trouble Mother, will you?"

Always this anxiety for the old lady. She was probably well able to take care of herself. (Formidable, Nan had called her.) What was wrong with her children, not to recognize this? Or was it that they kept secrets from her for their own ease of mind, because of her likely disapproval? What at first seemed protective affection could really cover a childish fear of authority. Still the martinet, did she insist on remaining in charge?

Josie seemed to assume she'd made her point. "Thank *you*," she said in return. "I'd better see what's happened to the others." She smiled, shrugged, and left the room.

"Doesn't she know," Mott asked from the window recess, "that it was simply a mugging? From what she said about her brother, you'd think he was the villain, not the victim!"

4

HARRIET had decreed that the policemen should come out to her in the garden. Christopher was apologetic about her rather bizarre request but, in view of the shock she had just received, Yeadings could understand she might need the reassurance of such surroundings. He found her sitting in the sunlight on a bench outside what appeared to be the potting shed.

She had topped the earlier purplish silky sheath with a disreputable oatmeal cardigan badly plucked in places and with several large holes gaping in its thick cable pattern. Her hair and much of her face were obscured by a floppy-brimmed straw hat. She was small, with a long, straight back. Her legs were made to look sturdy and truncated in a pair of green wellies.

As they approached she turned and fixed them with an authoritative stare from near-black eyes set in a sallow, bony-structured face. Yeadings noticed that she held a soil-spattered trowel in her gloved left hand and she tapped it impatiently against one thigh as she waited for them to reach her. When they did, she put off the moment of greeting by removing her hat. An elaborately swathed hairstyle had come slightly adrift and dark strands stuck out wispily giving her the appearance of a madwoman. But the look she gave them was level and completely controlled.

"Good afternoon, gentlemen. It was good of you to come."

An eccentric, Yeadings decided; and one determined to use the fact to her own advantage.

"My eldest son, Christopher," she announced in a high, clear voice, "insists that I should not go to see Joel."

"I would advise against it myself," Yeadings said. "It's better perhaps to remember the living face of someone you are fond of."

"Fond of?" she repeated, as though he had uttered some solecism. She gave a bark of mirthless laughter. "In any case I have changed my mind."

She indicated the empty places to either side of her, and the staginess of the gesture reminded Yeadings that Nan had spoken of her as having been 'an actress or something'.

"I understand that Josie has been entertaining you both. No doubt she gave you a vivid thumbnail sketch of each of us."

Yeadings wouldn't let her get away with that hinted criticism. "Yes, indeed. You have a very distinguished family, Mrs Sefton."

"My children are all gifted, but I'm not entirely convinced that they have made the best use of their talents."

"They all seem unusually successful."

"Sadly, you have come too late to appreciate the most gifted one." Quite suddenly they were at the heart of the matter and she had offered it unasked.

"Joel was your youngest?" Yeadings prompted gently.

"And most promising. Oh, the others are all rather clever, but Joel was exceptional, brilliant. A very good-looking boy. He had the greatest gift of all — true charm. I was forty-seven when Joel was

64

born — quite a miracle in every way."

"He took after you, I believe." Mott had taken over at a nod from his chief.

Harriet Sefton looked across at him, startled. "Yes. The only one who resembled me at all. He was small, compact, and he moved well. Dark, as I am — " she indicated her own black-dyed hair with its single dramatic white streak — "but he had his father's blue eyes. He could have turned his gifts to almost any career, but he chose to be an architect. He was just about to start his second year of study."

"And he lived here with you at Marisbank. So when did you last see him?"

The specific question shook her. Her eyes widened. She sat tense a moment, then answered abruptly. "Yesterday."

Mott flicked a glance at his chief and got the nod to continue. He went on more gently. "The attack on him happened yesterday too, sometime after dark. So we need to know where he was before then; what plans he had for the evening."

"It was Friday," she said harshly. "In the early morning Christopher looked in as usual before he left for the City. I passed Joel's room on my way to join Kit for breakfast." Her mouth tightened. "You haven't met Christopher's daughter yet. You will realize: she has an eating problem. I try to be with her at mealtimes. We had breakfast together and I drove her to school."

A lot had been covered in a few sentences, but she had moved away from the subject of Joel. Yeadings watched her as his inspector probed on. "You passed your son's room on the way downstairs. Did you speak to him?"

"The door was ajar. He called out to me."

"What did he say?"

"'Top of the morning to you, Mother mine.'" Her voice almost broke. "He used to imitate accents. He seemed in good spirits."

"When I returned from taking Kit to school he was dressed, had breakfasted and was about to leave. He intended calling on an estate agent he'd been helping during the long vacation. He had been quite successful at it. Mr Lever

66

was most impressed by the way he dealt with clients."

"He would have called in there on his way to college?"

"Presumably." There was a little hesitation there, as though she might have suppressed doubts.

"And later?"

"He didn't return for dinner last night. That wasn't unusual. He had given notice that he would be out."

"So the last time you saw or spoke with him was before he left the house in the morning?"

She bowed her head in reply. "At about nine-forty. Apart from visiting the estate agent, I had no idea of his plans for the rest of the day."

"Thank you, Mrs Sefton. We shall see if Mr Lever can take it any further."

She looked past him to where Christopher was approaching from the house with a middle-aged man carrying a slim attaché case. "Why is Philip Carter here?" she demanded of the empty air.

Her son picked up the vibes if not the actual words, and explained that he had phoned the doctor to suggest he called.

The new arrival nodded briefly to both policemen. "Mrs Sefton has suffered a shock," he told them unnecessarily. "If you can spare her I should like to talk to her for a few minutes. Indoors."

"You'll find the others in the drawing-room," Christopher suggested.

They all moved housewards, separating at the conservatory door where Dr Carter guided Harriet to a wicker chair and planted himself defensively opposite, delving in his case in a determined manner. The expression Yeadings caught on the woman's face was one of wintry scepticism.

In the drawing-room, besides Josie they found two women and the fair, slight man who had hovered in the background on their arrival.

Christopher made the introductions. "My sister Erica."

She was well-fleshed, tall and big-boned like himself, her blonde hair cut short and swept back into a modified drake's tail. Her strong features seemed uncluttered, with interesting planes, and she gave the senior policeman an instant impression of impatience.

On closer examination the other woman was no woman at all but a tall and ungainly young girl, her jutting, skeletal frame quite clearly revealing the anorexic condition her grandmother had suggested. She wore a stiffened sort of pale party dress with a sash, suited to a child younger than her eleven years. Her dark copper-coloured hair hung long over her shoulders. Her face was cavernous and uneasy.

Christopher Sefton waved towards her. "My daughter Christine. We call her Kit. That's Paul over there. He's number three, comes between me and Josie. Now you've met us all."

Yeadings faced them on his feet, introducing himself, then waving Angus forward. "My colleague, Detective-Inspector Mott, will explain how things stand and how you can best help us."

At some point while Mott was speaking a car drove away outside. A few moments later Harriet came into the room and took a chair. She had changed, looking diminutive in tapered black trousers and black pumps, but as if to deny the theme of mourning, her frothy lace blouse was pale turquoise. A triple choker of pearls hid the ageing neck, and her dark hair was now smoothly swathed close to her neat, small head. She already appeared affected by sedation but was forcing herself to remain awake. For her sake Mott was even more concerned to cut things short. There were one or two questions from the family when he had finished and he answered them frankly. "We'll tell you more later, when we know more," he closed.

Harriet swayed slightly and hooked an elbow over the wooden arm of her chair. There was a disturbing echo about the odd way she felt, as though a dormant part of her brain, used only once and long ago, had suddenly started to function again, and all she observed, heard, felt, thought, was now being channelled through it, distorting the familiar into forms of the past. She sat straight-backed, the fingers of her left hand, shrunken and fleshless under their rings, fastened tightly about the lace-bordered white handkerchief and deliberately she turned her mind back, seeking the source of the disturbing sensation.

70

It was when Eric had died. There had been the same awful suspension of normality. She'd felt breathless and numb, incapable even of grief. In near-trance she had gone through the medical checks, the cremation service, the funeral lunch, and then straight after, when the last car had left and the children were dispersed about the house, she had been bludgeoned into reality.

Mrs Dawes had come in from the kitchen. She had planted herself directly opposite, dumpily erect, clasped hands hanging flat across her white apron like a sporran. A self-righteous little woman with her sombre dress, powdered face and tight grey waves. And — enjoying it, but managing to sound aggrieved — she had given notice. After fifteen years of uncomplaining — if slightly disapproving — service she was going. Not ever a part of the family, but as familiar as the front door knob or the hall's waxed floorboards.

"I stayed on only because of the master," she said in her prim, old-fashioned way. "He was a good man, Mr Sefton, understanding, and a gentleman.

I would have done anything for him."

Meaning, of course, that she, Harriet Sefton, was anything but a good woman, no lady and therefore unworthy of such slavish devotion. Even of eight-till-one and six-to-eight adequately-paid service.

Dawes's little puckered face came back to her now, boot-button eyes hard with a newly overt malice, condemning Harriet out of hand. All the emotion pinpointed then and suppressed over the following years came flooding back.

Not a good woman, Harriet silently repeated to herself behind closed eyelids. Yes, I am hard, despotic, unforgiving. A harsh mother. Unloved. Barely respected; perhaps not even that by my children. All I ever valued is gone. There is really nothing left to live for now.

"Mother," Josie whispered, "would you like to go and lie down?"

Harriet sucked in her cheeks, held her breath a second before replying. "There is no call to fuss." And there wasn't. She looked round at her remaining family, all at that one moment anxious for her. Dawes was long gone. In her place sensible Mrs Lavender on an every-other-day basis. She had stood by the Seftons well today, surely the worst day of Harriet's sixty-six years.

Josie took one of her mother's arms and Christopher the other. The two policemen stood back to let them go by. Crossing the hall towards the stairs, she dimly saw the passage door to the kitchen open and an accusing aproned figure stood there.

Harriet's heart gave a little bound so that she found it hard to get the words out. "A pleasant lunch, Mrs Dawes. A pity perhaps that the beef was overdone."

Poor soul, this has really rocked her back, Mrs Lavender thought, returning to check that the cooling turkey remains were properly under cover.

With Christopher momentarily detained and the others making no move to see them out, the policemen made for the front door. "Incredible," Mott marvelled quietly as they reached it. "I thought this sort of set-up went out with Queen Victoria. Remember that musical *Bless the Bride*? Dutiful offspring and retainers in a full chorus of 'God bless the Family'."

Yeadings glared a warning and turned at a slight sound on the stairs. Harriet Sefton had paused on the way up and swung unsteadily round to face them. She shook off Christopher's arm, whispering harshly, "I may appear frail, but I'm not given to the vapours."

Yeadings walked back and addressed her gently. "You'd easily be forgiven a little frailty now," he allowed. "On your birthday too."

"One to remember," she said sourly. "Have you children, Superintendent?"

He inclined his head, inviting her to go on.

"Then you will know that there is a reverse side to the comfortable, supportive image. Children are indeed hostages to fortune. Instead of guaranteeing security, they — make one more vulnerable."

There was a deal of bitterness there. The woman had summoned resources to withstand their inquiry and she now used her anger as armour, would probably have some pretty lethal weapons honed to use against them if they overstepped the permitted bounds of her privacy.

"Like everyone else, I have read newspaper accounts of these muggings," she claimed. "But I should be interested to hear the full police version, Superintendent.

I am quite sure you must have made more progress than you allow the general public to know. Perhaps tomorrow you would call, and we can talk again."

Dominant from habit, Yeadings realized, she couldn't help herself. She had to attack in order to maintain an advantage which she felt to be slipping away. "I shall be in touch," he promised, and waited for her to have the last word, but she turned back wearily and looked up at the stairs that remained to be climbed. He left her to beat them.

"So?" Mott demanded as they regained Yeadings's car.

"So you watch it with this lot. Especially with Madam. She has sharp ears and a sharper tongue. Even as she totters drugged to bed."

"I goofed there."

"No real harm done. In fact an interesting reaction. *In vino veritas* has nothing on what slips out with sedation. In normal circumstances I think she would have made no comment. However, my duty's done as far as the CC's concerned. Now I return to my proper arse-worthiness, furnishing a desk. You and Beaumont can stir the action, keep the reports rolling in. What have you set up?"

"See this estate agent Lever who employed Joel in vacations; carry on from there tracing the youngster's day. His mother seemed uncertain about his going in to college, but you didn't follow it up."

"By this point in October he should be registering for lectures. PC Lavender informed us that Joel Sefton was a student at Oxford Polytechnic, so I rang through for a private word with someone I know there. It seems that Sefton hasn't yet signed on for this academic year."

Mott nodded. "So if he spent the whole of yesterday showing clients round houses his movements shouldn't be hard to trace. There has to be a day-book with addresses. All the same, that's unlikely to be relevant to the killing. I've more hopes of inquiries in the neighbourhood of the supermarket and Tandoori restaurant."

"Eye-witnesses are less common than Santa Clauses in real life, lad, and even less credible, but you might strike lucky. The Lord knows, we've been short enough of luck over the earlier muggings. Our man or men must have perfect night sight and a cloak of invisibility."

Back at Reading, Yeadings dropped his Inspector behind the caravan housing the temporary, on-the-spot Incident Room. Its outer office was a small space crammed with telephones, desk and two harassed uniform men checking lists. Beyond the central door halving the caravan's length DS Beaumont was interviewing a small dark-skinned man with a Charles Bronson moustache. The detective flicked up his eyes as Mott came in, tapped his pen ominously on the desk in front of him and growled. "Now you're for it. This is the boss."

The interviewee seemed to shrink further. He sat with both hands tightly clasped between his knees. His neck had receded between two sharply jutting shoulders. Mott wondered at the thinness of the man, and bracketing it with the foreignness of his appearance, found his mind leapt in a single bound to drugs. East, opium derivatives — morphine, heroin; west, cocaine and its newer more deadly mix of 'crack'. This man wasn't an oriental, so . . . ?

"Chummy doesn't appear to have any papers," Beaumont said in a menacing tone. "Not so much as a bleeding passport. No national insurance. Lives on air, it seems. Never been born. Pushed up overnight like a nasty fungus."

Mott walked past both of them and leaned against the reinforced frosted glass window. "You have a name. Let's start there."

"The bleeder suddenly doesn't understand English," Beaumont ground out. "Had no difficulty back in the caff."

"The Tandoori? But he's not Indian. South American, more likely. He nodded to the man. "*¿Es Usted cocinero?*"

"*No, señor, pero toco.*"

"*?Músico? ¿Qué toca Usted? ¿La guitarra?*"

"*Sí, señor. Y canto.*" Encouraged, he ventured into English. "Ay zing. And Ay play guitar. For peoples eat."

"Good," Mott told him. "I am not asking about papers, but a young man was killed last night. *Muerto*, you understand? *Matado.*"

The South American shivered.

"*Sí, un joven.*"

"You saw him?" Mott pointed to his own eyes.

"*Sí, muerto. He visto, y había lástima del pobre joven. Le tenaré presente por siempre jamás. Pues los agentes, los policías . . .* "

"But you saw him alive before that? *¿Una vez viviente?*"

"*Sí.*" The man frowned in concentration. "I see heem two, three days back. I zing heem *Brasil*. For the *señorita*."

Beaumont made a soft whistling sound and started taking notes. He waited while the Inspector teased out the information that the girl with Sefton had been young and pretty. The man paid to serenade her had not noticed her clothes. She had sat back in the corner, her hands under the table, so he could not tell if she wore any wedding ring. But a hat, she had worn a big, round hat. Invited to draw it, he had produced a lopsided version of a dark béret. She was the only lady in the restaurant with her head covered. This had been Tuesday of the same week, at about 7.30 in the evening.

It gave the DS ironic satisfaction, now that Mott had broken the ice, to record finally that the man's name was Luis Retortillo, his temporary home the local Youth Hostel; his home country, Colombia.

"Notta lotta use," Beaumont grumbled when he had left, Mott having impressed on Luis that he shouldn't leave town on pain of a hue and cry pursuing him to the ends of the earth. "Unless he's some kind of pusher and Sefton a user."

So the DS had jumped to the same hasty racist conclusion as himself, and didn't give it much credence either, Mott observed. "He's thin from malnutrition, not drugs," he gave as his opinion. "Rather an innocent. No need for you to come the heavy stuff."

"Bet you spent all your time at Torremolinos in the local library," Beaumont muttered. "All I picked up was how to, if you get my meaning."

"Let's see what you've learned so far," said Mott by way of distracting him from a threatened account of his holiday conquests.

"List of diners linked with car licence

numbers. Four lots interviewed, five to go. There were others, but the Tandoori folks didn't know their names and they paid cash, not by card. Two waiters due across any minute now. The owner's statement is in your tray. How about some coffee? I suppose you got some fancy stuff out at the big house?"

"By the time we got there nobody was thinking of food or drink."

"With Himself on hand I didn't get a look indoors. Begged a lift back with their doc. Rocked back, were they?"

"What would you expect? No hysterics, thank God."

"Up in arms, then? 'We shall all be murdered in our beds. What do we pay the police for? — why don't they get off their fat arses?' etcetera."

"No, but you can get off yours and fetch me the car park data. I want to see how it squares with the licence numbers of the Tandoori customers."

5

THE door bearing a black print legend DET-SUPERINTENDENT M. YEADINGS stood ajar, and occasional loud-mouthed groups who passed in the corridor, becoming aware of the silent figure hunched over the desk, lowered their voices and suddenly became purposeful. This was not totally lost on Mike Yeadings but entered an isolated compartment of his mind unconnected with present concentration.

On the cleared desktop he had dealt out the seven bundles of papers like a Tarot hand, the central pile topped by photographs of the recent corpse: Joel Sefton, aged nineteen years, struck down before his time, victim of — Of what? A simple mugging? Yeadings doubted that. Too much had been done to him, and in another way too little.

Where were the injured ribs and bruised kidney area, the stamped-on ankles, featured in other attacks? The split lips were there and certainly the bloodied cheeks, but the facial damage was more widespread and, as Littlejohn had remarked on first sighting, the wounds were now confirmed as probably caused by a single jagged-edged instrument aimed from one general direction. Except the first blow which, delivered slightly upwards from a blunter weapon and from the rear, had landed below the right ear, breaking the neck. After that the face and throat had been repeatedly slashed — not stabbed at — with a sharp instrument, presumably while the body lay on the ground.

Not the ground of the supermarket rubbish area, however. There the surface of scattered débris had been insufficiently disturbed, showed no bloodstains. And no weapon had as yet come to light. Examination of the dead man's clothes and shoes was not yet complete, but the soles had certainly not borne traces of mixed grit and spilt flour similar to that marking the footwear of the SOCO team. Which meant that however young Sefton had come to be found among the supermarket's refuse bins, he hadn't gone there on his own two feet.

Yeadings lifted the grey phone at his elbow and contacted the station Incident Room. "I don't have all the reports in. Where's the list of contents of the refuse containers? . . . Eh? Damn the computer, it doesn't have priority over me. Don't we still have photocopiers? . . . Yes, right now!"

When the information arrived four minutes later he had controlled the brief flash of impatience, sardonically eyeing the uneasy face of the WPC proffering the papers. "Relax. I've given up executing the messenger."

She risked a small smile. A doe-eyed, soft-looking little thing, they'd have chosen her deliberately, like music, to soothe the savage breast. (Or was it 'beast'? — he never knew.) "Is the scramble still on?"

Another slight smile. "Things are settling, sir. Actually it's going like clockwork now."

"Practised routines. You've not worked on Serious Crimes before?"

She hesitated. "Not this end of it, sir. On the street, yes."

His thick brows went up. "On which case?"

"I was mugged on the beat, sir. Fourth victim."

That WPC? So she wasn't as fragile as she looked. Mugged, recovered, and back on the job. "Going to get some of your own back now, is that it?"

"No, sir. Mr Atkinson thought I might be useful. Never saw their faces, sir, but I did hear two voices."

Yeadings tapped with his pen on the Sefton papers. "It's unlikely you'll hear them again on this case. It could be a completely different kettle of fish."

"Sir?" She was alerted, keen to know more.

Yeadings reached across for one of the six piles of paper surrounding the central one. *Rosemary Zyczynski.* Turning over the top page he read out, "Abrasion to rear of head below occiput; split lip and one incisor dislodged; general bruising to small of back; skinned knees."

He hummed briefly. "Apparently you were surrounded, kneed from the rear by one and punched by another as you fell."

"Yanked up and then punched again, yessir."

"They didn't stamp on you?"

"There wasn't time, sir. PC Finlay came back at the double when I squawked. We share the beat. The third man just snatched my radio and scarpered."

"Where was Finlay during the attack?" Yeadings had already memorized the whole business, but he wanted to hear how she told it.

"Gone for a leak, sir."

Which happens to us all, he thought. The man could hardly perform in front of the girl. And she accepted that.

Yeadings gave her a hard stare and she looked back levelly. "I think Mr Atkinson is right. You could be useful to us. Get back home and change. Nothing eye-catching, mind."

She had herself under control, and if he hadn't been looking for it he might have missed her eyes' sudden, brief illumination.

"Report to Inspector Mott at the Incident Caravan. It's in the supermarket car park. By then he'll be expecting you. I'll see to your cover at this end."

"Sir." So controlled, it was barely more than a murmur.

I remember, Mike told himself grinning inside. I trod a beat once too. God, a lifetime away. Nearly burst with pride the first time I was loaned to the Met CID. Made an idiot of myself. They nearly all do.

Rosemary took the plain-clothes role quite literally: grey and white houndstooth pleated skirt, white open-necked shirt, black jacket, grey bag over one shoulder. Almost uniform again, she thought, surveying it anxiously in the long mirror of her secondhand wardrobe. That chequered cravat and the band on her police hat must have brainwashed her unwittingly. But it would have to do. It was the tidiest of her outfits, and her only other suit was bright green.

With a skin-deep air of calm she rapped on the open caravan door and, given the nod, went inside. A uniform constable seated at a small desk said, still writing, "Name, please."

"WPC Zyczynski, reporting for duty."

"So it is." He stared up at her, grinning.

"Thank God I don't have to write your name down."

"But you do. I want it logged." She looked at her wristwatch. "At 16.03 precisely. I'll spell it out for you. Once you've got it right, you can refer to me as Z."

"Doesn't sound quite intimate enough somehow. There: are you sure that's right?" He scowled at the written letters she had dictated.

"Certainly. Is Inspector Mott through there?"

"Yup. Just go in. No need to knock while I'm on the desk here."

She pulled down the seams of her jacket, took a breath, opened the partition door and marched in on CID.

The Inspector and his sergeant were in the middle of a disagreement. "Anyway," the blue-eyed giant with the crisp blond hair wound it up, "we'll do it my way. And I'd like that list at once." He was seated directly opposite with Beaumont draped against the side wall.

"WPC Zyczynski? Good. Brought your shorthand notebook? You'll be coming out with me."

"Sir." After the first flick of her eyes towards the sergeant she kept them straight ahead. She'd have trouble with him, they'd warned her back at the nick. Fancied himself as a comedian — and a ladies' man to boot. She could feel the vibes of his sardonic amusement, as he well meant her to.

"Okey-doke," he said, sliding into the seat Mott had just vacated. Now she could hardly avoid eye contact with him and mentally he was running a tape-measure all over her, returning to stare at her face. "Which one is it?" he demanded.

She looked levelly back in incomprehension. He was certainly addressing her, taking the mickey.

"The falsie," gloatingly. He let a few seconds tick by before qualifying it. "Lost a tooth, didn't you?"

"Two," she said drily.

"Huh! Falsified report too."

"The second came out next day. It's mentioned on a subsequent sheet covering medical expenses." She turned to face Mott who was watching her intently. "I'm ready, sir."

"On our way, then."

In the car he handed her a list of diners known to have been at the Tandoori the previous night. "It's not complete, but we may jog a few memories as we go around. Mostly locals, after all. Those ticked have been seen by Sergeant Beaumont. I'll introduce you to him properly when he's recovered his manners."

She bent over the paper. He might have said he was pleased to have an extra hand, even if he despised the female arm of the law. For herself, she automatically mistrusted anyone so good-looking. With a comedian and an Adonis to deal with, she hoped the case would have compensatory interest. "How many diners haven't been identified, sir?"

"Possibly eight. A party of four woopies who paid cash; a middle-aged man, the same; then three casually dressed teens-to-twenties who were going to town on a stolen credit card."

"Didn't the manager check it at the time?"

"Unfortunately not. He seems to think all young whites have the golden touch."

The woopies — Well Off Old People — might be the easiest bunch to check on. She guessed they probably weren't as well-off as the Asian had inferred. Retired people round here often dressed up for their few special outings. And four of them together, perhaps two couples: that sounded like a celebration. A family birthday? One couple's wedding anniversary? They hadn't chosen to go to an up-market hotel. She could imagine her own aunt and uncle booking a foursome at a Tandoori for cheapness, and covering with a bright reference to 'going oriental for a change'.

"The woopies," she said. "Did they book?"

"Yes. The name as taken down is indecipherable. Could be Norris, Morris, Dollis, almost anything. Let's hope one at least of them is known to some of the other diners. How's your local geography? There's a street map in the glove compartment. We're looking for Castleton Avenue."

"That's off the Caversham Road, north of the station. No connection with our castle. Named by some councillor nostalgic for Lancashire, I expect. I'll direct you. Third exit here, sir."

"Part of your beat?" He sounded more casual now.

"No. I'm central. I have family out this way. Walked it all in reins as a tot."

"A genuine local? We don't meet many of those."

"Originally. We moved away, then I came back when my parents died."

Something hard in her voice made him glance at her. "How old were you then?"

"Ten."

A tragedy of some sort, he supposed. No call to pry now. If she wanted to open up about it she could choose her own moment.

"Left after fifty yards, then a quick right. Harper," she read off the sheet. "Donald and Marion Harper. Will he be in at this time of day?"

"I fixed it by phone. He owns a hardware store, has left his assistant to close up. He was tetchy at first, then intrigued. Murder has a sort of glamour for those who feel secure."

Her shorthand was more than adequate. She got all the dialogue verbatim. The

92

Harpers were an ordinary couple, had dropped in for a curry after seeing a Rambo film.

Rambo, Rosemary echoed silently. This seemed to confirm Inspector Mott's opinion that comfortable, unimaginative people leading dull lives needed a touch of the extravagant. "Did you enjoy the film?" She asked her only question of the woman as finally she replaced the elastic band round her notebook.

"Well, it was more in Donald's line, really," Mrs Harper allowed. "I prefer a bit more glitter and ritz, like. But it was his turn to choose. Mind, I won't say that Stallion's not a lovely man. All those muscles!"

Rosemary Zyczynski looked from the woman's wistful eyes to the wimpish little figure of the hardware-store owner. "Yes, I see." Her voice, Mott thought, was as soft as her big brown eyes just then.

It was only a few streets away to the next interview in the office of a Building Society. A rather pink young couple who had agreed to delay closing admitted to having gone on to the Tandoori the previous night after working late at the office. As the routine questions were answered they became increasingly embarrassed.

"Look, this doesn't have to come out, does it?" the young man demanded anxiously. "I mean, do you hand all this over to the local press?"

"It's unlikely they would get hold of your names unless criminal charges are eventually brought against you," Mott assured him. "Do you think that's at all likely, sir?"

"God, no! It's just that — well, I haven't been married long, and my wife wouldn't care to know I . . . "

"The first ten years being the hardest," Mott considered ruefully when they had regained the car. "Matrimony doesn't come easy, so they tell me. I'm engaged myself. How about you?" He looked sideways at the WPC.

"No. Nothing like that." It sounded definite, almost final. Got it in for men, Mott decided. Well, maybe that makes her better to work with. Can't have hearts and flowers getting in the way of hard graft. A good-looking girl, she'd have her hands full batting Beaumont off. But there was a barrier there, under the soft exterior, and his guess was that she wouldn't take what she didn't want.

Two more visits and they called it a day, Mott dropping her off at Valpy Street to get her notes typed up. Tomorrow, Sunday, he'd be putting her on the six earlier muggings.

She'd never seen the full evaluated reports and he'd welcome a fresh approach, the woman's angle.

"At the Incident Caravan?" she asked.

"Until we disband there. You're one of my team now, so don't take any orders from outside. Sharp on eight-thirty. OK?"

Back at the caravan he took out the Scene of Crime folder and studied the enlarged photographs of Joel Sefton's injuries as found. Then he compared them with those taken at the morgue when the young man's face had been tidied for his brother's visit. Identification hadn't been difficult then; but earlier? Under that mask of congealed blood and loose flaps of hanging flesh, would Sefton have recognized his brother Joel?

So had the disfigurement been an

unsuccessful attempt to hide who the young man was? If so, why were the hands not mutilated? Everyone knew about fingerprinting. Sooner or later Joel Sefton would have been reported missing and dabs would have been raised off articles in his rooms at Marisbank. Identification would have followed. The killer's only gain would have been one of time, never more than a day or two. Time to do what?

On the other hand, such mutilation could have been carried out in a frenzy of hate. Or fear.

And with this case alone of all the muggings, some attempt had been made to hide the body away. Because of where it happened or who the dead man was?

There was always the possibility of identifying the body through the car, as had actually been the case. So if the face had to be made unrecognizable and the body hidden, why hadn't the car been removed? Even a few streets distant, it could have remained unremarked and unassociated for some time.

What would that tell you of the killer's psychology? In a matter of days there would be no shortage of polysyllabic opinions on that subject from the eggheads. But right now what did common sense tell him? One thing or the other: someone trying muddleheadedly to cover up whose the dead body was; or a killer overcome by some ungovernable passion.

Either way death was already occasioned before the mutilation — according to Littlejohn's first diagnosis, by a single blow dislodging the third and fourth cervical vertebræ and damaging the windpipe. A mark of violence. Or could it in any way have been due to accident? Was it beyond belief even that someone unconnected with an accidental killing had later performed the mutilation?

He was making sweeping gestures with his hands when Beaumont slouched in, his raincoat shoulders dark from the recent downpour. "What's this?" he demanded. "Karate practice? Rather a limp wrist movement for your sort, Guv."

"The death blow," Mott said shortly. "The only way I can imagine it as an accident is a swinging boom catching him unawares."

"Boom as in sailing, rather than boom ta-ra-ra? Well, that's more in your line than mine."

"He wasn't dressed for sailing, and even with yesterday's fresh wind I guess the river boats aren't heavy enough to cause such damage. And we're too far inland for sea-going to be anything other than fantasy."

"Shall I ask the path lab to look for evidence of sea or river water on the skin?"

"They're pretty thorough, but you could offer the suggestion."

Beaumont made the call, then threw off his raincoat. "It's turning into a dirty night. Which reminds me, what have you done with Her Scrumptiousness?"

"WPC Zyczynski is back at the station, typing up her notes. I'm sure you accept that as a suitably female occupation? And you'd better cut out the silly bugger's act. She's Mike Yeadings's choice, and he knows what he's about. If you feel the need to taunt her, remember that means you accept she's bigger than you. I don't see you as any kind of child-molester."

"Has to be licked into shape, like any

98

beginner," countered the sergeant. "Don't spoil my fun."

"Murder," Mott said grimly. "And a serial of six muggings. Let's keep that in the forefront, shall we?"

Beaumont gave him a shrewd glance. The inspector's feathers were slightly ruffled. Maybe he didn't care himself for the responsibility of a weak link added to the chain of command, even at the lowest end. He needn't worry. As her immediate superior, Beaumont could find plenty of paper-shuffling to keep her from getting under their feet.

Rosemary sorted her typed and photocopied statements into three piles, checked that the numbered pages ran consecutively, and slid one set into a green file addressed to Det-Supt Yeadings. Then, having delivered the others, she went to leave his copies on his desk.

He was still ensconced there, browsing over computer printouts. "Hallo, lass. What's this?"

She told him and handed over the file which he riffled through. "In a nutshell, what does it amount to?"

LEABHARLANNA TAISTIL
MOBILE LIBRARIES
TEL. 8307749

"Not a lot, at least to my eyes. There's one thing, though. I thought maybe — "

"Yes?"

"The car park. If I went down there now and made a sketch, blocked in all the positions we know were filled, noted the times of arrivals and departures, we might get a better idea of when Joel Sefton's car first appeared. I know it had a ticket showing 22.57 hrs, but we can't be sure that wasn't put there to fool us."

"And in any case it might have been taken from the machine by any third person and thrown away, then picked up by the killer to cause confusion."

"Yes. It does get complicated. So many ifs."

Yeadings considered her. "If your idea can cut down the possibilities, it's a damn good one. I could do with a spot of fresh air myself. Let's go along now and look."

They didn't take his car but struck off on foot along Duke Street, Rosemary matching his long stride in a way that bounced her pleats like a Scotsman's kilt. The rain had previously turned to drizzle and died away leaving the wet road surfaces shining like black sealskin. Where amber pedestrian lights made reflections like barley-sugar twists, they crossed and took a turning off Queens, approaching the Goldbasket premises from the rear. The night sky was overcast, with a scent of more rain yet to come, and Rosemary — remembering coal-smoky autumn evenings of childhood — was strangely excited. To her, autumn — not spring — had always signalled beginnings: new schools, new uniforms, new houses, new towns; and of course her October birthday looming with promise. Leading up to Guy Fawkes, there had always been an unforgettable smell of adventure almost upon her, and it was here tonight, even in mid-town among the familiar scents of car exhaust, wet tarmac and aromatic drifts escaping the Tandoori as they passed.

By the uncertain light it wasn't easy to make out all the demarcation lines on the parking area, but she quickly drew in the inverted L-shape of the yard. On the right a single line was set aside for customers' cars, leaving a central clearway for large vehicles to approach the Goods Inward bay directly. On the left was a double rank for cars, a gap and then a final row against a brick wall of the adjoining property. Two-thirds of the way up, the horizontal of the inverted L supplied two lines of parking with generous turning space between. At least half of these positions had plaques attached reserving them for grocery reps and personnel of the supermarket or of offices on the two floors above it. Not that these spaces were sacrosanct. At busy times, such as Friday evenings and Saturday mornings, impatient shoppers would have parked up the Goldbasket flagstaff if their cars had allowed it. Rosemary had once used the reserved part herself, driving Auntie's elderly Escort in to save the old lady's swollen legs.

Mike Yeadings was enjoying playing the rookie, singing out the total of positions in each row while the girl marked them off on her sketch. When the grid was completed she frowned at it. "It doesn't seem such a good idea now. So many spaces and so little information to fill them. I'd like to ring everyone who's been interviewed so far and get a more precise positioning for their cars."

"M'm. Nobody seems to remember seeing the Sefton car, but then how often is one so observant when rushing off for an evening out? Once you pin them down to their exact position they may start recalling details which they half-noticed at the time. Good luck with it anyway. But get home now before the rain starts again. There's always tomorrow. Knock off and snatch an early night. Once information starts rolling in and the pressure's on, you'll need all the rest you can snatch."

But tomorrow, according to Inspector Mott, she was to be sidetracked on to checking the six earlier muggings. And the Superintendent had already doubted whether the murder was really a part of that series. Suppose she went back to her digs now and used her own phone? She could do it all there just as well, and avoid being accused of clocking up unsanctioned overtime. A little private research: no one could possibly object to that.

6

ROSEMARY furtively eased off her shoes behind the skirting of the desk and, left to mind shop in the inner sanctum of the Incident Caravan, settled to her study of the muggings as a series. Inspector Mott had gone off to Oxford with his comedy sergeant in search of Polytechnic staff likely to have known the dead man. The local police had provided names and addresses and Mott was hopeful of finding them at home on Sunday.

That she was shunted into a siding looked to Rosemary a clear case of male chauvinism, but she reminded herself that until the official announcement of her own promotion to uniform sergeant, she must seem like so much spare furniture about the place, albeit furniture with a more than adequate shorthand speed.

She was grateful that the Serious Crimes superintendent from Maidenhead had picked up Mr Atkinson's hint and borrowed her for CID. If she could pull her weight on this case and not upset anybody's established apple-cart, her posting might even be *Detective*-Sergeant when it eventually came through. Not Serious Crimes, of course, but at divisional level.

Right then, girl, what's holding you back? she asked herself and started making notes.

STREET ATTACKS, CENTRAL READING

Six victims of robbery with ABH, vicinity of central Reading (+ Joel Sefton, murder victim, found in car park of Goldbasket Superstore, Friday October 9th.)

1. *Patience (Pattie) Morgan*, retired schoolteacher, aged 72, after collecting two weeks' pension from Post Office, Thursday, July 16th. As customary, shopped around the Hexagon, took a bus up Coley Avenue, then walked across the park to take tea with crony in council flats, finally leaving to get home by six for the TV news, entering her road-end by track worn diagonally across housing clearance

area. Discovered conscious but unable to walk, by youngsters playing on abandoned earth-digger at a little before 7.0 pm. Estimated time of attack between 5.40 and 5.45 p.m. — still daylight and warm — and site overlooked by upper floor of row of terraced houses. No witnesses.

Single attacker wore stocking mask, never spoke. Gestured with 'truncheon', snatched handbag and carrier bag, struck victim's abdomen, then her head as she lay doubled up on ground. Description: height 5' 8" – 5' 10", slender, with fine wrists, small feet for a man.

2. *Thomas (Tom) Boyle*, 66, retired postman, widower, returning from local pub, ¼ mile from previous incident, confronted by 'masked youth' when turning into angle of path between neighbours' back gardens and allotments. 10.47 p.m. (registered by smashed wrist watch), Tuesday, July 21st.

Victim retreated when he saw the attacker ahead, stumbled and was struck on head by 'heavy object' from behind. Had not been aware of anyone following him. Lost about £23, notes and cash, plus

Building Society cashcard and Swiss Army knife. Weather overcast, dark. Single lamp in pathway too far away for description of youth, but 'average height, not heavily built'. No mention of voices. Found half-conscious some ten minutes later by courting couple and taken home, later by ambulance to Royal Berks Hospital. Police informed from Casualty. Slight concussion; bruising at waist and two broken ribs indicated kicking when down.

3.   *Jane Swallow*, 18, bank clerk, walking home alone from bus stop after seeing film with girlfriend, half-mile from both of previous incidents, attacked at 10.15 p.m., Saturday, July 25th. Street light then defective but reported functioning fully at 10.07. Heard steadily running soft footsteps behind, expected to be passed by jogger, stood aside against high garden wall. Two men running in step pushed her into wall. One twisted her round, pulled wrist up behind back and covered her mouth while second removed gold chain, bracelet and handbag. First man 'felt her over' indecently before banging her head

against brick wall. Slight concussion and shock but good recall of circumstances. First man of medium height, slight with bad breath. Second tall and thin, spoke with Midlands accent. Only words — 'Hey c'mon. Don't bloody fool about.' Lost only about £5 in small change; no bank cards or chequebook on her.

4. *WPC Rosemary Zyczynski*, 24, on beat Monday, August 3rd, waiting for partner (PC George Finlay) near public convenience, shopping precinct, 11.57 p.m. Watching approach of lone male ahead, jumped from behind, fell forward. Pulled up by collar and punched in face by first male who approached running. She screamed and PC Finlay came at the double. Third man appeared from shadowed doorway, about to kick or stamp on her but saw PC Finlay approaching, snatched radio and ran. First two had already made off in opposite directions. Two voices: one Afro, one 'flat and dead'. Dialogue: 'Hey, man, it's the Babylon.' 'Bleeding pigs!' First two wore pull-down woollen masks. Third, with nylon stocking mask, was of medium height, thin-faced,

'scrawny'. He wore blue jeans and dark brown PVC zipped jacket.

5. *John Southgate*, 59, partly crippled by poliomyelitis as a child, uses two sticks for walking. Early retirement from management of radio repair shop. Attacked in broad daylight, 4.12 p.m., Saturday, August 8th, returning from licensed betting premises with winnings. Used alley to reach side entrance to usual pub, the Silk Garter. No witnesses. Three attackers and same MO as with WPC: one ahead, one behind and one 'out of nowhere'. Sticks kicked away from behind; second man 'yanked him up and duffed him'. Third stamped on his legs. Serious injuries to legs and jaw; severe shock. No coherent description of attackers. No voices heard.

6. *Mrs Ada Farlow*, 68, slipped out to Lloyds Cashpoint at corner of Bosham Street, 100 yards from her flat over a newsagent. Attacked as she was attempting to put £50 in her handbag, 8.30 p.m. approx, Thursday, September 24th. Half-dark and drizzling. Streets deserted. Single

attacker swung her headfirst into wall, rifled pockets as she lay helpless on ground, snatched handbag and stamped on both hands as she tried to ward him off. Stocking mask, no description of size, etc. Victim now rather confused and unreliable as witness. Observer from neighbouring upstairs window, Horace Mellor, said attacker was 'on the small side and ran like a hare'.

7(?) *Joel Sefton*, 19, student of architecture at Oxford Polytechnic, found dead at rear of rubbish area in Goldbasket Superstore car park, central Reading. Anonymous 999 call by male voice timed at 11.12 p.m., Friday, October 9th. Injuries include broken neck, severe lacerations to face and throat probably inflicted after death. Pockets empty. Car parked normally, with ticket indicating arrival at 10.57 pm. same day, but no car keys in ignition or on body. Anonymous informant had local accent, educated manner but had probably been drinking. (Q. Used rubbish area to urinate before driving home, and wary of a police encounter in his possibly over-the-limit state?)

Quite a lot to pick out of that, Rosemary decided. Dates first: 1) Thursday, July 16th; 2) Tuesday, July 21st; 3) Saturday, July 25th; 4) Monday, August 3rd; 5) Saturday, August 8th; 6) Thursday, September 24th; 7) Friday, October 9th.

Analysis: Thursday and Saturday twice: once each for Monday, Tuesday, Friday. No Wednesday, no Sunday.

So why not Wednesday? Some alternative occupation then? Sunday was easier to guess at, because fewer potential victims were about the shopping streets after dark, and anyone lingering near the banks' cash dispensers would be noticed.

And the significance of distribution? Five days between the first and second attacks, then a gap of four days before the third, a gap of nine, and a gap of five. Then six weeks and five days when all was quiet on the mugging front, with the killing of Joel Sefton eight days after resumption. (Was it too ridiculous to assume that the muggers took a six-week break for their summer holidays? More likely they moved to warmer climes and easier victims on the thronged beaches of popular tourist

111

centres. That was something to bear in mind when she got round to the question of who.)

Meanwhile, how about the muggings' time of day? They were, taking them in the same order: approx. 17.40; 22.47; 22.15; 23.57; 16.12; 20.30; and sometime before 23.12. Four out of the six muggings took place after ten p.m. So did Joel Sefton's killing. The other two occurred before six pm., number five actually at twelve minutes past four, a time when most people would be at work. No, dammit, number five had been a Saturday, so it wasn't a workday anyway. In that case no room for a theory about the mugger or muggers being employed or otherwise.

She eased her back, stood and went to the caravan door. "Bloody bells," complained the duty constable when she opened it. Besides the rowdy tumble of St Mary's summons to prayer there blew in a flurry of rain. She drew a gulp of relatively fresh Reading air and returned to her task.

So who were these muggers, as described? Numbers, first. Taking the attacks again chronologically: 1) one mugger; 2) two muggers (one frontal attack, one from the rear); 3) two muggers in step, overtaking as joggers; 4) three men with a new MO (or was it two in collusion plus a third accidentally on their patch at the time?) This had been her own mugging and she'd need to go into it in greater detail.

Now that she saw it listed among the other statistics she at last began to feel almost detached. Strange, that she hadn't realized until this moment that although her face and scalp had healed, as had the bruises, part of her mind still cowered at the memory. Had cowered, she corrected. Now she could go for perspective.

5) Definitely three muggers using roughly the same MO as on herself. The muggings were reaching gang proportions, having started out as a single's enterprise.

6) One attacker, no description.

7) Victim dead, so no account of incident. Pathologist suggests one attacker with blunt instrument (broken neck) and same or a second using sharp weapon to slash face.

So what had she discovered? Nothing that a computer couldn't list more rapidly.

But she had the details fixed in her mind now that she'd looked for common factors. It was interesting how the lone operator appeared to have become a trio, and then, after the 'holiday' break, was again reduced to working on his own. She realized that that concept relied on accepting that the muggings were actually serial and not random. Dare she assume that the trio disbanded during their holiday break, two of the muggers finding more lucrative fields and one preferring, or being obliged, to return to base alone? She'd better keep such ideas under her hat or that laugh-a-minute CID sergeant would have a field-day with her.

So, with those details set on a back burner, what of the selection of victims? Why them? — vulnerable, not wealthy, any of them. How about the age factor? Four were elderly and/or disabled; the eighteen-year-old girl, whom one of the men had 'felt over', implied an added sexual motive; herself, most likely because she was both female and 'Fuzz'. Finally — an odd one out — Joel Sefton, young, fit, affluent-looking and self-assured from all accounts. He must have been taken unawares even as she was. And the first blow, with the blunt instrument, had finished him. He'd been no harder to tackle than the others, using the element of surprise.

Which brought one to weapons. In the first case a 'truncheon' was mentioned. The second victim had been felled from behind by 'a heavy object'. The young woman's joggers had assaulted her manually, but it didn't mean they hadn't a weapon along with them. She herself had been felled from behind and then punched. PC Finlay's timely return hadn't left the attackers any time for more, but she'd known in her guts that the Afro at least had intended to make a present of her to the Royal Berks Hospital. The crippled man had been felled by kicking his sticks away, then punched like herself, finally stamped on. The old lady at the cashpoint machine had been manhandled and her head bashed against the wall; no weapon used. Because the single assailant hadn't one, or its use was unnecessary? Finally Joel Sefton, killed by a single blow from a blunt instrument, then mutilated by a sharp one.

Up until then no mention of anything resembling a knife. But had her Afro attacker had one ready? She'd known he intended something special. Is that what would have happened to her if Finlay hadn't been a sprinter?

She could have ended like the Sefton boy, slashed and bundled into a shop doorway.

All the attacks had taken place in areas recognized by the police to be of reasonably high risk: two where money could be expected — near the cashpoint machine and the bookies' shop. And the first victim had drawn her pension from the Post Office, then followed a regular pattern of return home. Had the attacker known her, watched and followed, or was it serendipity?

And what of the gain from all this? How lucrative was the mugging business? Two weeks' retirement pension; £23; a Building Society cashcard; a Swiss Army knife; costume jewellery; a police walkie-talkie; betting-shop winnings of £55, £50 in new notes; and whatever Joel Sefton had had in his pockets: useful, but surely not enough for one villain to live on for twelve weeks, let alone stretch to a share-out! So perhaps these men did it for kicks as much as for profit. And did that mean that as time went on they'd need ever bigger kicks — and once having killed continue killing?

Well then, if the CID giants asked her, did she really think Joel Sefton's case was serial with the others, or one on its own?

Inspector Mott and DS Beaumont still weren't back at 12.30 and Rosemary was famished. She scribbled a note for DC Silver who should have relieved her, left instructions with the PC manning telephones in the outer office and quitted the caravan. It seemed a good time to investigate the Tandoori personally.

On weekdays luncheon customers were either of the dodge-in dodge-out kind or those who plotted exclusive business within a scrum of massive tweedy shoulders. On Sundays, however, the clientèle was more mixed and louder. There was no live musician, and by this stage in the rapid service the background wailing of a recorded sitar ensemble had been turned so low as to be rarely heard above the clatter of dishes and family chatter.

Ten tables, she noted, so customers might normally park up to that number of cars behind the Goldbasket at any one time. And what did the Tandoori staff do about transport? Would CID have looked into that? She wished she knew more about investigation priorities in this sort of case, because just now no one could spare time to put her wise. Beyond the classic textbook jobs of identifying the body, the weapon and the time of death — all of which had fallen to others of the team — she had no idea where to push her own inquiries.

So why not the waiter, a small Asian with a birthmark down one cheek? "Busy in here," she murmured. "I had trouble finding a place for the car. How on earth do you manage?"

"Bike," he said, grinning. "Other fellers live upstairs, all-in. Boss takes taxi. But bad for customers just now. No car park. Police take it all." He had a lemon-sucking expression as he mentioned 'police'. She blessed not being in uniform.

She let him advise her on a half-bottle of wine. Dawdling over her main course, she watched the other tables emptying. When the little man brought over the sweet trolley she tried again.

"I suppose you were here for all that fuss on Friday. Did you have to make a statement?"

He grinned. "No. I am emptying trash in the alley and see blue lights. My tables all cleared then, so I am jumping on bike and go like hell."

She smiled back. "Clever old you. No awkward questions. Still, I don't suppose you saw anything unusual earlier on? That rice cake thing looks nice. I'll have some of that."

Deftly he transferred it to her plate. "Oh, I keep eyes always open, but busy in here with Dolly lady. She laugh a lot so I make jokes with her. Special party for thirty years married."

"Dolly?"

"She tells me that her name — Mrs Dolly. I say 'Jolly dolly good'."

"I bet she laughed."

"They all laugh a lot. Very happy party."

Right, Rosemary told herself on leaving. I'll never get expenses on the lunch, but I'm one move ahead of DI Smarty Mott. Dolly wasn't on his list of diners. That must be the woopy family they're looking for as Norris or Morris. So do I report in now, or go one step farther on it?

7

THERE was no entry for 'Dolly' in the area phone book. Allowing for Asian mispronunciation Rosemary tried for 'Dorry' under various spellings, with the same result. So had these people no phone? The caravan didn't boast street directories for the outlying districts, and the Public Library was closed; which left only one alternative.

"I'm nipping out again," she warned the PC on phone duty. "Tell DI Mott to try my home number if I'm needed." Not that that's likely, she complained silently. The team appeared to be functioning lengthily elsewhere without her help.

She knocked on her landlady's sitting-room door and poked her head through. "Matty, could I scrounge your local paper?" she demanded.

"Of course, duck. It's somewhere under that lot on the sofa. Thought you was working today on that mugging murder."

"I am. Just had an idea the local rag could help."

It was in the personal columns that she found what she wanted. She might have arrived there more directly, without resorting to the Tandoori and an extravagant lunch: two separate entries — 'Love and congratulations to Mum and Dad on their thirtieth wedding anniversary, from Janet and Ian, Phyllis and Peter'; followed by 'Happy Thirtieth Anniversary, Gran and Grandad. Kisses from Gina, Johnny and Pip'. The name in block capitals above each entry was TOLLEY. Glowing with success, she ran back through the rain to log her first find.

As she stepped up to enter the caravan she discovered that the other two had just returned.

"What the hell d'you think you're doing?" DS Beaumont demanded, filling the doorway while she stayed under the drips. "Twice we phoned and there was no CID on duty."

"Now that I'm back I'd like to come in."

"I asked you a question, WPC Zyczynski.

Perhaps you didn't hear it. What do you mean by sloping off home?"

"I heard, but the answer isn't for broadcasting to the passing public. I wish to report to DI Mott. Inside."

"You report to me. I give you your orders."

She was breathing hard, not entirely due to the running. "My work for you is in the folder. This is something else."

Beaumont moved backwards, tugging at his own drenched raincoat. "Well, first you can make yourself useful. Tea for me with milk and two sugars. Black coffee and one for the DI."

Rosemary eased past him and hung up her waterproof. Her hair dripped wispily, runnels of water wriggling between the roots to trickle down brow and temples.

She went through to the inner office to switch on the kettle and Mott looked up from the desk as if he hadn't overheard the exchange. "Ah, you're back. Why the sudden departure at the double? Not a sudden distaste for CID, I hope?"

"Look," she offered, and pulled a notebook from her shoulder-bag. "I've found the four woopies of the Tandoori.

The two celebrating were a Mr and Mrs Tolley. And I've confirmation from the waiter who served them."

"So what have they to tell us?" Beaumont demanded, breathing over her shoulder.

"I haven't located them yet."

"Try the phone book," Mott suggested, handing it over. "Beaumont, fix the brew, will you?"

Rosemary ran her finger down the page. "There are two Tolleys here, both out at Caversham. Wait a minute, Peter could be the son who put in the greetings. That leaves W. S. Do you want to ring them?"

"It's your lead," Mott offered. "Carry on."

A woman took the call, surely the one the waiter had called Dolly. Her voice was plumply rounded, one easily turned to laughter.

"Yes, that's right, Friday it was. Married thirty years, just imagine! We had ever such a nice meal, foreign, but lovely for a change. Still, I can't think why the police should be interested. Nothing wrong with the restaurant, was there? *Our*

124

food seemed quite all right."

Rosemary assured her that it was a different matter entirely, more an inquiry about car parking facilities. She stemmed the next flow with a crisp request to come out and discuss it in person, at a time when Mr Tolley would also be available.

Mott gave her a nod of approval as she put down the receiver. "Coffee or tea for you?"

"Better not, I think. I'm going out there now, and she sounds the hospitable sort. Can I take the car?"

"I think I'll come along," Mott told her. "DS Beaumont has some pressing paperwork."

"Hey, Guv," he protested, "why not me? She can stay and type my notes up."

"We do our own."

"But you don't take any notes."

"That's right. As I said, we do our own."

Beaumont's lips tightened, but he slung the car keys on the desk. "I'll have another go at raising the clients Sefton was visiting Friday."

Mott was swallowing his coffee hot. He

grunted. "Look, Zyczynski, there's a towel through there. Get your hair fixed."

"Women!" Beaumont muttered at the closed door.

"You've never fought shy of them before."

"In their proper place."

"Which, according to Mr Yeadings, is here and now. Snap out of it, man. I won't stand for feuding on the job. When you grant her professional status I'll back your seniority. Until then you're both skivvies. Got it?"

He let her drive; might as well know the worst. But she was careful enough, maybe a trifle too careful, not the one to pick for a vital car chase. For chasing up the Tolleys' info, though, good enough.

She handled the interview well, steering the woman off irrelevancies and encouraging the man — a lanky, laconic plumber — to put in his own word here and there. But it was the woman who'd been observant, savouring every small detail of their special night out. She could pinpoint exactly their position in the car park; had noted as they left the restaurant that they'd be back home by

11.20, with nice time to make tea and slip into a dressing-gown before the late TV film; saw the young man operating the supermarket timing machine, so marked him down as a newcomer to the district. No, she hadn't a clear sight of his face, but her husband confirmed the make and type of car the lad had taken the ticket back to. It was Sefton's all right. And the time just a few minutes short of eleven.

"Does that get us any farther?" Rosemary asked anxiously as they started back.

"They left the car park just minutes before the killing, so everything they noticed — even noticed then and have temporarily forgotten — is vital. Tolley managed to identify three cars there besides his own. That helps fill in your grid. A good idea, that. The SOCO team should have done it. Although we know now for certain about the Sefton car, we'll want everything else we can get on possible witnesses. And we fell down on the Tandoori interviews, letting that waiter get away without questioning. He may help identify other customers we haven't traced. He knows you now, so I'll send Beaumont in to take a heavy line."

"Was the killer waiting in the car park, do you think?"

"He can't have been far off. It could be our lone mugger again, lurking for a chance encounter, or else someone Sefton had arranged to meet there. In which case there wasn't much time to develop an argument serious enough to end in blows, unless the killer had it in for him already."

"Someone Joel had upset. That gives us a better chance, if we check on everything he'd been up to recently."

"Don't forget it was a single blow that killed him. That could have been a sudden, wild swipe by someone temporarily inflamed by drink or drugs. The killer could even be the unknown who phoned in to report finding the body. And the weapon hasn't turned up. A blunt instrument, which reminds us of the 'truncheon' of the early muggings. Working from descriptions given, I think we have to accept that its user, the first lone mugger, is the one who has resumed on his own since the summer break."

"About the other two who took part in

the intermediate muggings," Rosemary said tentatively, "I was wondering . . . Suppose they all went on holiday abroad, for richer pickings and a good time thrown in. They apparently haven't come back. So did they decide to stay on longer while our solo mugger returned for some personal reason, or . . . "

"Go on."

"Or did they fall foul of the local police, say in Spain or some island in the Med, and are being held in jail there? It's two months since their last combined operation in Reading, but they could languish in a foreign jail for twice as long again without us knowing, especially if they wanted to keep a low profile."

"Interpol," Mott said tersely. "Yes, I'll ask Mr Yeadings to follow that up. A list of Brit undesirables detained abroad might provide some local names to look into. And we'll put uniform men on contacting travel agents for clients who failed to return."

Either way, Rosemary reckoned, slowing in the Sunday evening church traffic as they entered the town, progress has been made and I know the next moves.

We look for a quick-tempered close acquaintance of Joel's who has recent reason to be annoyed with him and at the same time we check on the two missing muggers, who certainly knew the identity of their remaining partner. A double-pronged Inquiry; and she knew which part she'd rather work on.

"Sir."

"You'd better make it Angus. What do I call you?"

"I'm Rosemary, but maybe Z's better. Less feminine. I don't need to get up male chauvinist noses."

Mott grunted. "I hope that dig wasn't aimed at me, because it doesn't fit. I'm putting you from now on in close harness with DS Beaumont, to get the fireworks used up more quickly. He's a good jack who can teach you a lot, but he's wasting energy at the moment. You'll have to make out as best you can."

"Yessir, Angus. I was going to ask — after I've written up the travel agencies idea, can I work on the Sefton lifestyle?"

Mott grinned. "I was going to switch you there in any case. But for God's sake don't call it that in your reports: 'Personal

130

background', Z. Original thought by all means, but document it under established headings."

"So where do I begin?"

"At Mr Yeadings's update briefing tomorrow morning. Nine sharp, at the nick. Have your notes there at eight-thirty in a form he can read through quickly. Then I'd better take you out to meet the dead man's family. No, dammit; Monday they'll probably have dispersed. It will have to be today. I'll give them a ring and find when's convenient."

The older daughter answered the phone. They were all still there, supporting Mother. Josie had arranged to stay on for four days anyway, but tomorrow everyone else would be back at work. Yes, if DI Mott had anything to tell them he could certainly come tonight. As they intended having an informal meal at seven, soon after eight was best.

"And knock off duty on the dot of nine," Mott stipulated. "There will be more than enough overtime accumulating soon with a murder case. Meanwhile we should get ourselves something to eat. Beaumont and I usually opt for a pie

131

and a pint." He sounded doubtful.

"Suits me fine. I ate at the Tandoori for lunch, so I don't want food. And by the way, I stick to soft drinks."

This — no surprise — earned her a look of disgust from the DS, who called the first round. "Felt sure you were a Baby Cham living it up on vodka Martini."

"Don't judge a sausage by its skin," she warned him. "I mix a mean Tom Collins when I'm roused."

He stared at her poker-faced, then seemed to relax a little, even dropped a bag of crisps in her lap when she refused solid food. They broke up at 7.40, Beaumont going to hand in his report on the Oxford interviews.

Mott directed Rosemary out to Callendar Lane. "Impressive," she said as the house, windows ablaze, came into sight after the walls of evergreens.

"The whole family's impressive, in their different ways. All very gifted, to quote the old lady herself. There will be no prizes for guessing what line she was in once you've seen her."

"Can you give me a quick rundown?"

He listed their names and ages from memory. "Erica's a high-powered lady in producing garden equipment — majority owner and MD of Florafaun Frames. Christopher's in insurance in the City. Paul directs TV films and writes. Josie's a Civil Servant, considers herself rather dull but she's warm and human. The dead Joel made up the five. Their father died about eight years back, ex-solicitor and JP. Mike Yeadings could tell you more about him."

Their arrival at the front door was the signal for curtains to be pulled at all the downstairs windows. A well-built woman with stylishly cut, corn-coloured hair came out on the steps to greet them. "I hope you're prepared for the Grand Inquisition. You won't get away this time with asking the questions."

Rosemary looked at her curiously. She had put on a dark dress with random white spots but she displayed no other signs of mourning. Her voice was crisp, half-jocular with a cutting edge to it. Aggressively on the defensive, the WPC decided; Erica had no intention of anyone reading her feelings.

Christopher, on the other hand, had a crumpled look. His distress was overt, a hovering unease on behalf of everyone else present as though he feared some breakdown of nerves and was steeling himself to cope with it when it came. "Er, my daughter goes to bed shortly, Inspector. She has been told the circumstances, but if you prefer she can go up with Mrs Lavender now."

"Perhaps she might stay for the present, sir. I should like WPC Zyczynski to meet the whole family. She will be working in the CID team throughout the case. She was, in fact, one of the earlier mugging victims."

"Come in, both of you. Sit down, my dear." Harriet Sefton came forward, offering her hand. Rosemary smiled, as much remembering Mott's reference to the lady's profession as from politeness. No one who had ever worked through junior ballet classes could miss the practised poise of the small, dark woman, so distinct from her towering children.

But after the statuesque Erica and overweight Chris they had compromised on size. Paul was of medium height, lithe, taut, with a neat, almost lizardy head, cool eyes, and a mouth too that was reptilian, the closed lips in a permanent half-smile. Someone to be reckoned with sexually, she felt. He was both a warning and a magnet. Josie, a little shorter and willowy in a navy silk dress, had wide-spaced eyes, small nose and the sweet mouth of a Renoir model. Pleasant, Rosemary thought; and clearly under stress although trying to seem normal. What could be normal under such circumstances? Surely not this stagey family tableau.

Harriet moved back to her seat on a chaise-longue and took the hand of a thin, hollow-eyed girl who sat hunched there silent. "And this is my grand-daughter Kit. Kit, sit up straight, dear. That's better. Now, Inspector, what have you managed to find out?"

The woman's attempt to control the interview didn't put Mott off, Rosemary noticed. She took a seat offered by Paul, beside and just behind the DI, and took out her notebook.

"We have interviewed a considerable number of people and now have witnesses to your son's arrival at the supermarket.

135

Which makes us wonder why he should choose to leave his car just there. Can any of you tell me whether it was his custom? If, indeed, he had ever done so before?"

There was a silence while the Seftons looked round at each other. "I can't imagine how we could answer that, Inspector," Harriet concluded. "He was a free agent, you know. He may well have gone there at some time for a private purchase, but he was never expected to do the household shopping. In any case we normally buy from Sainsbury's."

"But he appeared to know the parking space was available." Mott turned to Christopher Sefton. "Did you, for example, sir?"

"Never heard of the Goldbasket before, Inspector. But then I don't circulate in Reading to the same extent. Not of late, anyway. I think it must have appeared since my young roistering days."

"Would you call your brother a young roisterer, sir?"

"Oh Lord, you know what I mean. He was nineteen. At that age you have spare time and a need to be seen everywhere and see everything. It's part of the cult

136

of being young. He didn't need a map to get round the town, you can be sure."

"Thank you. But no one actually saw him with goods or a carrier bag from that store?"

There was a negative mumble all round. "At what time was Joel seen at the car park?" Harriet pursued.

"Shortly before eleven, Mrs Sefton. So our main concern now is to fill in the time between your last seeing him here in the morning and that last known sighting Friday night."

"More to the point, surely, is what happened after his last sighting," Erica insisted crudely.

"That too. A very short period, and possibly only his killer can tell us about that. But I hope that at least one of you can offer suggestions of where we should look to fill up the blanks in his day."

"The estate agency," Harriet said shortly. "I told you that before."

"We have contacted staff there, thank you. We shall be interviewing them tomorrow."

"He used to get a pub lunch usually," Christopher offered. "Unless he went through to Oxford. You could ask at the Poly there."

"He doesn't appear to have gone to the college. I saw the Course Secretary this morning."

"Actually," said Erica, "I suppose I'd have been the last of us to set eyes on him. Elevenish, he looked in at the office. Eleven in the morning, of course."

"What on earth for?" This sprang spontaneously from Josie who stopped, flushed and put one hand to her mouth.

Erica was looking frostily amused. "Meaning it was the last place he'd choose to drop in for coffee? I'll admit I was somewhat astonished myself to see him. But it was a special occasion, or the next day was going to be. He wanted to be sure I knew of all the arrangements for Mother's birthday and wouldn't be throwing a spanner in."

"That was — thoughtful of him," Harriet said in a low voice.

Rosemary, glancing across, caught a glance of disbelief exchanged between Josie and her brother Paul. *Question*

Ms. Erica S, she wrote in the margin of her notebook.

There was a marked pause and Rosemary thought Mott had caught the vibes, was going to follow it up himself then and there, but instead it heralded the opening of the door to the hall and Mrs Lavender's entry with a service trolley. Mott's fair skin darkened at the interruption.

"I ordered tea and coffee," Harriet Sefton said graciously. "Kit, you can take your milk up with you. Mind you clean your teeth *afterwards,* dear."

The girl stood up and looked round wildly. Her father was preoccupied, taking filled cups from his mother's hand. Josie was separating a nest of side tables. "Shall I come up with you?" Rosemary asked on an impulse.

The girl nodded. "'Night, Nana, 'night, everyone," she muttered. There was an answering rumble. Halfway up the stairs she stopped abruptly and turned to the policewoman. "Were you really mugged?"

"Yes. Two months ago. I was the fourth one. We think your cousin — "

"Uncle."

"Sorry; we think your uncle may have been the seventh. We want to make sure nobody else gets hurt. That's why we have to ask so many questions."

"But none of us saw it happen."

"Just in case it wasn't an ordinary mugging," Rosemary said cautiously, "we need to know if anyone wanted to hurt him."

"*One of us?*" Kit cried in horror. She was shaking from head to foot. Rosemary took the tumbler of milk from her tight grip and put an arm round the thin shoulders.

"Of course not you. But he could have mentioned something. Some quarrel with one of the other students, anything that could lead us to whoever did it."

They had reached the girl's room. She pushed the door open and went in to switch on the bedside lamp. Rosemary put down the tumbler on a glass shelf above the hand basin and kept her back to Kit while the girl dropped her clothes off. Briefly in the mirror she saw the jutting bones of the child's emaciated body.

"Don't forget your milk." She crossed to the window, found the cord to

140

close the heavy curtains and turned back. Suspiciously fast the milk had disappeared. A semi-circle of white lay in the groove of the hand basin plughole. Kit reached for her toothbrush and began ostentatiously to brush her teeth.

Josie Sefton appeared suddenly, full of apologies for leaving the visitor to take over. "Mother and Mrs Lavender were busy. I didn't notice Kit had left us."

"That's all right. I'm the dogsbody anyway. I'm glad to be able to help."

They both said good night to Kit who promised to read for only fifteen minutes before switching off the light.

"I'm afraid the milk . . . " Rosemary said when they were out again on the landing.

"Went down the drain? I think it most often does. Just as well, perhaps. If she's made to drink it she brings it back. We all have enough on our minds now without a scene with poor little Kit. Thanks again for jumping in. She seemed quite taken with you. You should be honoured."

Rosemary made no comment. In Kit's

eyes, she guessed, one thing only had made her acceptable. She had been mugged, as the child knew her uncle was. Possibly as figuratively she felt herself to be.

8

ERICA SEFTON saw them to their car. Ten past nine, Rosemary noted as they left. DI Mott had fought off the social entanglements, emerging slightly ruffled but dominant. His questions had been put without any great revelations resulting. Everyone, it seemed, had been about their normal occupations on the day Joel died, and none of them could supply any certain information on where he went after leaving Erica's office at a little before midday. The suppositions offered were: a pub lunch, his student circle, various properties offered for sale by Lever's agency.

Mott wound down the passenger window as Rosemary turned the ignition. "Would you care to change your statement, at all, Ms. Sefton?" he challenged. "Or add to it?"

Erica gave a low chuckle. "I thought you'd cottoned on. Couldn't be tactless

143

in front of Mother. Even I admit to limits. The truth was that Joel didn't come to socialize, much less to ensure I was *au fait* with arrangements for the birthday. He complained he was low in funds. Not an uncommon situation, but he usually knew better than to approach me about it. He said he needed a sub to get Mother's present, but I wasn't having any. I reminded him the birthday had a way of being pretty regular. He'd had all of twelve months since the last one to save up and buy something within his price range."

She stood straighter and ran a hand through her hair. "No regrets. I still think I was right. A pity he wasn't brought up the hard way I was."

"So you turned him down. What was his reaction?"

She hesitated. "Couldn't do anything about it, could he? Went off with his tail between his legs, but he'd have bounced back in no time and found himself a sucker."

"I see." Mott's tone was wooden. "And how much did he suggest you should give him?"

"Loan, Inspector, not give. That's what he called it anyway. Fifty pounds. A nice round sum to complete payment, he said, on an antique ring. Anything more I can help you with?"

"Not for the moment, thank you. We shall probably need to see you again."

At his nod Rosemary slipped in the clutch. Before the first bend in the drive she looked in the driving mirror. Erica Sefton was standing, legs astraddle, hands on hips, staring after them. "You've made her uneasy, Guv," she said.

"A late surge of conscience, perhaps. Could she have a soft centre after all?"

"If he did eventually raise the necessary somewhere else, and bought the ring . . . "

"It could have been on him when he was attacked. Something to trace; it could lead us to the mugger. First thing tomorrow, straight after the briefing, we'll need to contact all local jewellers, see who if anyone sold an antique ring on Friday."

"If she was telling the truth this time."

"Why shouldn't she?"

"I've no idea why, but I had a funny feeling. No love lost there. The way she told it: 'to complete payment, *he said* . . . ' It sounded sceptical. As though she thought the idea of a deposit already made, or else of the ring's existence at all, was probably a try-on."

Mott grunted. "You could be right. Not a case of *nil nisi bonum* by implication, even though her brother is dead. What age difference was there?"

"If she's thirty-four, fifteen years. She was at a precarious age when the newest baby arrived and he the light of her mother's life apparently."

"What age isn't precarious? But there is hostility. Based on jealousy, m'm. She's got where she is through hard slog, mental ability and sex, while he gets what he wants by holding out his hand. Could be galling. And she's a woman of strong feelings."

They drove some way in silence. "I don't think she was alone in resenting Joel," Rosemary suggested, "although the others didn't come out with it. Little Kit was different, of course. Another petted child — fussed over, anyway. She seemed to see her uncle in the light of a cult hero. So she was more ready to accept me, because I'd been another of the mugger's victims."

"You could have dropped me in it, going off with her. Did you learn anything?"

"It confirmed my suspicions. She's been anorexic for some time. They have a real problem there. I get the impression as well that her other aunt, Josie, might know more about things in that household than seemed obvious at first. If so, she could be useful to us."

"If she'll part with it," Mott agreed. "When I went there first with Mr Yeadings she let something drop. She was chary of us delving too far in brother Joel's affairs. Protective, but she gave me the impression she regarded him more as an inadvertent villain than a victim."

Rosemary turned into the Oxford Road. "Mr Yeadings will want a full report on this visit by the morning, won't he? Can I type it up at home?"

"No. Come in early, leave it on his desk by eight-thirty. I'll be ringing him tonight, so he'll have a good idea of its gist before he gives the briefing."

Mott turned sideways in his seat and

for the first time gave her his famous melon-slice grin. "Don't worry. I'll give you credit where it's due. Now drop yourself off where you live. I can drive myself home."

Next morning the hall off the Incident Room was already crowded to the doors when the Nobs came in. CID had collared the front seats. Many of the uniformed house-to-house inquirers arrived last and were still on their over-exercised feet. Mike Yeadings pointed a finger to the floor near his blackboard, and the last row came from leaning against the farther wall, to sit at his feet like a kindergarten class. Through the open doorway could be seen the bank of twelve VDUs, and on a bench below them the printers of the computer system. Telephonists and the Receiver were still working at their desks.

Yeadings broke straight into a summary of the mugging series, " — in which this death may or may not be the latest example." He then listed precisely the case's similarities to the previous incidents and what set it apart. "We may each of us lean to our own preferred opinion," he told them, "but let's all keep an open mind: this is either a serial mugging *or* an individual murder. Until one is proved beyond doubt.

"However, because it is indisputably a violent death aggravated by robbery, we need to go very carefully into the dead man's recent behaviour. Particularly important are his activities on the day in question, the people he spent time with, any unusual incidents observed in his vicinity.

"The family has been interviewed, and they have pointed us in several directions. Due to the intervening weekend, not all the persons needed for interview have been readily available. Today DS Beaumont and DC Silver will tackle the Oxford Polytechnic end, mix with the students and pick up whatever associations of Joel Sefton seem relevant. DI Mott with WPC Zyczynski, temporarily seconded to CID, will follow the estate agency trail. Mr Atkinson will instruct the rest of you on individual visits.

"There will be further inquiries at the Tandoori restaurant and information is still required on cars and their owners using the supermarket parking space. Selected teams of two officers will visit all jewellers and shops selling antiques, for particulars of any second-hand rings sold last Friday, including any previously reserved. I stress *visits*. No corner-cutting by phone. I want discretion maintained, which means plain clothes for uniform officers employed on this duty. No discussion in the hearing of customers or other uninvolved parties. Impress on those questioned that the success of the hunt for our killer depends on his remaining in the dark about our moves. And certainly no action is to be taken against anyone offering jewellers a second-hand ring for resale. The ring is to be retained for 'preparation of an estimate' while we are notified. Keep your ears and eyes open too for any such article being flogged in a pub. Observe only and report back. We are a team, so no lone-ranger heroics and no sudden moves. You all know of the TIE follow-up — Trace, Interview, Eliminate. Leave that to the experts.

"Finally, if I hear there's been any leak

to the Press, whoever is responsible will live to leak like a colander before I'm through. Understood? Right. Questions, then."

The questions came: the pointed, the idle and the smart-alec. Detective-Superintendent Yeadings dealt with them all, succinctly and equably, photographing the faces of the questioners in his mind. "I don't need to remind you how badly we want to get this killer, and what a string of violent incidents we stand to clear up if it does prove to be a serial crime. Go to it, then."

Rosemary had taken it all down verbatim. DS Beaumont shifted his haunch from the table alongside to look over her shoulder at the shorthand notes. "Some folks are gluttons for it," he told her. "Still, keep it up, gal. No knowing when you'll be needing a desk job again."

It didn't rattle her. "My first overall view of the battlefield," she claimed. "Useful to remember when you have your head down, blindly firing."

He made a hen squawk back. "She begins to sound just like the Old Man.

D'you think she writes his homilies for him?"

There was a titter as the room began to clear. Rosemary caught sight of Finlay, her former partner on the beat. He looked quickly away, then thought better of it and came across. "Make the most of it, matey," and he gently punched her on the shoulder.

"It's because I heard the muggers' voices," she said quickly. "And then I think they needed a woman, to help get the family talking."

"Good luck, anyway. We'll all be watching."

"So lay *off* my guv," Beaumont put in slyly. "And remember he's a half-married man."

This time the taunt reached her. She found her hands were trembling as she stuffed the notebook away in her bag. Finlay was scowling after the man's departing back. "That's about all *Beaumont* is at present. That's what's souring him. Take no notice. Suddenly he's right off women."

"Half-married? How?"

"Cathy's left him, taken the kid. 'Gone

to look after her sick mum,' he says, but it seems there's nothing wrong with the old girl. And Cathy's been heard asking around for a good brief."

"I didn't know. Thanks for warning me."

"So long as you don't think he's got anything personal against you."

"Oh, it's that too. Make no mistake, it's chemical. My hackles rise just like his do."

"Z!" Angus roared from the doorway. "On the road!" She pulled a face and bolted.

This morning Mott drove. The office and school rush hour was over and housewives hadn't yet clogged the in-town parking. He found a space in the lane behind the estate agency and as they left the car a green Rover going past tooted them. "That's Mr Yeadings," Rosemary recognized.

"He had a fancy to check on something for himself," Angus told her, grinning. "He complains the shine on his suit can't take much more sitting."

"So where . . . ?"

"The local office of Florafaun Frames. Where else? Last known visit made by the dead man."

He nodded at a fascia board opposite. "Brockham Estates, here we are. I'll tackle the manager, Lever, while you have a quick look through the properties list and their daybook."

Yeadings was in luck. A delivery van drew away just opposite the double gates to Florafaun's yard and it offered him a space. He left the car unlocked while he went across for a quick glance through the area behind the high walls. On the side at right angles to the loading bay were several cars, one of them the red BMW he had seen on his first visit to Marisbank.

So Erica Sefton was in her office. A pity, but at least his intuition to seek the rear entrance had given him warning. Unless she went out on foot by the front way he would know when she left. Surely she wouldn't spend the whole morning at her desk? Give her time to go through the post, dictate some letters and issue a few instructions. Time for him to snatch a coffee and Danish, maybe look at the leader in today's *Times*.

He went back to make the car secure and passed the meter maid on his way, warned her not to stick a parking ticket on his window if he overstayed the limit. Then he allowed himself an hour for refreshment and a welcome chance to ponder the case.

The best lead to come out so far was the dead man's intention to buy the antique ring — if Erica Sefton was to be believed. Of course 'antique' sometimes meant no more than 'second-hand', which could imply Joel knowing a man who knew a man who had one going cheap. Would he have risked buying something of relative value on those terms, or — since it was for his mother — would he have gone to a more reputable source? In any case it was unlikely he picked up the ring at all unless he succeeded in raising the cash required. Who, then, would he have approached next?

Joel had left Erica's office just before midday on Friday, and one of the family had suggested he would go for a pub lunch. Yeadings brushed doughnut sugar

155

off his finger ends and decided that later he could do worse than tour the locals at the same hour as Joel. Somewhere in the area would be a yuppie rallying point, a familiar face to put a bet on with or to touch for fifty quid.

More calories! he thought guiltily. Coffee and doughnuts followed by incalculable pints: Nan would be horrified if she knew. Ah well, all in the line of duty. Meanwhile, back to Florafaun Frames and anyone who could recall young Sefton calling in on the last working day of last week.

There was an awkward atmosphere in the Brockham Agency. Rosemary thought DI Mott had picked it up too, because he started moving and speaking just that little bit more slowly, allowing time for impressions to trickle in.

The manager, Lever, was definitely uptight. Two female assistants — one middle-aged and dealing with a client, the other pretending to be busy among rotating boards which advertised properties — were as interested in his reactions as in the visitors themselves. Since the interview had been arranged in advance, the man couldn't plead pressure of business to put them off, but clearly he would have preferred retreat.

They were ushered by Lever into his private office. Before closing the door he looked back at his two assistants. Silencing them with a scowl, or appealing for relief? Time would tell.

"I — er, didn't know young Sefton very well personally," Lever plunged in. "I had done business with his mother on more than one occasion, and it was with her in mind that I — er, made an offer to the boy. A student of architecture, after all. That would go down very well with some of our clients. Oh, do sit down, won't you?"

Rosemary took out her notebook and observed the man's increased unease.

"You know Mrs Sefton, you say? In the line of business? I understand that she had lived for many years in Callendar Lane." Mott sounded amiably curious.

"Oh, quite. No question of her selling Marisbank. Though if and when she does, of course it would be a great pleasure to handle the sale. No, she had other property to dispose of, within the town limits. Some by outright sale, others for rental. The Brockham Agency was able to be of service then."

"So on the strength of that association, Mrs Sefton asked you to employ her son as an assistant during his summer vacation?"

"Not Mrs Sefton, no." The assurance was hurried. "Young Mr Sefton approached me direct. He seemed quite knowledgeable, very persuasive — which is an important qualification — and we were under some pressure then. Our books full, you understand, and my regular helpers all taking their holidays in a bunch."

"So, in view of his background, and without references, you decided to take him on?"

"Er, exactly. And, indeed, he did seem quite gifted in customer relations. Through him we actually moved several large properties which had — er, hung fire. Of course, it was the height of the season. He could hardly have enjoyed such — er, success between say November and February."

"Right. You mentioned customer

158

relations. I imagine there's more to the business than that?"

"Oh indeed, Inspector. If you have ever been a party to purchasing property . . . "

"I understand it can be a lengthy and hazardous business."

"One requires such patience to humour impractical expectations. Clients can become quite frantic over the many pitfalls encountered. And then practical experience does not come overnight. There are legal requirements to be observed, ethical standards. One essential both buyer and vendor demand is — er, integrity."

"You are trying to tell me something." Mott's quiet voice was innocent of sarcasm. Rosemary bent over her notebook, visualizing him with tongue in cheek.

Lever seemed to have run out of steam. He flicked a switch on a box beside his phone and demanded acidly, "Where's that coffee then, Miss Simmonds?"

After a squawked reply there was a short wait and then the door opened to admit a tray and a third girl looking wildly for a free space to deposit it. During the manœuvring to supply this

159

Rosemary caught Mott's hard stare and a quick flick of his head in the direction of the door. She rose apologetically and appealed to the girl. "I wonder if there's somewhere I could — er, tidy up?"

"Course," said the other. "Cummalongamee."

The client was just leaving the front office. Rosemary went through the door indicated, shot the bolt and laid her ear flat against the panel. "Lotta baloney if you ask me," girl three was grumbling. "Silly old fool."

The rest of the conversation was inaudible. Rosemary waited, flushed the loo and came out. The two original assistants were leaning together over their desk.

"I expect you knew Joel Sefton quite well," she said sympathetically. "Awful shock for you, and all that. Was he nice to work with?"

The older one pursed her lips. "Quite fun in a way," said the other. "Went out with him twice, but he'd got his eye more on the clients. Not a snob, though. I liked him. He shouldn't have ended like that. Nobody should."

"I wish I'd known him," said Rosemary wistfully. "I suppose you couldn't give me any help? I'd like to feel I'd done something to help find out who killed him. Background stuff, you know."

Out of sight she crossed her fingers. "My boss gets all the breaks, makes me feel a right wally. I'd like to come up with something he didn't know."

"We-ell . . . " It was going to take time to get her going.

"Look, are you busy after work tonight? Can I hang around?"

Suddenly the girl made up her mind. "Meet me down at Patty's Pantry. Quarter to six sharp?"

"I'll be there. Thanks."

"And if you don't mind, so will I," said the older woman. "There's something I've had on my mind ever since . . . I'd be glad to hear what you think."

Rosemary nodded. "Another thing I need is a full list of properties Joel Sefton dealt with since he came here. Could you manage that?"

When she returned to the private office, knocked and walked in, Lever and the DI were talking about motorways and her

161

coffee had gone cold.

A second reconnaissance of the Florafaun trade yard satisfied Yeadings that the red BMW had now gone. With it, he fervently hoped, its mordant owner. He went round the block, presented himself at Reception and was duly downcast when told sorry, he had just missed Ms Sefton by a mere fifteen minutes. In her absence he asked to see her secretary.

"Girl Friday," she corrected him confidingly when he'd taken the lift to her office. "We're pretty modern in our outlook here." She examined his card. "What can I do for you, Superintendent? How about a nice strong cage for your villains?"

"I've not come as a customer, he admitted, "though I'd be more than happy to take one of your catalogues on fruit protection. This year the damn blackbirds had more of my loganberries than we did."

Girl Friday — May Barling by name — produced the required literature and a current price list. "Order direct by mail," she advised. "It's quicker than going to a retailer."

"And cheaper?"

"Depends on quantity. How many acres?"

"You're cutting me down to size, lass," Yeadings appreciated. "Nice try."

"Sorry. I get used to having to keep my end up here."

"Hard job, is it?"

"Pushy. It's 'on your toes or out'. That's what enterprise is all about, after all."

"Your boss seems a very successful lady. I've met her. Over the matter of her brother's death."

"I thought you must have come about that." May Barling had shed her sparkle. "I was appalled. He was so — alive. Quicksilver, if you know what I mean. And to think he was here that very morning. So full of bounce. The sort to charm the birds right off the trees."

"He was in a happy frame of mind when he left?"

"Full of fun, a real tease. I never knew anyone could get round Ms Sefton the way he did that morning."

"You amaze me."

163

"Funny, isn't it? Especially since she caught him — "

"Up to his tricks?"

"Going through her desk, actually. It wasn't my fault he'd got into the office. Ms Sefton rang through for me to bring some invoices down to her in Dispatch. When we came back he was reading her correspondence. She was livid."

"But he won her round?"

"Must have done. Eventually. He was pleased as Punch when he left. Suggested I went in and asked for a rise, because it was his sister's giving-away day."

"So did you?"

"Not on your life! I couldn't charm her like *he* did. And after the way she went on at him at first! I could hear her out here. She doesn't usually raise her voice when she's wild, but wow! Still, she soon quietened down."

"He was having you on. How could he get anything out of her after she caught him snooping?"

"I was just as unbelieving, but then he waved the notes at me. Fifty pounds! It was true. I checked the petty cash later in her box. Ten fivers were missing, and this morning she put them back."

"What it is to have charisma! I don't suppose he's done that sort of thing before?"

"Sorry, couldn't say. That's the first time I ever saw him. I've only been here five weeks."

And won't be much longer, Yeadings thought, when Erica Sefton discovers what you've spilled. Girl Friday maybe, but never a confidential secretary.

"Well, I mustn't waste your time," he said, rising. "No need to mention I dropped by. A bit thoughtless to try and catch her at work perhaps. Just happened to be passing. I'll give her a ring sometime at home. There's no news to report anyway."

9

AT the Brockham Estate Agency Mr Lever was seeing his visitors to the door, Rosemary tucking under her arm the square envelope containing particulars of the houses for sale which Joel had been expected to check on last Friday. Two were new on the books, the other had once been withdrawn and was now back 'under fresh instructions'. Joel had never reported back on Friday's properties, nor had the firm's expensive camera been returned.

"Something more to try and hook the killer with?" Mott demanded of himself aloud as they made for his car. The camera had been a recent Japanese model; possibly not a lot of them yet in circulation locally. "Might as well let the Incident Room have its particulars before we go on to see the three houses. While I look in there, you can grab something for us to eat *al fresco*. Crunchy rolls with a filling. But avoid canned fish for me."

"Right, sir."

"How did you get on with the girls in the front office?"

"Promising, I think. One agreed to tell me things on a personal level. Then the other volunteered that something about Joel had been slightly bugging her. I'm meeting them after the agency closes this evening."

"No idea what that last thing was?"

"None. Some irregularity, I'd guess. She looked a stickler for doing things according to the book. Maybe he tried his prentice hand on a gazumping exercise and took a cut. I wish we could be sure what sort of person he was."

In the outskirts of Oxford DS Beaumont, with DC Silver struggling over his shorthand notes, was finding it slow work getting a clear picture of the young man so recently done to death.

Tapping his front teeth with a silver propelling pencil, the Academic Secretary had referred to a slim folder containing an assortment of papers of varying colours and sizes. "Somewhat sparse," he complained pettishly. "During the

167

past term Joel Sefton appears to have been economical of his presence." He paused thoughtfully. "Nevertheless, however inadequately he filled his place here, his removal does guarantee a vacancy for one new student, and at an opportune time. Second Year Architecture, h'm. Even at this late date one should be able to find a suitably qualified person among our disappointed entrance candidates."

He looked up, half-moon spectacles gleaming. "I can modestly claim that there is considerable competition among young people anxious to enrol, and here at Oxford we have an enviably low drop-out rate for all subjects."

"That's nice," Beaumont appreciated. "But we still aren't applying. Now what can you tell us personally about the late Joel Sefton?"

"Personally?" the Academic Secretary echoed with distaste. "Nothing at all. For that I must refer you to some member of staff in the discipline he studied. Phyllida, take this folder and show these gentlemen to Mr Howard Dent's room, will you? Good day, gentlemen. It has been a pleasure to be of assistance."

"Thanks for nothing," muttered Beaumont as the door closed after them. The tiny girl alongside entrusted with the few forms available grinned from under her freckles. "Got a touch of down-the-road, Mr Shorthouse has. You know: thinks everything in Oxford is University. Still, so do some of our students. You ought to hear the way they go on outside. 'Up at Oxford' and all that. Dead rotten, I call it. As if the Poly can't stand on its own for what it is!"

"Thank you, lady. You make my three O-levels feel quite respectable after that."

"Only three?" She tossed her head. "You wouldn't get in here with that, I can tell you!"

"Cleaner, lavatory attendant? Surely there's something?"

She gave him a withering glance, thrust the folder on him, knocked at the door they'd stopped beside and left him to it.

Howard Dent belonged more to the world the two policemen inhabited. He expressed regret at the early death, and also that there was little he could offer as funeral eulogy.

"What we're after is a balanced

background, sir," Beaumont told him. "We have the family's views, but they're biased. I'd like to know how he struck you as a person, how he behaved, the sort of friends he made, the sort of things they got up to together."

Dent's bespectacled glance kept going to a half-constructed model of city buildings on a table at the room's far side. He sighed. "I'd recommend the refectory from twelve-thirty onwards. That's where the real chat is, where they dig the dirt, so to speak. But I can certainly give you something to be going on with."

"I interviewed Joel Sefton myself when he applied as a sixth-former for a vacancy. And frankly I was impressed: all the signs of a good beast, as a farmer would say. Clear-eyed enthusiasm. Actually listened to what I had to say. Asked original questions. Definitely possessed of a brain, and with a helluva lot of presentation."

"Presentation?"

"Sold himself well. Put it all up front."

"Confident?"

"Better than that. Confidence overlaid with what I took to be natural modesty. Superb combination. But, as I later discovered, phoney as they come!"

"Go on, sir."

"A robot system. Like adverts' lighting. Brilliant when needed; but when the purpose is served, programmed economy shut-down."

"And you accepted him for the course."

"Recommended him, yes. I confess I bought the glitter. I wasn't personally involved with him during his first term, and such complaints as I came across I was inclined to overlook as based on prejudice or possible envy. Then it was my turn to fit his nose to the grindstone." Dent leaned back, mouth opening and shutting like a fish.

"And?"

"He — bloody — patronized me. Lots of pleasant waffle. No call to be so demanding. Come out on the town with us. See a bit of life before you go brown at the edges. Where, in heaven's name, did he think I'd been while he was cutting his teeth?"

"Bit of a Hooray Henry, you think, sir?"

Dent sat brooding. "More than that," he said at last. "Just an old-fashioned bad hat. No respect for anyone, anything." He stood up and went slowly across to the half-completed model and stood considering it, his back to the others. "No eye for — anything but himself."

"Did you get all that down?" Beaumont demanded of Silver afterwards.

"Everything except the last bit, but he was only talking to himself then."

"Add it on. It's important. So's the list of Joel's fellow students. They may all have to be interviewed eventually. We could get from them what Dent wouldn't be specific about. We'll do what he said; sit in the refectory and mingle with the kids. When his fellow students hear we've come about young Sefton they'll probably fall over themselves to get in on the act."

"More likely clam up."

"In that case there's always one, mate. There just has to be one."

When Silver went across to collect two coffees he was asked for his student ID. He pulled out his warrant card. "How about this? Inquiries re Joel Sefton deceased. Which tables do the architecture lot settle at?"

The refectory manageress nodded to a corner where several chairs were tipped up. Only two students were already sitting at the farthest table, both lean as rakes, the girl with cropped bleached hair, the man with a straggling reddish beard.

The two policemen went across. "Architecture?" Beaumont inquired. "If so, may we join you? We think you could help us."

The pair stared back unblinking, looked at each other for reaction, then simultaneously shrugged.

"John Cole," said the man heavily. "Do we have any choice?"

"Police," the DS explained, offering their names and avoiding a direct answer.

"You didn't have to tell us," said the woman. "Your fame has gone before you. I'm Jane Warren."

That pert little clerk spreading the news, Beaumont thought, and this was confirmed as the woman demanded, "Which three GCE subjects were they?"

Beaumont seated himself opposite and gazed at the ceiling. "Aramaic Cuneiform, Brain Surgery and Bathos. But when *you* answer *me*, I'd like the truth."

173

The other two looked sheepish. "It's about Joel, of course," John Cole supposed. "Not our year. We're one ahead. But the second years will be here any moment now. They knew him better."

"But you at least noticed him. You formed an opinion."

"Cocky," said Cole. "He thought he knew the lot. Anything else was bilge."

"He was like a little boy stuffing cream cakes," Jane offered at almost the same moment.

Again they glanced at each other and looked more sheepish still.

"We seem to have two separate and quite different reactions here," Beaumont observed cautiously. "How come?"

"Jane's a woman," Cole accused. "He did gobble up whatever he could get from that direction."

"And John's a dedicated intellectual snob," she flared back.

Beaumont thought he saw. "He was out for what he could get, er, socially; but he wasn't as open to others' ideas; is that it? Would you say Mr Dent had much the same opinion as yours, Mr Cole?"

"You've been listening to gossip. But

yes, Dent's a decent old codger, experienced and professionally as sound as they come, maybe a trifle nervous of the *avant-garde*."

"And over-sensitive about his pet projects?"

"Ah, the Marvell Development. I'm amazed he mentioned it to you. Yes, Sefton ragged him unmercifully about it. Wouldn't admit that you have to meet the customer's requirements. I mean, you wouldn't push the Post Office Tower on the Prince of Wales as an alternative to Highgrove."

"Even I would see the folly of that," Beaumont admitted.

"It wasn't that Sefton necessarily admired the structurally kinky," Jane reasoned. "He varied his argument according to the antagonist. Argumentative oneupmanship. He just went straight for a natural victim and took the opposite stance."

"And now he's a victim himself." Beaumont swung round in his chair as a stream of ravening young poured through the refectory doors.

"I'll arrange a sort of seminar for you," John Cole offered with faint condescension. "We might get more sense out of them that way."

Joel Sefton's classmates were quite eager to be heard. Murder had a rare allure. All had admiring anecdotes or complaints to air, depending, it seemed, on how long they had been in the dead young man's close company. DC Silver's wrist grew heavy over the notes, and when finally the two policemen left they encountered the refectory manageress again.

"Funny you should be here today asking about that young fellow," she observed.

"Only natural, seeing that he's been killed," Beaumont countered.

"Not here, though. Miles away, and a mugging at that. But it was only on Friday that someone else came looking for him. Fellow about your age, Sergeant; medium height, sandy, slight. Smooth sort normally, I should think, but something was really gnawing at him inside."

"So what happened?"

"He asked around among the students and finally decided they were telling the truth; Mr Sefton hadn't been in that day. I saw the man drive off outside. Nice car, dark blue Saab."

"Doesn't ring a bell with me," Beaumont said. "Better put all that down, Ted. About what time would this be, ma'am?"

"Round about now. Bang in the middle of the lunch rush."

"Well, thanks," said the DS with satisfaction. "That's the most promising titbit so far. Unless, of course, there's a couple of plates of that lasagne stuff going begging."

Issuing from Erica's showrooms in Reading, Detective Superintendent Yeadings looked for the place where Joel might have gone for lunch. After the third pub visited he was ready to call it a day. A ham and cress roll, two pork pies and three halves of bitter had failed to help him pick up the trail of the dead man on the previous Friday.

He was crossing back to go for his car when he spotted the bistro, *Aux Trois Jongleurs*. Well, of course, that smacked more of the right generation. *Crevettes* and white wine, and surely a bright, brittle clientèle.

The pottery plates were cheerfully peasant. He covered one with an assortment

of colourful *crudités*, acquired a glass of
Sancerre at the bar and looked around
for a seat. There appeared just room on a
continuous padded bench that ran across
the room's far end. He made for it only
to see it swooped on by a thin woman
with greyhound tendencies.

"You've gotta grab what y'want here,"
advised a diminutive man at his side.
"Here, mate, stick yer wine on the shelf
while y'tuck in."

"Popular place," Yeadings commented,
twirling his fork in bright shredded
carrot.

"S'all right if you get here early. I got
a bit hung up terday. Mondays they only
use this front room. After midweek they
open up the back. Get a bigger crowd in
then, lot of young Ruperts and Melanies.
A right fruity crowd, they are."

"That so? I imagine Friday's the big
day."

"I should say so! — pay day and all.
Know what they was up to, end of last
week?"

"I can't imagine."

"No, well, you wouldn't. Cutting up
their credit cards. Right little ritual they

had, all sitting round in a circle on the floor like Red Injuns, chanting and making up rhymes. Clever, some of it." He sounded wistful, as if his youth hadn't included much that was carefree.

"Sounds like quite a party. I wonder the manager didn't damp it down."

"Not he! Likes a bit of fun himself. And they're good customers. Borrowed a big steel bowl from the kitchen for the bit at the end, and the cards were all snipped to pieces. One of the lads was High Priest, dressed himself up in a tablecloth."

Yeadings looked suspiciously round. "I don't see any tablecloths."

"They have them for evenings. More upmarket lot comes in then. Different grub. The cloths are kept under the back-room bar."

"D'you know," Yeadings declared, setting down his empty plate beside his wine glass, "this sounds just the sort of thing my young nephew would get up to. He told me about this place but he isn't in here today. Probably you know him. Got a snapshot of him somewhere. Hang on."

He put on a show of patting his pockets

and finally extracted the photograph of Joel Sefton given him by Josie. "Handsome young stallion, isn't he?"

"Lordy, that's him! That's the one I was telling you about."

"And this was Friday? If only I'd known. I wasn't far away that lunch-time. Missed all the fun." His voice expressed regret while mentally he kept his fingers crossed that the man hadn't yet seen the newspapers with Joel's face under the banner headline 'Local Man Murdered'.

"Well, nice meeting you. Guess I'd better get back to the grind," said the new friend. He deposited his empty plate and glass, then eased off through the crowd.

Give it half an hour, Yeadings decided, and they will have thinned enough for me to get through to the manager, ask for a fuller account of Friday's cult scene. Meanwhile — he raised his glass above the heads and nodded across to the barmaid — "Sancerre, when you've a minute, love."

DI Mott and Rosemary Z shared their picnic lunch in the car between the first and second properties which Joel had

180

been expected to check on the previous Friday. There was no way of knowing in what order he had visited them, so they took the farthest first, a gentrified pair of thatched cottages on a hillside near Pangbourne.

Alterations to turn them into a credible single unit were almost complete and the harassed owner, who had persisted in staying on during modifications, began pouring out a string of complaints against the Brockham Agency. It took time to persuade him that Mott's questions had no connection with the intended sale. Finally, however, when he had been almost bodily pushed into one of his dust-sheeted bamboo chairs and the warrant card thrust into his hands, he did gather that a police inquiry was behind the visit.

"Lever's young man?" he asked. "You mean he's been *murdered*? And I was one of the last to see him? Oh my God! I needed this! I really needed this!"

Reassured that he was not immediately at risk of arrest and soothed — this Mott left in disgust to Rosemary's more tender approach — Mr Frobisher eventually recovered sufficiently to tell them that not one but two of the Brockham staff had arrived to view progress on the rebuilding, but the young lady had stayed in the car. No, he hadn't seen her face, couldn't describe her. Mr Sefton he had met before, in the shop. Not a very helpful person, in fact damn offhand and barely stayed long enough on Friday to say howdo. Taken all round, the attitude of the firm left much to be desired. He heartily regretted letting them have sole agency rights on the sale.

Time? — he looked wildly round him as though it was something he'd never heard of and was unwilling to encounter. Oh, it had been some time in the afternoon. Two, three, something like that. No, he didn't wear a watch when he was working, and the grandfather clock was covered over until the last of the plaster had been cleared away.

"You meet them all in this job," Mott claimed, laughing in spite of himself as they drove away. "Next, Orwell Close, Caversham Heights. People called Dunbar."

The Dunbars were not at home, but

their next-door neighbour came scuttling up the drive to see what it was they wanted, hunched against the blustery wind and holding her hair on with one hand while she shouted information.

Dot and Harold, it seemed, were both working, couldn't easily take time off without giving prior notice, but they'd both managed to be there on Friday all day. After all, selling your house was a big thing. And then the wretched estate agent never came. As bad as the plumbers, always letting you down. But you'd think, with all the fees they take, and the little they ever do, house agents would be a bit keener. Well, wouldn't you?

"Not much farther, are we?" Mott asked Rosemary. "Apparently these clients weren't given a precise time for Joel's visit, so we can't tell in which order he intended taking the properties. Maybe the next call will help to clarify."

It seemed unlikely when they arrived. The house, large and detached, was clearly empty. The Brockham *For Sale* board swinging above the gate offered viewing by appointment only.

"Joel would have had a key to get in,"

Rosemary said. "This is the one that was taken off the market, then put back with fresh instructions. That usually means a cut in price. I suppose he was coming just to check everything was all right here."

"And we're going to do the same," Mott declared firmly. "Just turn your innocent eyes away while I find a window open at the rear."

She heard a faint groaning of wood followed by a click of metal on glass. "Right. Fancy that, now. Looks as though someone's tried to break in. We'd better check through the house, then let Lever know. You up first. I'll give you a hoist."

Mott rolled over the sill after her. They were in a downstairs cloakroom. The door was unlocked and opened directly into a square hall. Together they went from room to empty room. Apart from junk mail that lay over the floor behind the front door and a faint pervasive smell of mould, there was little worthy of note.

"Upstairs?" Rosemary asked. "Is there any point?"

"Might as well. It's rather a nice place,

really. Pity it's been neglected. It's harder to sell a place once the furniture's taken out. I wonder what happened."

The master bedroom and its dressing-room were bare. So were the next two. In one bathroom a ring of sand marked where the lavatory water-level had originally stood, but in the farther one this had partly cleared. Mott looked at it consideringly. He nodded to Rosemary to keep behind him, then went forward quietly to the last, closed door.

When he threw the door back — anti-climax. Nothing there but an old single bed with mattress and a grey army — surplus blanket hanging off the near side.

"Did you think someone was in here?" Almost absently Rosemary lifted the blanket and put its corners together. Mott came over beside her to stand looking from the window, and his toe struck against something hard on the floorboards under the bed.

"Someone was here lately," he said. "The loo's been flushed." He stooped, making a sweep with one hand to find what he had kicked. It came out with a compact Yashika camera in it.

"And I guess we know who."

"But how did he come to leave that behind?"

Mott frowned. "Damn. Now it's got my dabs on." He laid it on the bed, took out a handkerchief and lifted the camera inside it. "Walk round the outside of the room to the door, Z. Then go down and radio in for the SOCO team to come out. I want this place gone over with a fine-tooth comb."

When Rosemary returned and halted at the door Mott was still standing there. Correct according to the book, she noted, amused: hands safely in pockets, eyes and ears open. Blood and/or a weapon, she guessed, were what he hoped a scientific examination of the house and garden would throw up.

"Mr Atkinson's sending the experts right away," she reported. "We're to wait for them to arrive." She put her own hands in her jacket pockets. "So is this the scene of the crime?"

"Not necessarily. There are aspects of bed that can make a man walk away forgetful of more mundane matters, even

186

an expensive camera. If valuables can be left in taxis and on trains, how much more likely when pushed out of sight in post-coitus circumstances like these."

She regarded the mattress. "Aren't you reading a lot into it? All we know from that camera is that he was here."

"And started out with a girl companion."

"Do you think it was a girl who struck him, perhaps in self-defence, hit too hard and killed him, then mutilated his features in a fit of rage or panic? That's possible, I suppose. But how about getting the body down into the car and transporting it to central Reading?"

"She didn't have to do it on her own. Maybe there was time to drive to a telephone-box and summon a friend, someone who'd be angry enough at a story of near-rape to help cover up. Then she could have gone elsewhere to establish an alibi. It's only one possible scenario, but I must say I fancy it. What are you smiling at, Z?"

"I'm just waiting to hear Mr Yeadings say, '*Cherchez la femme*'!"

The smile Mott returned was slow

to develop. She sensed in him a new tautness. "You may be a step ahead of him there. Haven't you arranged a meeting later with the two girls from the Brockham Agency?"

10

THEY left as the scenes of crime experts started to arrive, and on their way back received a message that Detective Superintendent Yeadings wanted them both in his office at 19.30 hrs.

"That gives us time for a bite of something beforehand," Mott considered. "Now, about your meeting with the estate agency girls. If you're not expecting trouble there, it may well break out: Sod's Law. I want you covered, just in case. They've seen me, so it will have to be another officer. How about your uniform partner? Would he be suitable to lurk alongside unnoticed?"

"He'd give his eye-teeth to be in on the case. And he lives close enough to get home and change."

"Right. I'll set it up. Whatever happens, don't let them change the venue you've arranged. Got that?"

"Yessir. Guv."

"God. You can drop me near the Hexagon and I'll walk through. Park by the caravan and get your notes made up while you're waiting. Mr Yeadings will want to have all the details piping hot tonight."

As the lunch-time customers thinned in the bistro Mike Yeadings had made his way by stages towards the man in charge. "Nice place you have here," he commented, handing over the price of a fresh cup of coffee. "Seems popular."

The man looked him over as Mike reached inside his jacket for the warrant card. "No need to flash that. I know one when I see one. What's up, then?"

"Like to join me?" Yeadings invited, indicating his cup.

"Why not? Choose a table. I'll be across in a minute."

He came with his own coffee and two globes of something amber-coloured on a tray. "Since you're not in uniform, I'm not risking my licence with this. Barry Whitaker's the name. Now, what's the trouble?"

"This young man." Yeadings put Joel

Sefton's photograph on the table.

Whitaker picked it up and nodded. "Often comes in. Not regular, but four, five times a month. 'Came', I suppose I should say."

"You knew he was dead?"

"Saw his photograph in the paper. Not this one, though. A studio portrait. This one's more him. Mugged, it said."

"Maybe. The newspapers don't always get it right. When did you see him last?"

"Friday. I know that because I worked it out when I read the bit about him. It was the same day he was killed, Nineteen, eh? Bloody waste. He was a fireball, all energy. Had a right little harem of his own used to gather. Fellows too, but he was the pack leader, the guru or whatever. Full of it, he was, kept them happy with his tricks and stories. A performer. Should have been on the stage. Or in my business."

"And on Friday — they were up to something special?"

"I couldn't help sympathize. They were all grouching about overspending on their credit cards; how once they got straight they were going to pack it all in. So he said, 'Why not now? Let's do that thing. Let's scissor the lot and then burn them.' Little Dave was sent off to get his shears — he's in the rag trade — and they all sat round on the floor in the back room having a party over it.

"Lot of silly giggling at first, then it took off, Guess Who in the chair. Started making rhymes. One went, 'Access, Visa, Lloyds, Natwest, Let's do what we know is best.' Then they all screeched like a lot of witches and threw their charge cards into the centre."

"One of the girls got on her knees and stirred them all up together, squawking, 'Hocus pocus, fiscal focus. Pox on all the banks that soak us.' Then more squawks and screeches. One of the lads did that *Macbeth* bit with eye of newt and something of toad, but all muddled up with debt and Barclaycards.

"It wasn't just them by that point. Some of the other customers had joined in, old enough to know better, but they like a bit of fun. The cards were all put in a bowl we keep back there, passed round, and each of them in turn ceremonially snipped one in two. They were going to set fire to the remains but enough's enough. I checked that all the cards were useless by then and finally we binned them."

"Ritual slaughter of the credit system," Yeadings appreciated. "A lot of people feel that way. Certainly I did after last Christmas. I expect your little lot all popped into their banks first thing this morning and applied for a new card to replace the 'lost' one."

"A bit of harmless fun," said Whitaker. "At least the lad enjoyed his last day. That part of it anyway."

Yeadings watched the long, flat face displaying evidence of sorrow, and suspended judgement. He wasn't satisfied that Whitaker had seen it all as harmless fun. The man's grey eyes stayed cold and wary. He was careful of his licence and premises. Towards the end of Joel's fun he had stepped in, stopping them short of setting fire to the plastic.

It wasn't beyond belief that he would pull the young man in, once on his own, and deliver a strong warning. If so, could this have gone farther and led to blows? From all accounts Joel Sefton had a robust ego and wouldn't take kindly to personal criticism.

The wine bar was only a few streets away from where the body was found. And when it came to disposal, weren't jumbo-sized refuse bins just the solution that would occur to a man involved in the catering industry?

'Suspect everyone' was a maxim he constantly drilled into CID. To Yeadings it was as much a part of him as his avuncular approach and expressive eyebrows. Nothing that Whitaker had said, in words or body language, eliminated him from the role of suspect.

"How about the lads and lasses with young Sefton?" he pursued, offering a new angle for comment.

Whitaker shrugged. "Regular customers. We get a lot of youngsters in, but mostly evenings. The lot that were with him on Friday come and go, in pairs or groups, sometimes singly. I don't know their names. They don't use their plastic here. We operate on a cash only basis."

"You must occasionally pick up a name. Joel Sefton himself — "

"I told you. I read about him in the newspaper, recognized his face. Actually I had heard him called by name, but I thought it was Joe."

Reasonable, Yeadings thought. But the man was getting just a little nervous. "You did give me one name," he reminded him. "Young Dave, who was sent for his shears. I take it he didn't have far to go to get them?"

"Oh him, sure. He works in Samuels', the tailor round the back. It's an old-fashioned firm, still does some handsewn suits, but mostly finishing and alterations locally for the multiple stores. Number twenty-three, if you want to go and see him. A door between the Health Stores and the greengrocer. Just ring and go up the stairs."

"You know it well."

"Old Samuels makes my waiters' uniform trousers. Gets the cloth wholesale from Finland."

"And when the party broke up on Friday, what time would that be?"

Whitaker took time to reply. "It would be one-twenty, one-twenty-five, when I stopped the fun. Most of them stayed on

195

another half-hour, I think."

"And Sefton?"

"He — left rather sooner."

"Alone?"

"No. There were three of them. He left with Dave and a girl, the one who'd stirred all the cards up."

"And whose name you don't happen to know."

Whitaker appeared to think about this. "It could be Myra. Something like that."

"Thank you." In any case he could have got that information from 'Young Dave', so Whitaker hadn't made much of a gift there. "And a very pleasant cognac, that," Yeadings conceded, making moves to go.

His visit to the tailor's shop was brief, and questioning yielded only the fact that Myra was a student. Of Reading University, Dave thought; subject and faculty unknown. And no, he'd never heard her family name. Yeadings had the impression that he thought her rather upmarket and was accordingly too in awe to be familiar. On their being *chucked out* of the wine bar he'd left the two others at the end of the street.

Which is where I'd better leave this and get back to base, Yeadings decided. I've strayed far enough on others' preserves. Time now for them to take over my findings. I'll get Angus and his team in together this evening and we'll see what the day's dredged up.

They crowded into the Superintendent's office; Angus and DS Beaumont, DC Silver and Rosemary Z. Angus listed the directions inquiries had taken, then left it to the others to report individually. After Beaumont's résumé of his findings at Oxford Poly there was general discussion.

"So," Yeadings recapped, "that seems to confirm the general impression of a heartless charmer who could excite pretty extreme reactions, but it was a no-go for filling in his last day. The one point of interest is this anonymous man who's on his trail. Did he catch up with young Sefton, and if so, what occurred? I want the refectory manageress's description circulated and all officers to be on the lookout for him. He's not particularly distinctive but, if not the actual killer, he may be peripheral to the action elsewhere, so stay alert for anyone remotely like the description."

"DI Mott will be referring later to a brief visit Sefton paid to the Brockham Estate Agency on Friday morning soon after leaving home. As it happens, I can account for his movements myself for the time between then and about one-twenty-five p.m." And Yeadings gave details of his own visit to the Florafaun Frames showroom, followed by the reported incident at the wine bar. At its end he asked for DI Mott's comments.

"It covers the gap," he agreed. "Several questions arise. First, was the 'borrowed' fifty pounds a gift, a loan, or extracted by menaces from his sister? If either of the first two she must be a great deal more kindly, or simple-minded, than I had judged. Those who knew Joel Sefton longest all seem to mistrust his motives. And Erica Sefton is outstandingly practical — especially, I imagine, in matters of finance. I should very much like to know what Joel discovered by searching his sister's desk. While she was detained down in Dispatch, had she left some private papers open to prying eyes? Some delicate matter she preferred not to have bruited abroad?"

"Blackmail," Beaumont said. "Why not? According to the Oxford lot, oneupmanship was the name of his game."

"Secondly," Mott went on as the others nodded agreement, "what happened to the fifty pounds? Did Joel actually purchase an antique ring on which he'd already paid a deposit? Or did he blow some of the money on food and drinks with, or for, his friends in the wine bar?"

"Sorry, I should have mentioned," Yeadings said. "They all paid for themselves at the counter as they took what they wanted. I checked that with the girl on duty."

"Or did he still have that amount on him when he was attacked and robbed?"

"Make a note, Z," the Superintendent put in. "To find out if a list was kept of the numbers of the petty cash banknotes."

"And finally," Mott went on, "I'd like to know whether this Myra of the wine bar and Reading University could be a girl seen with Sefton later that afternoon on the house calls he made for the Brockham Agency."

"Ah," said Beaumont, leaning forward. It was his voice which, with relish, uttered the expected, "*Cherchez la femme.*" Mott caught Rosemary's amused glance on him and smothered a smile.

"Which brings us back to your report, Angus." Yeadings prompted.

"In the morning we interviewed Mr Frank Lever of the Brockham Estate Agency who was cooperative about the properties Sefton would have visited during the past seven weeks or so, while he's been helping the office out. Not so forthcoming or frank about the sort of person he found him. He was certainly disillusioned, but felt himself under some kind of obligation to the mother. More than a little in awe of her. WPC Zyczynski contrived to make an appointment with both the girl assistants for this evening. We then visited the three properties Sefton was expected to call at on Friday.

"Unfortunately we didn't know what order he would take them in, but if he left the wine bar at one-twenty-five p.m. it's possible we started off at the same house he did. The vendor, a Mr Frobisher, was very vague about times. Two or three o'clock was the nearest he could get, but he was considerably annoyed by the briefness of the visit and Sefton's offhand manner. He also mentioned a girl waiting outside in the car, whose face he hadn't seen. No description, except that she had a lot of fair hair. Which might have described the younger girl employed at the Brockham agency.

"Our next call was at a property in Caversham Heights, where Sefton had failed to turn up at all on Friday; but at our third we hit pay dirt, so to speak. An empty house, with one upstairs room having a bed-frame, mattress and ex-army blanket. Forensic are doing tests. We thought this worth while because hidden under the bed we found the Brockham camera used to photograph properties coming on the market. There were no evident signs of a struggle, nothing broken, no visible bloodstains, no weapon."

"But you thought the killing could have happened there," Yeadings said slowly, measuring the others' reactions by their expressions.

"Yes. It was isolated enough for no one to hear shouts or notice cars leaving. And we don't know how long Sefton and the girl stayed on there. Long enough, probably, to make it out of the question to go on to the third call. Or else, of course, he couldn't go because he was already dead."

"Time of death," Yeadings put in, "is something I'll be dwelling on later. Leave that for the moment. Obviously reports will be coming in from forensic to confirm or otherwise what you think went on at the empty house. There's one more report. Right, Z?"

"I met the estate agent's assistants at the buttery as arranged," she said, "with PC Finlay in plain clothes covering my back in case there was trouble. There wasn't.

"The younger one, Pat Morphew, wanted to tell me about a brief affair she'd had with Joel and how heart-broken she was when it faded out. She denied being the blonde in Joel's car when he called at the first house, having been at work all day. The other, Enid Bowyer, was older, more of a dedicated spinster. She was worried because she suspected Joel had been up to something professionally questionable.

"An assistant from the locksmith and security-alarm shop in Silver Street had been in to tell her that Joel had taken in half a dozen keys to have duplicates cut. Obviously estate agents have to be very careful about that sort of thing, because new people moving in don't always change the locks on their doors immediately although advised to. Well, he'd not have thought much about it except that payment was made by Joel's personal cheque. I suppose he felt safe from suspicion or got careless. Anyway, the man started worrying and took his fears to Miss Bowyer. She said she would deal with it, but she had put off speaking to Joel until she'd decided just what he was up to. She didn't report it to Mr Lever either, but she thought we ought to know in case it was relevant. I think she was afraid Joel would take clients around privately and make secret deals with them outside the firm. But, in view of what we found today, it could merely be that he needed venues for his fancied dalliance."

"Thank you. Comments, anybody? If not we'll go on to what I mentioned before. Time.

"Time, as ever, is our taskmaster. Whatever hour it was when Sefton left that empty house, either alive or dead, there remains a gap until late on that night. I'll remind you of the chronological order of things then.

"We know that at ten-fifty-seven a ticket was taken from the car park machine and left in Joel Sefton's car. At 'a few minutes before eleven' according to witness Mrs Tolley, she saw someone roughly answering to the dead man's description taking the ticket and walking with it towards a car which her husband described, and which was identical in make to that of Joel Sefton. From this we can, I think, safely assume that there was no trickery in the obtaining of the ticket. It showed the correct time it was actually left in the car."

"Indicating that Joel Sefton had just driven in, alive." DS Beaumont insisted on pushing it one step further. Yeadings merely raised bushy eyebrows at the interruption. He resumed.

"The anonymous 999 call reporting the finding of the body was booked at eleven-twelve p.m. We have a lapse here of only fifteen minutes. Can we believe that during that short time — " He was interrupted this time by DI Mott thumping the table with his fist and muttering between clamped teeth, "Should have seen that."

"Hold on just a wee while, Angus. What should he have seen, Silver?"

"Fifteen minutes seems a bit short for Sefton to have locked the car, the Tolleys to have got into theirs, clipped on their seat-belts and driven away, then someone to have crept up on Sefton, slugged him, slashed his face, removed him to the rubbish area, rifled his pockets, hidden him, and gone away *without being noticed* by the person — a man — who phoned in sounding drunk."

"Anyone can work fast when he has to," Beaumont objected.

"So do you think," Yeadings pursued, giving Rosemary the nod, "that in our informant we have a potential witness to at least a part of the crime?"

"Or the killer himself."

"DS Beaumont, how d'you like that?"

"Better. Ted left out something important that also had to be crammed into the time-limit. The man who made the 999 call had to get to a phone-box. The nearest is functioning now, but I checked and it was out of order all Friday and Saturday morning. Even by car it would have taken — I timed this — three and a half minutes to get back to a car, unlock it, drive out, try the first box and then get to the next. Allow possible extra time to urinate and recover from the shock of finding a body, let alone get fuddled wits working. Working backwards, the latest he could have sighted it is 11.08 — eleven minutes after Sefton took that ticket from the machine. Small wonder our appeal for the man who phoned to come forward hasn't had any result. He had to be the one who did it. Or else people were bobbing in and out of that car park like a West End farce."

"So your scenario has a distant phone-box in it? There's an alternative. Not the majority of car owners, but a growing number, have car phones. Even more business men carry their own cordless one. The communications firms involved are already helping us with a list of local names. Not that the man in question is necessarily from these parts.

He looked round at the others. "Anyone else have something to add on the witness/killer option before I ask DI Mott to drop his bombshell? No? Right then, Angus. Tell us now what it is you ought to have seen."

Grim-faced, the DI took over. "We don't yet have the full report from the post-mortem, but I was at the on-site examination with Dr Littlejohn. The body was cool, but actually so was I — on the surface; the wind was freshening. Littlejohn took the initial temperature reading, rectal of course, and kept it to himself. But he did make one comment, to the effect that I should observe the early signs of rigor. I left it to him to elaborate on and didn't include it in my notes. In fact it never properly registered.

"At that time the Tolley evidence of Sefton's arrival wasn't to hand, but in view of it and the early onset of rigor there's only one conclusion to be drawn. The young man who took the ticket and returned with it to Sefton's car was not the one killed. The body must have been already dead, whether stashed behind the bins or not. I'm sorry, sir — everyone — I've wasted time over this."

"But Mrs Tolley's description!" Rosemary objected. "Quite unprompted, she described the dead man, even to the style of dressing."

"So, unless she was badly out over the time, perhaps we have a description of the killer. Almost certainly of the person who drove the car there. Do we believe he also brought the body in it?"

Yeadings sighed and picked up some papers from beside him. "We do now have the preliminary report from the post-mortem. The time of death given has wider margins than usual: between four-thirty and eight-thirty on Friday afternoon. Certainly nowhere near eleven p.m."

There was a general stirring as they took in the new estimate. "Why so wide an estimate?" Beaumont demanded.

"Because possibly the body was kept artificially warm before being dumped in the open; near a boiler or open fire, or if in the car then wrapped in some way. Examination of post-mortem staining and other flesh marks is continuing."

"Friday afternoon," Rosemary marvelled. "It all turns on where he went from that empty house. Or on whether he was killed there."

"How about our unknown from Oxford?" asked DC Silver, breaking his silence. "The one asking the refectory manageress for Sefton, Friday lunch-time." He opened his notebook to the last page of entries. "Medium height, smooth, sandy. Could that be the one seen parking Sefton's car? In Oxford he was seen driving a dark blue Saab. Flashy, that. Might well be the sort to have a car phone."

"Could be." Yeadings nodded. "A warning, though. So far we're just letting our imaginations run loose on this. Remember there are a lot of options. Go first for what your nose tells you, but still keep sniffing over your shoulder."

11

AT his chief's nod Mott stayed behind while the others dismissed. "God, I boobed over that time of death."

"Bad, that. Still, we all make 'em, lad. If life was fair our new cases would arrive with the new day and not when we're already worked half silly. Tell me, how's young Z shaping up?"

"She's sharp. Increasingly keen as she gets the scent."

Yeadings's face eased into a leathery smile. "Sounds as though she needs a dog-handler rather than you."

Mott shrugged. "Now that you mention handling, she's got on the wrong side of Beaumont. I meant to team them together, but I haven't fixed it yet."

"It might be a good thing to make the change now. Until there's some news of chummy with the Saab, you'd better take the University end, look for Sefton's girlfriend Myra. Also check at the bistro,

Aux Trois Jongleurs. Join in the student fun, all-kids-together stuff. Don't tell me you're too adult, Angus. One of your famous grins and you're the answer to every Sloane's prayer. See what you can pick up. In the info line, I mean. Is DC Silver up to pairing with you?"

"If he isn't he damn well should be."

"Better not put too much on Z. We don't really know what that mugging did to her nerve. She has yet to prove herself in action. Send her out to Callendar Lane with Beaumont. He can run a second check on the dead man's affairs. With a house of that size I very much doubt Joel kept all his belongings in a single room. Which leaves Z free to have another woman-to-woman with the younger Sefton daughter — Josie, isn't it?"

He swivelled in his chair to look up at Angus. "So what about Beaumont? Not nursing an ulcer, is he? We didn't get a single flat pun out of him this evening."

Mott hesitated. "I heard there's a bit of domestic trouble. He hasn't asked for leave, so until he does I'm acting deaf Nelson. His humour's certainly gone sour on him and he doesn't miss a chance to beef about women."

"Nice for Z. Can she cope with that?"

"It's like water off a duck's back. You'd think he wasn't there. That's partly why I want them teamed together, to force her to react, because there's a lot she could learn from him, and you don't lift much from an invisible man."

"Right. That's it, then. I'll see that Action Allocation knows what's what." Yeadings tapped his teeth with the end of a ballpoint. "I think I'd like a private word, if Z's still around. You can send her along with some papers."

Mott nodded. He could guess what Yeadings had in mind, the canny old codger.

Rosemary appeared shortly, bearing not only a file tucked under one arm but a carefully balanced coffee. "The Guv looks a bit down," Mott had told her. "Get him a mug of instant with two sugars. Better take some papers with you as an excuse. Can't make it look as if we're cosseting him."

He did look jaded, she acknowledged. The strain of the job wasn't all on one's

212

feet, or a matter of slammed car doors and haring off at an instant's notice. Much of the stress was back here at base, in uncounted hours of sieving and collating, searching for the one significant drop in an ocean of facts.

"Back again?" he asked, with apparent surprise.

"Something DI Mott thought you should have," she said ambiguously.

"Half the offering is very welcome. Papers I have a surplus of. Thanks." He cleared a small space on his desk. "Well, how's it going, Z?"

She knew he didn't mean the case progress. He, if anyone, had all that sussed. "It's great."

"M'm. The thrill of the chase. It gets to us all. There's something else, though." He leaned back and appeared to be searching for words.

"At some later point it can hit you: that they're *people*. It's a man-hunt and what you feel is bloodlust." He was watching her under the bushy brows. "I thought I'd warn you. Your first murder case. Tell yourself thank God we don't hang them any more. Then keep right on at it. OK?"

213

"I'll remember. Thank you, sir."

" 'Boss'. You're one of the team now."

"Boss, sir. Yes. Can I ask a question, Boss? DI Mott's sending me out to the Sefton home again tomorrow."

"So?"

"If I'm asked about this crime in relation to the muggings, do I let on that we're now treating this murder as something quite separate?"

"If that is your personal opinion, why not?"

"But it's not yet the official line?"

"For my sins, Z, I've two appointments tomorrow morning. One is factual and detailed, with the Chief Constable, but the second is with the press. In their case some of the leads we're following will have to be hinted at — just enough for the media to weave their own assumptions into. If you take much the same line with the family they will then be better prepared for what they later read in their newspapers."

She gave him a long, hard stare. What he also meant was that if she went too far it would be on her own head and he could later deny any part in it.

214

As though he read her mind he nodded slowly. "If the family — or even one member of it — finds you sympathetic, then you'll have their confidence. Feel your way, Z. Give a little, but always get a little more back. And keep me informed how you get on."

He watched her go thoughtfully out, then cleared her from his mind. He had hoped to get home tonight before Nan put the children to bed, but already it was too late. Tomorrow's meetings required him to be familiar with all the new material and to know exactly where he stood on the investigation so far. Then at least another half-hour to get his next moves set up.

There were times when he wondered which of the two was more his adversary, his senior officers or the media pack. Both seemed equally ready to gun him down if progress wasn't at the rate expected.

He rubbed a hand wearily over his eyes and pulled the next bunch of reports towards him.

It was something to be grateful for that the Chief Constable was to come down from Kidlington, saving Yeadings from any need to break off contact with the case while he brought the Old Man up to date. Weighing against that advantage was the fact that Chief Superintendent Minns could now act host, sitting in on their interview like the acidic chairman of some television quizz show.

The CC was perfectly capable of reading reports for himself. He could get at what lay between the lines every bit as well as Yeadings could sow the hints there, but his presence in the flesh was two things more: it signalled officially that he was expecting results, and that quickly; and it was his opportunity to see for himself what sort of form Yeadings was in — flagging, flummoxed or flailing.

For this reason Mike Yeadings took great care with his turnout next morning; second-best grey suit, maroon and white striped shirt, and — after consulting Nan — a plain maroon tie. There hadn't been time to sit about at the hairdresser's awaiting his turn, so he'd got her to trim the bits over his ears and above his collar.

It was galling after all that to realize,

as he seated himself in the Chief Super's room and nonchalantly crossed one knee over the other, that his socks weren't a pair. He pulled his feet back under his chair; gone his sangfroid. He scowled at the immaculate senior officers facing him, conscious that discomfort was the message that had gone screaming out in his body language.

"I don't know why you should look so fierce, Superintendent," the CC remarked mildly. "I thought that in a short time you had thrown up one or two promising leads."

Minns's thin face took on a spinsterly look of echoed approval only to wipe it off as the Chief went on. "I need hardly stress that since this case now seems unrelated to the earlier muggings, over which we've shown conspicuous lack of success, it's essential that it should be cleared up rapidly. Particularly as the dead man's family is one respected for service to the local community — and therefore of special interest to the press. Perhaps you would indicate the direction in which the main thrust of your inquiry is now being made."

What the hell, Yeadings asked himself, do socks matter? If I'd come bare-toed in Jesus sandals, I'd still be the best jack in the bunch. The Old Man was a good one himself in his day, so — copper to copper — here goes . . . "

DC Silver drove into Reading University precinct on the dot of nine, decanted DI Mott before the main administrative building and went in search of a legitimate parking space for visitors.

Having an LL. B. to your credit made a difference, Mott admitted. True, his had been gained the hard way, as an external student, and he'd missed out on the social ambience of student life, but it did mean he hadn't an exaggerated respect for academic set-ups. Nor did he suffer the opposite reaction which Beaumont, for one, displayed, implying that intellectuals were incapable of common sense or of recognizing any need to speak the truth when questioned by the arm of the Law.

Accordingly Angus grinned cheerfully at the porter who inquired his business, waved a vague arm and followed the arrow indicating College Office. There he met with cautious helpfulness. "I should think it's possible, depending on the computer," a middle-aged lady informed him.

Depending on — the terminal not having hiccupped or not already being queued upon? Or on its having successfully reached familiar forename terms with its students? Surely the lady was being over-cautious. He followed her advice and sat back while a printout was requested.

Fourteen Myras in an undergraduate student population of roughly five and a half thousand, of whom fifty per cent were female! He'd had no idea the name was so popular. He hoped Yeadings's informants had been right, and that it wasn't a mispronounced Mary he was after.

Eight of the names on his list were personally known to staff in the office, being senior students who had had repeated problems over courses or grants. He held up the bureaucratic machine while staff gathered round, providing descriptions for these eight, the personal details quoted becoming more bizarre as routine was evaded and hilarity grew. None of the Myras quoted sounded particularly like the girl whom Dave, the apprentice tailor, had sketched for the Boss. Of the six remaining Myras two were freshers that term, and although Joel might have known a local schoolgirl before the university term started, Mott considered that a student of only a few days would hardly yet be roistering in a town wine-bar at lunch-time. He therefore determined to seek out first the remaining four. On a fresh sheet of his notebook he listed — Myra Hennessey, 2nd year Mathematics; Myra Hope-Gore, final year Business Studies; Myra Jones, 2nd year English; Myra Withers, 3rd year Law. Under each he added her local address and left a gap for description and report.

Chasing them up and interviewing them all could take him well past midday, but if he hadn't run the right one to earth by then he would get back to the *Trois Jongleurs* area and see who turned up of the Joel Sefton fan club.

WPC Zyczynski took an early bus to work, so when DS Beaumont called for her at her lodgings he had a lost journey. He arrived at his desk scowling and ready to cast blame.

"You should have told me you intended lifting me," she said coolly when he complained.

"Look," he ground out, glaring with his face too close, "we have the one car between us, right? So whoever drives picks up. Time you picked up a few ideas about how things are run in CID."

She stepped back, head tilted, letting her gaze rove over his flushed face, not missing the square centimetre of bloody tissue stuck on the edge of his jaw where he'd nicked himself shaving. His shirt was clean but hadn't been ironed and she recognized the storm signals. "I'm not psychic," she told him equably. "I'm sure you can put me wise to your ways as we go along. Who better?"

He looked uncertain whether to shout her down or shrug it off. In the event he turned on his heel and made for the door. "Come on, then."

There was no call, Rosemary thought, to make pleasant conversation on the way. He was a more than adequate driver. She sat back to give him a clear view when turning, but halfway down Callendar Lane she swivelled in her seat to look after a car they had passed head on.

"That was the mother," she said. "Mrs Harriet Sefton. No passenger, so we'll probably find Josie on her own."

"Red Mercedes, this year's registration?" Beaumont queried.

"I wouldn't know. I've never seen her car before, but I'm sure it was her." She didn't need it spelled out that in the DS's view she was being observant about the wrong things. The damn man wasn't going to admit she could do anything right. Well, if he wanted it that way she could play too. Rivals, not partners.

She slipped out of the car first, giving the impression to Josie who had come out to meet them that Beaumont was just her driver.

"Hullo," Josie greeted her. "You've just missed Mother, I'm afraid. She won't be back until tea-time. Is there any news? Oh sorry, do come in."

They went through to the kitchen where, in Mrs Lavender's absence, Josie started up the coffee machine. It was a room out of a glossy advert, with gleaming teak and stainless steel, double ceramic hob, swagged muslin at the two wide windows. Rosemary smiled wanly; she had to go down one landing to fill her electric kettle, but at least she used the same brand of ground coffee.

"There's nothing worth reporting yet," she admitted, "but we have two or three useful leads, arising from your brother's activities that last day."

Josie stopped in the middle of lifting crockery from a dresser. "But — do you mean it was someone he knew who killed him? Why should you think that?"

Rosemary sat on a stool and frowned down at her hands. "I'm supposed to be the one asking the questions, but I will tell you one thing. It's more complicated than it seemed at first. We think there was an attempt to cover up some of the facts."

"Well, there would be, surely. I mean, this time it was murder — much more serious than a mugging. Whoever did it, whatever the circumstances, went too far. He'd be scared stiff of being caught, wouldn't he?"

"And so more likely to cut and run. But this one kept his wits about him, tried to cover his tracks."

"And that's all you're going to tell me? What about Joel's activities that day? Mother said he would be calling on Mr Lever before going on to Oxford. Did he?"

"Yes, but it seems that afterwards there were some visits he had to make for the estate agency, so in the end he didn't get to the Poly. We don't know all the details yet. Miss Sefton, did he ever confide to you how he felt about his course there? Was architecture his first choice for a career?"

Josie gave a little grunt. "Confide? That wasn't a thing Joel ever did. Whatever he thought or felt he always kept inside."

"You make him sound insecure."

"Secretive certainly. Maybe it *was* defensive. He had a habit of ferreting out everyone else's private concerns while making quite certain no one could find out anything about him."

"And making use of the information? As leverage?"

"Oh God, he's dead. What does it matter now?"

"Because by ferreting around as you

224

say, he might have upset someone enough for them to — "

"To want to *kill him*?"

"It's possible to kill without meaning to. A single blow did it this time. It just took someone to be furious enough to lash out once."

Josie turned a white face towards her. "That's awful. It's somehow worse. He could be infuriating. I should know! I could have done it myself before now."

Rosemary watched her intently. *Before now*, she'd said. What was so different about now? "Was he the reason you left home?" she suggested softly.

"No! Well, partly. Yes. He was a good bit younger then, more of a — a tease. He knew the sort of thing that really got under my skin. He — "

"He went too far."

"Maybe it was silly of me. I don't think it would have mattered to me now. Not so much, anyway. I'd have found some way to pay him back, but I was younger then, touchy about — personal things."

"What did he do?"

Josie hesitated, then shrugged, her hands busy pouring coffee. She kept

225

her face turned away but Rosemary saw the flush staining her neck. "We — had rooms on the second floor, with a bathroom between, which we shared. He thought it was funny to bore a peephole through from his side. More than three months later he actually showed it to me. That's all. I told you it was silly of me to mind. I should have squirted soap through when I knew he was watching there, but instead — when he told me, jeered at me — well, I just curled up inside. I wanted to die."

So, a Peeping Tom, on top of any other dubious habits. Or just a knack of discovering others' vulnerable points?

There was a tapping at the kitchen's outer door and Beaumont was there, hands plunged in the pockets of his anorak, his face plaintively registering caffeine-starvation. Josie let him in and was persuaded to find him a large mug which he could take outside again.

"There's a sort of annexe down the garden. Would there be any of your brother's stuff in it?" he asked as she poured for him.

"Joel's? I expect so. As teenagers we

used to call it the Rave Cave. Since Paul and I left home Joel's had it to himself, as a sort of studio."

"Did he paint?"

"No. Sometimes he did sketches of buildings, but I meant a photographic studio. He turned one end into his dark room."

"I'd like to take a look. Do you have the key?"

Josie went across to a cupboard and started looking through bunches of keys that hung on hooks inside. "There doesn't seem to be a spare. I expect he had his on him when — "

So no one else used the place, and presumably no one had been in there since his death. Rosemary watched controlled alertness flicker across Beaumont's face as he turned casually away. "Never mind. I'll take a peep through the windows." He picked up the steaming mug and went out by the back way — bound, Rosemary was sure, for a little manipulation of a lock. Well, she would keep Josie occupied while he had a good look round.

The phone began cooing and Josie excused herself to take the call elsewhere.

Through the half-open doorway the WPC could hear her level voice answering, then a sharpened tone of alarm, interrupted assurances. Finally the receiver was replaced and Josie came running back, her sandal heels clacking on the tiles of the hall.

"Look, will you help me? I haven't a car, and they've just phoned from Kit's school: the headmistress, Mrs Capelin. Kit's had a spat with some girls and locked herself in a loo. One of the senior girls tried to climb over to release her and Kit went for her, scratched her face badly. Now they're leaving her there to cool off until we can pick her up."

While Josie fetched her jacket Z ran down to Beaumont for the car keys. He had just opened the studio door and was about to search the place. "Fetching the kid from her school," Rosemary said briefly. "Some kind of emergency."

He nodded. "Good. Gives me time to root around."

Josie was waiting in the passenger seat. "Has Kit ever threatened to hurt herself?" Rosemary asked as she switched on.

"Not that I know of. D'you think she

might? Oh, hurry! It's left into the lane and second exit from the crossroads. She's never *threatened*, but then she doesn't volunteer much at all. Keeps everything inside herself. That's why I'm afraid. She's been in such a weird mood, worse than usual. Shock over Joel, I suppose. I didn't think she should go to school for a day or two, but Mother's pretty stiff on discipline. She does have a point, but — "

"Try to relax," Rosemary counselled. "You'll need to play it very cool when you get there." She sat tight and concentrated on the driving. As they pulled through the school gates she offered, "I'll stay in the car. I don't think she needs reminding of the police just now."

The senior games mistress had taken over, a stringy, taut person in a PE kilt. "In view of the recent family trouble," she told Josie, hurrying her away, "the Head preferred not to put pressure on Kit." It was clear that she herself would have winkled the girl out sharpish.

Z waited. Somewhere inside the buildings an electric bell sounded and she felt an instant wash of nostalgia at the muffled hum of voices and slam of desk lids that followed. She looked at her watch. If Kit didn't make her exit soon she could be caught up in the changeover between lessons. Already a swarm of grey-skirted youngsters was pouring from the side of the building as Josie came out from the front with her hand on her niece's elbow. Kit was walking slightly apart, her body disdainful, her face a zombie's. Rosemary let out her pent breath and left them to get in behind. In the driving mirror she saw Josie shake a white face at her.

"Just missed the crowds," she said casually and started the car. She felt, rather than saw, the girl become aware of her. Would she think of her as police, or as the muggers' victim?

Kit sat forward on her seat, fists balled. "I hate them! They're pigs, all of them! I'll never go back there, never, never, never!"

Josie continued to stay silent, appalled, and unable to make any promises on her mother's behalf.

"I suppose that was the gym mistress," Rosemary offered again over her shoulder. "You can't miss it, can you? 'Down with a bounce and a bounce and up and . . . '"

There was no answer, but a quick glance in the mirror showed that the two in the back were sitting closer. By the time they drew into Marisbank drive the girl was sobbing in Josie's arms.

Once in the house she stood hunched and hopeless again. What comforts did you give an anorexic? None of the customary offers of food or drink would do. "Hot bath?" Z suggested. "Then get out of those school clothes?"

Kit moved in silence towards the stairs, mechanically obeying commands. "I'll go up with her," Josie said. "But don't go away, will you?"

Rosemary Zyczynski watched them turn into a passage off the gallery, and then slipped out by the back way left unlocked on their hasty departure. In Joel's studio she found Beaumont hunkered beside a heavy, old-fashioned safe.

"That's more than you bargained for, isn't it?" she demanded.

"There's nothing for it but the right keys," he said with disgust. "Or plastic explosive. We'll have to ask permission to open this."

"Is it that important?"

"Anything locked is important. There's nothing else here that helps, and it could be that someone other than Joel had a doorkey, came in and cleared up. There are ashes over in the grate there and they smell fresh. Could be photographic paper in among it."

Peeping Tom, Rosemary remembered. Maybe Joel's schoolboy interests had continued beyond puberty. If so, she could imagine the sort of things that might have been burnt. And one person at least who would want to destroy them.

12

YEADINGS had been right about Mott. Now, switching on a look of sprightly insouciance under the cap of crisp blond hair, he could pass for a student, of the athletic, good-looking sort not over-endowed with brains. Followed closely by the genuinely less mature Silver and seeming to fill the width of the doorway with shoulders well muscled at water polo and rugger, he advanced on the wine bar.

But fruitlessly. No sooner was he over the threshold than a mocking cry rang out: "My God, the Old Bill! Whitaker, you're being raided!"

Rushton the bookie with wheezing laughter waved to Mott from his smoke-filled corner. "What'll it be, Inspector? This is on me."

"Not on your life," Mott told him over watchful heads. "I take a big plateful. So does my friend. Can't make inroads on your puny profits. See you sometime."

And, whenever, that'll be too soon, his eyes signalled above the broad grin.

A path opened as he moved towards the service area, but at least nobody made any effort to leave unobserved. Joe Public, Mott told himself; no professional villains, just an average crowd of urban tax-evaders and pocket-liners.

It being only Tuesday, the back room wasn't in use. Having heaped his plate and been served a glass of chilled Chablis, he surveyed the social scene and made for a group of youngsters, mostly teenage girls. Reluctantly they shifted a dump of handbags and outer garments from the wall-bench, moving along to make room for the two newcomers.

Their reception was mixed: curiosity, barely veiled prejudice and in one case open hostility. The two detectives could have done without the bookie's introduction.

A girl with small dark eyes like currants in a sparsely fruited bun ventured the inevitable comment on a policeman's lot.

"Oh, it has its moments," Mott allowed.

"He wasn't kidding, then? You really are one?"

Mott nodded, busy forking salad and keeping an ear on Silver's efforts farther along, which had opened with the old favourite, "Do you come here often?"

It appeared that they were regulars, but only on Tuesdays: a class reunion that met to share romantic records and complaints about their several employers. None of them, which included the two low-key male hangers-on, had even heard of the Sefton-Myra-Dave group.

Half-heartedly Mott pursued a chatting-up routine with the most likely of the girls, refused a dessert and signalled Silver with his eyes to cut the cackle and join him outside.

"We'd have done better to keep on at the university end," he said as they emerged. "If that fails and the addresses yield nothing, the only thing is to come back on Friday. People seem to eat here on a daily rota."

Beaumont, having completed his examination of the annexe at Marisbank, had turned to the garages sited beyond a shrubbery on the house's north side. There were two of them, each a double. Tracks in the gravel showed that the nearer one was the more regularly used, although empty now, with its doors unlocked. Presumably it normally housed the mother's Mercedes and whatever the eldest son drove up to town in.

The first time Beaumont had come here there had been a red BMW at the front door, and Yeadings had spoken of one at Florafaun Frames. So that had been Erica Sefton's, left out front because she had no permanent place here to garage it. So who had been using the second double garage? Not Josie, who had no wheels, so presumably the other two adults then present in the house — Paul the film-maker, and the visiting housekeeper Mrs Lavender. It seemed probable that she drove the elderly Vauxhall sometimes seen delivering PC Lavender to the nick.

The doors to this second garage were padlocked, but through the window he could make out that no cars were at present in it. One space for the dead young man's car (still with Forensic) and only one left for a visitor. Not that this knowledge was worth a tinker's cuss one way or the other, but he liked to have every detail about people he'd an eye on. He made a mental note to check what cars the surviving Sefton brothers drove.

He made his way back towards the kitchen. Somewhere nearby he could hear water gushing in a downpipe and he caught a waft of scent. So the aunt was bathing the kid sent home sick from school. Which left Rosemary Zyczynski free.

He put his head in at the back door. "Have you finished farting about? I've got all I want from here."

Rosemary dug her heels in. "I'm staying on. Radio in that I'm still here before you take the car, will you? Say I could be getting somewhere with Josie."

Beaumont scowled. "Does it matter?"

"Mr Yeadings seemed to think so."

"How will you get back?"

"A pick-up at the drive end if someone back at the nick remembers. Otherwise I'll walk to a bus stop."

"Any coffee left?" Beaumont went across and peered in the percolator, then switched it on again. "Damn, I've left the mug behind. Get it, Z, would you?"

She eyed him evenly. "Why? Suddenly

legless? Or coming the senior officer? I'd love to help, *of course*, but my job's right here and I won't risk breaking contact."

Beaumont's eyes went to slits but he controlled his tongue, counted to ten, then commented, "You ought to get married, Z. You could make some poor chap really miserable."

"Like you are." Before she could stop it the words were out. Well, perhaps kinder than just staring him out and clearly thinking it.

She thought he would have hit her but unexpectedly he dropped on to a chair at the table and sucked in his cheeks. Slowly she went across to the line of mugs hanging on hooks at the dresser and took another down. She filled it with coffee, added milk and pushed it across with the sugar bowl. "Tell me, then, how badly she misunderstands you." Her voice was calm and unstressed.

The DI spooned sugar. "That's the trouble. She understands me too bloody well."

Rosemary let the silence build up. "Are you so different from the man she married?"

"Some. It's inevitable with the job. Not more than she's changed, though, having the kid and so on. No, it's not her or me exactly. Just that it's a thoroughly stupid institution."

"I've sometimes thought it might be. And then at other times it's the grass on the other side of the fence."

"You'd best stay on the side you are, Z. Get thee to a nunnery for preference."

She smiled, and watching her he thought what an unsuitable job she'd chosen. She met his eyes with a droll acceptance of what she'd read in them. "I can't quite see you in an all-male block-house yourself, B."

"B?"

"I'm not much of a speller for long names either."

He nodded. "Fine, we'll leave it that way." He sounded more cheerful. "I'd best get back to real crime. Good luck with the gossiping."

He was at the door as Josie came back in, a wet bath towel over her arm. He turned. "Oh, Miss Sefton," he addressed her chattily, "I understand you don't drive."

"I can, but I haven't a car."

"Sensible of you, living in London. What does your brother drive up in?"

"Chris? A blue Bentley. He's had it about eight years now, a beauty."

"Well, why change a good car when it suits you? Your mother and sister both go for red. Is your other brother's a blue?"

"Funnily enough, it is. I never thought of them going for the same."

"Not another Bentley?"

"No, a Saab, newish. Does it matter? I mean — "

"Sorry, I shouldn't bother you. No, it's a private theory of mine, disproved as often as not. About the sort of cars different people choose." He glanced at his watch. "I have to rush now. Thanks for the coffee. See you later, Z."

Rosemary gave a mock salute to a model example of interrogation by stealth. In one minute flat he'd discovered maybe — who had asked for Joel at Oxford Poly last Friday. Now it was up to her to take it farther. "Is your brother Paul often here?" she asked Josie.

"Very rarely. I hadn't seen him since Easter until last weekend. I doubt if he visited Mother more than twice in that time."

"Still, I suppose the brothers are closer, meet up on occasion?"

"What makes you think that? Maybe men are more gregarious, but not family wise. That's more the women's world. My brothers are so different that they've little to talk about when they can't escape meeting." Her hands were busy crumbling an Oxo cube in yet another mug and pouring on water. "Kit thought she might manage to drink something salty," she explained, "so I'm trying this."

"How does she seem now?"

"Hasn't said much since we went up. I thought I'd leave you to find out what went wrong. She seems to have taken a liking to you."

"Because I was another muggers' victim."

"And then you have a knack."

"We'll see. Do you think I could have another coffee?"

They were still sipping when Kit sidled self-consciously in. She had wrapped herself tightly in a thin cotton robe and her wet hair hung wispily on her shoulders. She sniffed at the mug she was offered, stared reflectively in and finally ventured to taste. She seemed disinclined to talk.

Josie continued telling the policewoman about her flat in Putney. " — but I have a feeling Gaynor has set her sights on something rather better."

"I just have a room," Rosemary confessed, "with use of my landlady's bathroom and kitchen. But at least I have it to myself. I can shut the world out when I need to." She put her cup down and looked at Kit. "Were the girls really awful at school this morning?"

Kit nodded. "Pigs."

"Asking questions." Rosemary sighed. "Sometimes people gloat over the most hideous things."

Kit had muttered something more with her head lowered. Rosemary, straining to catch the last words, heard " . . . wasn't all."

"Something worse?" she hazarded.

Kit continued sitting hunched with head bowed, hands covering her mouth as if fighting against speech.

"Who . . . ?" Rosemary offered, gambling.

More incoherent mumbling, but this time surely a name? Betteridge, was it?

"We had RE before break," Kit said, suddenly audible. To her it seemed to explain everything. And she wasn't going to say any more. Her mouth set stubbornly. More to stem her own emotion than to cut the other two off Rosemary felt.

The girl took a tentative sip at the Oxo, seemed to choke and slammed the mug down, shaking her head. "I can't. My head aches."

"Well, I'm not giving you any aspirin," Josie said doggedly. "You'll have to wait until Mother gets back. Why not go and sit quietly in the garden now it's turned warm, but give your hair a good rub first or you could catch cold."

Now her reply was a resentful glare as the girl stood up; and something else muttered between sniffs that included the word 'pneumonia'.

After she'd gone, "You'd think she was deliberately trying to — " Josie began, then cut off.

Damage herself, Z completed for her silently. Or even kill herself? In Kit's case was anorexia ultimately more than a wish to halt time and put off growing up? "When will your mother get back?" she asked Josie.

"Not until five. She has some wretched committee meeting this afternoon. Should I ring her, do you think?"

"Either her or Kit's father. It's too much for you to tackle alone."

"You're right. They both ought to know. After all, it's not certain the school will take her back. She really damaged that older girl's face. Will you stay on till Mother gets here?"

"I think I'd better. Maybe I'll follow Kit into the garden, get a little sunshine." The last chance to get her to open up before the old dragon clamped down on things, she guessed.

Beaumont was in no great hurry to radio in; he would report to Mott when he arrived, or the Super if the DI wasn't back.

Detective-Superintendent Yeadings was expecting him. He nodded him to a chair and demanded, "Well?"

"There's a single-storey brick-built

annexe in the garden which Joel Sefton used for a studio. I found a lot of photographic stuff there and a dark room. He had quite an eye for the artistic. Mostly landscapes and buildings, as you'd expect with his career in mind, but besides that there were a dozen or so portraits."

"Dress and undress?"

"Both. Nothing a modern vicar could object to, but in the grate were ashes, including paper used for photographic prints. Worth a glance by Forensic, I think. One of the family could have been cleaning up the boy's image. I risked picking out a few pieces." He produced a manila envelope and laid it on the desk. "Which makes me all the more curious to know what was in the half-exposed film in the Brockham Agency camera left at the empty house."

"That's part of my little collection," Yeadings told him, removing a dozen or so glossy prints from the folder in front of him. "As you say, he had an eye for the artistic."

The photographs included three interiors of what must be the house under conversion which Joel had first visited that last afternoon. The rest were nude studies of a vibrant blonde posed by an open casement.

"This could be the Myra Mott's gone after," Beaumont appreciated. "One's very good of the face. Has he seen these yet?"

"No, they've just come in. Take them along. You could catch him at the *Trois Jongleurs* if you look sharpish. Now what of the WPC?"

"She thinks she's getting somewhere with the dead man's background. Through the younger sister. Picked up the kid from school with her this morning — flaked out or sick, it seems. They've got problems there. Have we anything yet on the unknown man who asked for Joel at Oxford Poly on Friday?"

"Not a whisper."

"Well, it might be pure coincidence, but brother Paul runs a blue Saab."

"I'll send someone along to see him. Might go myself." Yeadings looked at his watch. "That's the lot? If so, get a lift now to the wine bar. If necessary, a bus after that out to White Knights for the University. Then stay on with Mott until Z's ready to rejoin you. I don't want her rushed."

Rosemary found Kit on a bench by the potting shed, eyes closed and her face turned blindly up towards the fitful sun. She seated herself at the far end, nursing one knee in her clasped hands, letting silence soften the fact of her intrusion. It was the girl who spoke first.

"Were you — very frightened?"

She was thinking of the mugging incident. Z turned her head to watch her. "Yes, but mostly afterwards. There wasn't time when it was all happening."

"What had you done?"

What *had* I done? Did the girl mean what did I do next? No, she wasn't verbally inept. She meant precisely what she had said.

"I mean — why was it you?"

"I was there when the thugs came along. Unlucky, I suppose."

"An Act of God," said the child tentatively. "You were 'struck down' too."

"No," Z said shortly. "It was an act of villains. They were out looking for someone to beat up and they happened on me. More fun for them, probably, because of my uniform. And they thought a woman would be easier to tackle. Cowards *and* villains."

She saw the doubt clouding Kit's eyes. She was looking for a parallel between the dead Joel and the attack on Z. And in her RE lessons she'd been taught to recognize the hand of the Almighty in happenings around her. It would be very easy to say quite the wrong thing now.

"It was the same for your uncle," Rosemary suggested softly. "Somebody rough and wild caught him unawares. That's all. There's no reason to look for anything more in what happened. There are bad people in this world, you know."

"But Joel wasn't! Not really bad, no!" A desperate cry for reassurance — because she was afraid of *Joel's* badness? Terrified because he had brought down divine retribution on his head?

Z was suddenly conscious of her own heartbeat. Surely there was a reason she felt herself reliving the past but at one remove. Something about the child echoing something she herself had experienced at the same age. An encounter with evil. She held her breath a moment, then risked an enormous step. "He didn't — abuse you?"

The girl's face was turned away, invisible. She made no movement to suggest denial. At eleven could she have avoided learning what the word meant? It covered so much: once a general term of officialdom, now hideously specific and a household word. "Kit, do you know what I mean by abuse?"

An audibly drawn breath, a pause, then an impatient nod of the head.

"So — did he actually abuse you?"

"No." It was a hoarse whisper. She was trying to get more out but seemed to have lost her voice. "No — it's wrong."

Wrong? Good God, it was wrong all right. But what did her recognition of that imply? That of course Joel wouldn't have done anything wrong? — or that because it was wrong, *she* had prevented him?

Inside herself Rosemary felt a cold void. She didn't want to pursue this inquisition. It was too fearsome. Despite the denial she could smell something horribly amiss.

And whatever she was told would most surely have to be passed on.

But the girl was religious, wasn't she? Or at least influenced by others outside the family who held to a strict moral creed. So was she seeing sin where others might brush it off as peccadillo? And was she so scared that she denied to herself that it ever happened? Wrong, therefore impossible; and the physical truth pushed back into the dark corners of the mind, there to fester and infect?

I don't want to pursue it, Rosemary told herself. It's too intimate. Too near my own story. Her own blood uncle abusing her. Eleven, just as I was when that man —

"He was — so — beautiful," the girl managed to get out.

Rosemary bit on her lips. This at least was a new part of the old story. "You loved him," she said quietly. The belief came to her at the exact moment of speaking.

"Everybody did."

Was that true? Behind the horror over what had happened to Joel Rosemary had surely detected a marked coolness towards

250

him from his siblings. Had that been the result of bad experiences with him, or merely a reaction against their mother's clear preference for her youngest?

But Kit was only a child, struggling with the complexities of early adolescence, only recently coming to live in close proximity to this golden youth accustomed to having his whims indulged. To her he could have seemed godlike in his perfection.

At least it could mean that he seduced — not forced — her. In fairness to him, had he in his turn found the emerging woman in Kit so overwhelmingly attractive that he was powerless to resist, and so made sexual advances to her under the family roof?

She looked at the girl now. The strangely pallid flesh was pulled tight over her skeletal frame, and in places showed the veins through, mauvy blue. Her face had a decadent, ethereal beauty. Earlier, before she lost weight, she must have been quite breathtakingly lovely with that rich tumble of dark red hair. And apart from their shared beauty, there was closeness in age: two young creatures against the rest of the older, alien world.

"You used to talk together," Rosemary said slowly.

"You could tell him anything. He understood. He explained."

"What did he explain?"

But she had gone too fast. The girl screwed her face up and the thin body became more angular still as she gesticulated impatiently. "Oh — things. You wouldn't understand."

Rosemary waited, holding her breath, then, "I think you may be wrong there. You see, you're standing where I once stood. Things I shall never forget happened when I was your age. But I survived. Whatever else is wrong, I know a worse thing: that's opting out."

Kit uncurled enough to raise her face and stare hostilely back. For the first time her eyes were fully open. "I don't care that you survived. Joel is dead. *Joel!* He was struck down, and it isn't fair. It was my fault. He's dead, and all I got was the curse!"

What curse? Involuntarily Rosemary reached out a hand to her. "Kit, have your periods begun?" The girl was only eleven, but tall, perhaps well fleshed before she began starving herself.

"It's come back. He got rid of it, but now he's dead it's come back."

Anything I say, Rosemary thought, could be fatal now. She could go right back inside herself and I'd never get near her again. "Thank God it did," she said with quiet fervency.

Kit's chin came up scornfully. "Thank God? You don't believe in God. You're swearing."

Do I believe? Rosemary closed her eyes. She'd like to believe. Right now she'd better. And if the right words came, then perhaps she would go on believing. At least until the next crushing victory of evil.

"Yes," she said clearly, "I do believe in God. Otherwise it would all be too awful."

When she dared to open her eyes again Kit was sitting staring down at her hands. She didn't appear to have moved, but she had a new calmness. Her pent breath came out with a soft whoosh.

"Kit, you do look tired."

"I am. I think I'll go to bed now. I

don't want anyone to come up. Will you tell them?"

"How about a hot drink?"

"All right. Josie can bring it up. Not milk, though, and she must leave it outside. I don't want to see anyone just now."

It was a risk. Youngsters of that age could do very silly things. But her last two words had sounded unforced: " — just now." If she couldn't face the world for the moment, hadn't she implied she'd need it at some later time?

"I'll explain," Rosemary promised. Explain was what Kit had said Joel did. What in heaven's name had he explained to her? And was that at the back of the anorexia everyone attributed wholly to her parents' break-up? It was unlikely Joel had advised starvation, but had he played lover-priest and presented his exploration of her young female body as a form of prophylactic, offering a contraceptive pill as a means to avoid her periods? It didn't quite make sense, but she was sure she wasn't far off the actual truth there.

"I've got a phone number," Rosemary

offered. "You can have it. Here. My landlady takes messages when I'm not there. Tell her if you need me."

Kit took it limply, without a word, then she turned and walked back into the house. Rosemary followed at a distance, watching her go up the centre of the grand staircase, moving like her grandmother, with the same upright carriage, each flat-heeled foot passing the other and planted centrally ahead, angled outward. Of course; Harriet would never have permitted any female child of her family to miss early ballet training.

What was Kit going to make of herself, so overgifted with others' interference? And now this intrusion by WPC Rosemary Z?

13

ROSEMARY spoke to Josie about the hot, non-milk drink, and stressed that Kit wanted to be left undisturbed. "Why not, poor kid?" her young aunt agreed. "I'll try her again with some Oxo. Mind, she'll never drink it. It will go down the loo or out of the window. I suppose it's progress that she lets anyone bring it for her."

Rosemary could have used the phone there at the house but she preferred to walk down the drive and do it from the call-box at the crossroads. Beaumont, as it happened, was out on a job with Inspector Mott and the call was put through to Mr Yeadings's office. He answered in person.

"Z? Y here." She could picture his rubbery grin at the mock espionage jargon. "I understand you're stranded without transport at Callendar Lane. Everyone's scattered at present but if you can wait, I'll pick you up in ten minutes."

She spent the intervening time debating just how much she should pass on of what Kit had revealed, and what could safely be inferred from it.

To start off, she, WPC Rosemary Zyczynski, was in the wrong. A child of that age should never have been questioned without someone present *in loco parentis*. But where did sympathetic conversation end and interrogation begin? When she had followed Kit into the garden it hadn't been her intention to extract such disturbing implications, but to give comfort. Not really a part of her police job. True, she'd still been trying to flesh out the family background, but it had got out of hand. She had stumbled into forbidden territory. There had been altogether too much flesh.

Yet if she hadn't talked then with Kit there wouldn't have come that intuitive knowledge of what truly lay behind the child's strange aberrations. Not simply grief at her parents separation and later her uncle's violent death. Much more: guilt over actions and feelings of her own that she could not understand nor relate to the sex theme underlying both her lost

257

mother's and her uncle-lover's behaviour. She had known joy perhaps, but without happiness. And now — such a confusion of misery, guilt and abject fear.

"Ravenous because you've had no lunch, I guess," Yeadings greeted her cheerfully as he drew up. "Hop in. Down by your feet there's a box of Danish, and a flask of coffee Nan put in this morning for just such an occasion. It usually keeps good and hot. Cups in the glove compartment on your side."

He drove on and pulled off the road into the yard of a small pub, through the frosted windows of which they had the impression of a surprising throng of drinkers. From an opened fanlight their voices came out in sudden, enthusiastic waves and holy silences. "Darts match," Yeadings surmised. "The extended hours seem to have taken on. We're lucky to find a space. Now, lass, help yourself first and then pass me the doings."

She poured for them both and sank her teeth in the sticky pastry while Yeadings burrowed in his pockets for a tube of sweeteners, then stirred in two with the end of his pen. She became suddenly aware that his eyes were on her, studying her face. Suspecting something of the chaotic thoughts his arrival had cut into?

"Who did you talk to?" he asked.

"The younger daughter, and the little girl, Kit."

"Not so little heightwise."

"But young for her age. At least, in some ways. In others, I'm not so sure. She's had a strange upbringing."

"And today, I understand, she was unwell at school. You took her aunt out to pick her up?"

"It was an emotional upset. She's had a lot to face up to in a short while."

"Broken homes are pretty common these days."

"I was thinking of the sudden change. She wasn't important enough to her mother to be taken with her when she left Christopher Sefton. That could mean that Kit is accustomed to being overlooked and alone. Then being absorbed by the Sefton clan. They can be pretty swamping. I found them formidable."

"Not all of them normally living at the

family home, though. The child's father is there only at nights and weekends. The oldest, Erica, has a flat in Reading and a cottage in Sussex. Paul visits, every two months at most: bit of a lizard — basks, flicks his tongue and darts away. Josie, the gentle one, spends the odd weekend there, but her interests are all in London. Which leaves Grandmother Harriet and the dead young man to share with her what time she's not busy with school and homework."

It surprised Rosemary that Yeadings should attempt to see the household from the child's viewpoint. She wondered if he had noticed anything special about Kit, apart from the obvious state of her health.

"They seem to have been quite close." She looked across to see him watching her. "Kit and Joel, I mean."

"Almost the same generation," he appreciated.

She hesitated. "I'm wondering if there wasn't more to it. I don't want to suggest anything yet, because I've really nothing to go on. But she has said some curious things. There's guilt there. Of course, I know it's a dodgy subject. Children's consciences . . . "

"A very serious matter," Yeadings said slowly. "Is that what you mean? How does she react to his death?"

"Appalled. She spoke of him being 'struck down'. She has religion, you know." She shook her head impatiently. "I'm sorry, I made it sound like a disease."

Yeadings was looking worried. He stayed silent for a while. "Have you any experience with this sort of thing?"

Rosemary looked stonily ahead. "Not professionally."

He had picked up her meaning. "And personally?"

"Some. Not the same, though. I think Kit was strongly attracted to Joel. Romantically. Hero-worship."

"And you think he may have taken advantage of that? Made it sexual?"

"That's what I strongly suspect, but I've nothing to substantiate it. Mere gut-feeling. Anyway I was a bit out of order. Talked with the child without Josie being there. Not really asking questions. Just letting it all come out."

"Well, there's certainly not enough for me to request a medical examination. The poor child has enough trouble already."

"It would terrify her. She's a private child, and sensitive. Joel Sefton must have made a very gentle approach to get through to her. Anything else . . . "

" 'Tread softly, because you tread on my dreams,' " she heard the Superintendent murmur. "What a frightening thing being young is."

He hadn't picked up the personal bit about herself, Rosemary marvelled. It wasn't because he hadn't noticed: nothing seemed to escape him. He'd noted without comment or prurient curiosity. No unwanted sympathetic noises either.

She hadn't expected such fine feelings, though it went with his quoting Yeats. Intuition had given her the courage to hint at her own childhood's horrors: an instinctive near-certainty that she could trust him. And now she was glad. She couldn't have confided in the younger Mott. And never, under any circumstances, to the mocking DS Beaumont, even since he'd momentarily weakened to admit his own troubles.

"This is the family's worry," Yeadings said slowly. "I wonder who among them knows the truth. If anyone. They'll have to know, and to see the girl has professional help, but let's keep this conversation to ourselves for the present. We don't want to start up the sort of hare that can get a lot of innocent people chased by mistake. You have something more concrete for Inspector Mott — young Sefton's comings and goings, dates and times, that sort of thing?"

"Yes, sir. I'll make a full report, apart from Kit's trouble. But I'd like to talk to Mrs Lavender at her own home, maybe go there when her son's present, in case she has exaggerated scruples about loyalty to her employers."

Yeadings grunted. "A view from outside the family. Yes, follow it up. Well, if that's all, we'd better buckle up and get back to our paperwork."

Harriet leaned over the phone desk and the tremor of her hands ran up her arms, invading her chest. She felt sick with fear. They had been back again; the girl with her soft, brown eyes, ingratiating herself with Josie, and the man — It was the idea of that man that really frightened her. Something about his Pinocchio face, round and fresh with an impudent nose — he was surely meant to be a friendly, helpful sort of person who mended things and made not unfunny jokes. But the expression when she'd first seen him waiting outside, after Chris had been to identify Joel's body — so coldly watchful; almost resentful. Out to make trouble, and God knows there was trouble enough for the family as it was.

This morning she had had a ridiculous feeling that if she herself was out of the house it would remain inviolate, but in her absence the police had come back.

The police; always so respectful when Eric was alive. But no one showed respect any more. This was no longer the world she had grown up in, grown old in. Well, if she didn't belong any more, did it matter what others thought? And shame came from inside you, not from any outside opinion.

But this policeman, sneaking about by the garages, as Josie had unwittingly admitted — what was he looking for?

264

Checking, he'd told her. Checking what? By what right? And the policewoman too, still sitting on, waiting in the kitchen for her to return, so *suspicious*!

Harriet tried to take three deep breaths before going on. Instead of remaining calm to cope with Kit's trouble at school, she had let the police presence fluster her. That was why she had now rung Erica and Paul as well, insisting they come in, so that when Chris arrived there would be a complete family gathering again. And why not? They were, after all, a family beleaguered. It was right that they should support each other. When Dr Glenister, the specialist, came tomorrow he might insist on a nursing home for the child.

With Josie's help Harriet prepared a cold buffet for when the others arrived. She had given Kit half a tablet of the tranquillizer prescribed for herself before the funeral, and the child was still asleep.

Predictably Chris was the first to arrive, in early afternoon, followed by a strangely alarmed Paul. Erica, steely-eyed and sceptical as ever, came after office hours. When they were all together

Harriet asked Josie for her account of what had happened at the school.

"And you say that break-time came straight after RE? That wretched Betteridge woman!" said Harriet tightly at the end. "It's due to that religious nonsense she's always filling the child with. Morals lifted straight out of the Old Testament. So Kit sees Joel struck down by God! It's preposterous. As if the child's not unstable enough already."

"Not unstable," Christopher demurred. That was surely going too far, accepting the irreversible. "Precarious, perhaps." His voice died away, unsure as he was that his correction had been any improvement.

"She's a sensitive child," Paul offered. "For which you should be grateful. We're short enough of artistic creativity in this family."

"Create certainly is what she does," commented Erica sourly.

Josie fidgeted impatiently on her chair. "Sorry. I'm completely in the dark. Who is 'that wretched Betteridge woman'?" she asked. "And how come she has so much influence over Kit when no one else does?"

"Last year's form mistress, thin as the proverbial lath," Christopher explained. "Kit despises the rest of us as elephants. Except Mother, of course."

"Even I," Harriet complained, displaying her own thin wrists and forearms for their appreciation, "have been accused of obesity. It's the most insulting thing Kit can imagine saying when she wants to wound."

"She actually dared — ?" Erica was fascinated.

Christopher stumbled in his haste to defend his daughter. "It's a disease. Anorexia, I mean. Doctors all agree it's officially a disease. Kit really believes that being anything more than a skeleton is seriously overweight. She won't eat because she's scared of becoming bloated."

"Scared of growing up," Erica fired back. "They do it to stay immature, don't they? To avoid menstruation. Dead scared of sex because she knows you and Martine — "

"Erica! This offensive talk must cease right now. I will not have it." Harriet sat bolt upright, her eyes hard black stones.

"You were the one who asked us to

rally and help, Mother." Erica rose from the chaise-longue and looked sardonically round at them all. "The mystery to me is why Kit needs anorexia. In this mood Mother can do all anyone needs to arrest development, don't you think?"

She shrugged elaborately at the aghast faces and made her exit, pausing momentarily to sketch a bob curtsey before Harriet's chair. Then she was gone. They heard the front door close deliberately, not slammed.

"I don't think," Christopher said to break the appalled silence afterwards, "any of us has ever behaved so badly as today. I'm sorry, everybody."

The other two mumbled reassurances while Harriet sat on, not frozen now but grimly ironic, running her eyes over them. Open hostility had given her something recognizable to work on.

Paul looked down at his own hands for shame that she should have read in his face the fierce leap of unholy delight as he recognized a perfect dramatic climax. If he could only reproduce it transposed . . .

Harriet rose and walked to the window, speaking over her left shoulder. "We have to remember," she said with throwaway calm, "that Erica has always been more successful with steel tubes than human relationships."

She turned back and sat down again, having gained control of herself through movement. "As for Kit's behaviour, I am partly to blame. It's true, as Christopher says, that she has scant respect for anyone she considers overweight — which is virtually everyone. But I do still have some influence with her, and over the past few days my mind has been so full of other things that I have overlooked her needs. I shall do all I can now to comfort her."

Comfort, Josie echoed in her mind. Mother as comforter? As leader, teacher, martinet, judge, yes. But when did she ever pick up one of her children to cuddle and soothe away its tears? But didn't she? Wasn't there actually a time in the twilight past when Josie had experienced something of the sort? A warmth, a presence, and her mother's scent. Then a fearful grief lifting.

But whatever the occasion had been, it was gone now almost completely. Perhaps it had only been wishful thinking, part of a child's lost longings. Baby Joel had been the cosseted one, and even then one could recognize a distance between mother and child, as though Harriet mocked her own fondness. Perhaps to prevent herself becoming wholly absorbed into the act of loving?

So what Kit was doing, this rebuff of everyone, denying the very need of human contact — that was surely a parody of her dominant grandmother's attitude.

Harriet drummed with her fingertips in the glass-topped table. "Josie, you're dreaming. Fetch the brandy, will you? I fancy we could all do with warming. No Paul, Josie will go. Perhaps you would ring for Mrs Lavender to make some fresh coffee."

The interruption for refreshments gave them more time to consider Kit's situation. They finally were agreed that as strong a case as possible should be presented to the specialist to keep her within the family, particularly in view of the shock she had received over Joel's death. From now on medical treatment would have to override all other considerations for the child, but to send her away alone was out of the question.

They must all keep in closer touch to give the child reassurance. Chris would arrange to take a week or two off work, and Josie offered to stay on longer, commuting daily. Paul, diffident about any advantage his presence might supply, would try to call in every two days or so, his rehearsal schedule permitting.

Afterwards, when she'd realeased them, Harriet went upstairs to knock on Kit's door. It wasn't locked because some weeks ago, as a precaution, she had had Mrs Lavender remove the key, but now a chair back was wedged under the knob — not with such expertise, however, as to prevent Harriet's forcing the gap wide enough to insert a wrist.

Josie, watching unseen from along the gallery, waited for the child to slam the door shut on the delicate bones. Instead there was a short silence and then the sound of wooden chair legs dragged back over the polished floor.

Harriet straightened, appeared to take a deeper breath, and made her entrance.

Josie wished she could be sure that all the offers of help just made had been for the child's peace of mind rather than Harriet's.

14

"**I**F I'd thought I could really help I'd have come in sooner," the man said wretchedly. "The truth is I was totally pissed, didn't know where I was or what day it was until suddenly I found myself staring at that body. I'd never seen anyone dead before."

Yeadings sat on, waiting and watching. The man — Joseph Santer, insurance broker — had been seated, white-faced and apprehensive, in Reception when he arrived back with Rosemary Z. Now, having been ushered into an interview room, he was doggedly making his belated confession while the WPC took shorthand notes.

A delay line of nearly four days, Yeadings considered grimly. Santer was probably correct in his estimate of his own usefulness, but that didn't excuse him his public duty. "When did you first hear of our need to interview you?"

"Next morning. My wife — said it was

on the early news. Of course, she didn't know it was me that — I mean, she'd waited up so she knew — "

" — the state you were in. Yes."

"I wasn't so bad by the time I got home. I'd dropped in at the Abbey House in Connaught Road to douse my head in cold water. There was some kind of party going on and no one took much notice. That's where I made the 999 call from."

"How long would that have taken, between viewing the body and getting through?"

Santer groaned. "Eternity. I was sick in between times too."

Which meant he could even have been in the car park when the Tolleys left and as the unknown man took a ticket for Joel's car. Yeadings spoke over his shoulder to the constable at the door. "A cup of tea for Mr Santer. Or should I make that coffee?"

"Tea would be fine. Milk, no sugar. Thanks." He shook his head at Yeadings's proffered cigarettes. "I have my own. Low tar."

Suddenly considerate for his health,

274

the CID man noted sardonically. But then we're all inconsistent, the normal ones.

When the man had lit up and taken a few pulls at the tobacco, Yeadings started again. "I think you may have noticed more than you've so far remembered, Mr Santer. I'd like to go through it slowly with you, in detail, right from your being in the pub talking with your friends. To simplify things we can leave out any reference to being in charge of a car that evening. Now, what were you all discussing?"

Beaumont had missed Mott and Silver by little more than a whisker at the bistro, but the inner man still required satisfaction. He piled his plate of cold cuts with four kinds of salad, added two rolls and butter, then found he couldn't cope with juggling cutlery, paying, and also taking on a glass of Beaujolais. Somehow he'd missed the pile of trays at the start.

"OK," the girl at the cash machine reassured him. "You find a table. I'll bring the rest over." Which she did, and stayed to chat, the lunch-hour press having magically cleared on the stroke of 2.30.

It set him up: food, drink and attention. Despite his present disgust with all things female, he felt cheered at being recognizably pick-upable. And a good bellyful now would mean he didn't have to plunge again into the already depleted freezer stock tonight. He concentrated on the moment, congratulating himself that he adapted well to a returned bachelor existence, even rediscovering its advantages.

Replete and comforted, he eventually went out into the first sunshine he'd noticed for days, and queued for a bus out to White Knights, arriving on campus in time to see his quarries escorting a blonde girl to their unmarked car.

"Room for a small one," he assumed breezily, opening a rear door and sliding in where the girl would sit beside him.

It wasn't the girl in the photographs. This one was bigger-framed with blotchy skin, and she wore her long fair hair in a single heavy plait over one shoulder. Beaumont left the packet of glossies in his pocket for a future occasion. "Well, introduce us," he invited the DI.

"Miss Hennessey, this is Detective-Sergeant Beaumont, for what it's worth. Myra Louise Hennessey, second-year Mathematics, Reading University."

"And friend of the late Joel Sefton," Beaumont perkily assumed.

"I'm not at all charmed to meet you," she told him sourly. Silver drove in a general silence until they reached Reading Central.

While she was being shown into an Interview Room Mott brought Beaumont up to date. "She admits being at the bistro with him. Later sat in his car to talk but denies going out in it afterwards. Come and join us on this."

Beaumont took an extra chair in with him, sat and listened while DC Silver read out his notes so far. At the end, "I believe her," Beaumont declared.

The girl's scornful look was replaced by one of suspicion, then calculation. "You didn't exactly part as friends, though, did you?"

"I wouldn't have attacked him, if that's what you're insinuating!"

"Tell us more about the credit card dodge."

She snorted. "Dodge is right. Joel Sefton ought to have joined the Magic Circle!"

"Sleight of hand, eh? D'you mean he managed to keep his own card back from the general slaughter?"

"And mine. Wouldn't give it back to me, what's more. Threatened to lend it to a girlfriend who'd go on a shopping spree. I had to rush to the bank before it closed and get the bloody thing cancelled, didn't I?"

"Now why would he do a thing like that?"

"Because he was that kind of tyke, liked to show off how clever he was and what a dope everyone else was. I don't suppose he really would have done what he threatened, but with Joel you couldn't be sure. And he had it in for me."

"Because you'd annoyed him beforehand. In front of the others. Is that it?"

"Ribbed him a bit. About not getting into a university. It really got his goat that he'd only managed a Poly."

"We can't all be clever."

"And you're no better!"

278

"Well, let's get all that written down and signed, shall we? And after that maybe you'll remember that he told you where he meant to go next."

Mott left them to it, more amused than exasperated at the way Beaumont had taken over. At the end of the corridor he saw Yeadings seeing a man out. He walked back with him and put him briefly in the picture about Myra Hennessey's statement.

"Did Beaumont give you the other girl's photographs? The ones from Joel's camera."

Mott swore gently. "So that's how he knew Myra was telling the truth. Sly bugger! He could be back on form, Boss. What's your news?"

"Our 999 man's just shown up, four days late. A Joseph Santer. Very foggy recollections, but he'd just got back into his car after sighting the body late on Friday night, time unknown, when a group of four or five came into the car park and drove off in two cars from the far end."

"The Tolleys and their guests?"

"It seems so, because while he was keeping a low profile from them another car came in right alongside. The driver left its door open, walked off and then came back almost immediately. I asked him to locate where he'd parked, using Z's grid, and guess what?"

"Right next to where we found the Sefton TVR. Did he get a sight of the driver?"

"Too busy lying low without actually throwing up, it seems. But at least we now know for certain that the body was delivered to the car park first; the dead man's car later. Which is borne out by Forensic's tests on the car interior. Plenty of different latents, some overlaid by smudges; but no traces of blood or shoe dirt in the boot. So the killer or another delivered the corpse, then thought to lead us astray on place and time of killing by making it seem that the dead man had driven himself there at a later hour."

"Leaving us to decide which of several hundred anonymous cars parking there from four-thirty p.m. onwards had actually had the body in it."

"Quite so. While we're on the subject of Forensic, they rang through with an initial report on the mattress from the empty house. Definite semen stains, two or three days old at most. The DNA identification will take much longer, of course, but I think we can assume it will link up with Sefton, since his dabs were found in the room. So we still have two people to find," Yeadings summed up. "The girl who was with Joel Sefton at the empty house; and the man, possibly his brother Paul, who was asking for him at Oxford Poly on Friday at lunch-time."

"Why Paul?"

"Because Josie Sefton told Beaumont that Paul's car was a blue Saab, and the personal description fits him. I was going to question him myself but I think I'll leave it now to you and Silver. There's a joyriders' RTA reported in by Traffic, so later on I must follow up on a pair of dead teenagers.

"When I rang through to Sefton's film studio I was told he'd been called away — an urgent summons from his mother, they admitted when I pressed a bit. He'd been filming on location in Burnham

Beeches, making the most of today's sun. Although he's in our locality now, I think we should leave the family in peace. There's rather a crisis over the anorexic child. Better put off questioning Paul until tomorrow morning. He'll be out at the Beeches from ten onwards. If you look out for a white canteen van when you get there they'll direct you on to the site."

"And how about the girl with Sefton at the empty house?"

"Finding her could be a long business. We'll leave that with DS Beaumont since he's become attached to the photos. With Z in tow, of course."

When he had concluded his questioning of Myra — 'for the present', as he warned her — Beaumont went looking for Mott, and his search took him past Yeadings's open office door. "Sir," he said, putting his head in, "did DI Mott tell you we now have another girl to find?" And he repeated the outline of Hennessey's statement. "So, as Myra's not the one who was out at the empty house with Joel Sefton, do we ask the Press to help?"

"Hand them the photos? Page three stripper stuff? No, we haven't anything against the unknown girl and even if we lifted the face off the rest of the picture, she'd still know where we got it. Could be too embarrassed to come forward."

"Someone else might recognize her."

"Have you no lead at all to her?"

"Only guesswork. Myra said Joel turfed her out of his car because he had an overdue appointment. To pick up a birthday gift for his mother. That would have been at about one-thirty p.m. At 'two or three o'clock', according to the Brockham client, he had driven out to the first property, accompanied by this second, much prettier blonde. So did he pick her up at the jeweller's? — I ask myself."

Yeadings grunted. "Or could it have been a private transaction? We've had nothing in yet from trade sources on that antique ring, either sale or purchase. It's not beyond impossibility that Joel bought the ring from, or through, this unknown girl — a minor heirloom, say — if she needed to raise some hard cash. It was *cash* he was after at his sister's office, remember. And from what your Myra said, we know he still had his flexible plastic on him."

"I could go along with that," Beaumont agreed, "but it doesn't help us trace her. She could still be anyone."

"Several sets of the photos have been printed, for the team, but not general issue. Maybe the Seftons will recognize her. DI Mott will be going to interview brother Paul on location, and he'll try for an identification from him. She could be a young actress."

"Or anybody's daughter. Still, I could take a look at *Spotlight*, see if she's advertising herself in it. She's certainly photogenic; could be a pro."

"Take Z along."

"Is she back?"

"Tucked away somewhere with a typewriter. You'd better get your own report done pdq as well. Is there anything else I should know about right now?"

Beaumont hesitated. "In Marisbank annexe there's a locked Chubb safe. I'd like to see inside it. It could be relevant stuff, and I doubt Joel would have allowed anyone a duplicate set of keys."

Yeadings shifted his weight in his chair, tapped his front teeth with a ballpoint. "All right, maybe take a locksmith along. But wait until I've tackled Mrs Sefton and received her permission."

"Dodgy," Beaumont remarked. "Rather you than I."

Harriet Sefton's voice was sharp as she answered the phone. Yeadings was aware of the silence building up after he made his request.

"There *is* an old safe in the studio, although I cannot see how your man could know about it, Superintendent. Everything out in the annexe belonged to Joel, so of course he had the keys." She wanted it left there.

"You do realize, Mrs Sefton, that in a murder investigation we are obliged to search in every direction, under every stone? That safe may contain evidence of something we cannot guess at, evidence linking your son to the person who killed him."

"I can assure you, Mr Yeadings, that it

doesn't." She hesitated, then rushed on. "I have already looked myself. If your sergeant cares to come out tomorrow I will, naturally, allow him to examine the contents. As it happens, I do hold a second set of keys."

He thanked her and replaced the receiver thoughtfully. If everything was so straightforward, why had she tried to brush him off at first?

Before he left for High Wycombe morgue to look at the two fourteen-year-olds who had killed themselves and a van driver on the M40 near Booker, Yeadings had another word with Beaumont.

"Twice in one day is a bit much for the Seftons to endure you and Z, so I've made an appointment for you both to view the safe's contents tomorrow. Since Mrs Sefton admits she's already been into the safe herself there's nothing to lose, and probably nothing for us to gain by now. I'm pretty certain she's the one who burned papers in the annexe grate. I sent your charred pieces of glossy to Forensic, but it'll be a day or two before they get anything off them. When you've put your report in, knock off. Things are about to hot up; I feel it in my bones. Get a bit of rest before the pressure builds. Look out Z and tell her to do the same."

He found her clipping the sheets of her day's report together. "Finished?" he asked gloomily. "I thought you might like a bite out somewhere. The Great White Chief says go home when the paperwork's done."

"Well, mine is."

He grimaced, gestured with his notebook. "Mine's still in indecipherable scribble. Did anything of interest come up for you?"

"Read it and see. If you like, I could start yours off while you're at it. As an exception to the rule, that is."

"Twist my arm." They exchanged reports.

Beaumont read slowly through, then went back again to the beginning. While Rosemary transcribed his notes he sat rubbing his chin. She was the first to ask a question. "This safe — what's to be done about it?"

He told her. "So if the mother's opened

it already, there's little chance we'll get a lead from anything left in it."

"But why should she suppress evidence? She must want to find out who killed her son."

"She won't see anything as evidence when she's whitening sepulchres. She's out to preserve his good name and save the family from scandal. And we're of the opinion, even on such short acquaintance with young Joel, that he was no spotless lamb. It makes him more interesting as a victim."

"You've seen what Myra Hennessey says — that he liked to be one-up, even to playing spiteful tricks on the friends he took his fun with. The picture of him as a schoolboy Peeping Tom you got from his sister is another key to what he became later. He had everything his own way. No corrective influence, and so instead of growing out of petty trickery he got more skilled, went for bigger targets. With what we've picked up elsewhere, isn't it reasonable to suppose he did have some hold over his sister Erica and through that extracted the fifty pounds? You'd agree she isn't the sort to be easily won over by charm alone?"

"You're implying some form of blackmail."

"Z, grow up. It's something we all do. He had fewer inhibitions than the rest of us. He was a gifted con-man."

"I wouldn't disagree." She considered the observations she'd omitted from the report. If her suspicions were correct — and Kit hadn't denied anything — Joel had been a whole lot more than what Beaumont thought him. She sighed, comforted that Yeadings at least was warned of what might eventually come to light. "Well, B, your report's done. Better check it. Its a pity your Myra Hennessey wasn't the girl he took to the empty house. It just seems we take one step backward for every one we go ahead."

"Fancy a pizza at my place?" Beaumont asked, abruptly switching the subject. "Funny thing, but I had a damn good lunch today at that wine bar, and I'm ravenous again. It's as though eating makes me hungry."

Rosemary smiled. "I can't think that my being observed by nosey neighbours crossing your threshold would help your domestic situation. And I've no proper kitchen at my digs. Let's toss for a pie and a pint, against two courses with waitress service at the Silver Skillet."

15

THE post came early in Beaumont's street. He heard the click of the letter-box as he was filling the kettle, but it would only be unsolicited junk mail so he left it until he was almost ready to leave. Then it meant going back and sitting down to take in properly what the daft woman was on about. But at least it wasn't from a solicitor — which would have required double time and a dictionary as well.

Bloody woman couldn't spell foresight. If she'd had any she wouldn't have married him: nice, that. So now he knew why they were in the present stinking mess; because Cathy hadn't had a crystal ball. Well, whose fault was that?

It was a long way for Stuart to walk to school, so she'd have to get herself a little car, but there was a chance of a good job coming up which meant she'd probably be able to put something towards it herself. You bet she would. Going off with the boy like that had been her idea. He didn't see why he should be made to suffer for it more than he was doing at present, with never a hot meal ready and the place already looking tatty.

Too true, she would need a job. Her mother was a determined, houseproud woman with no patience for anyone sitting around all day on their backside. And while at first she'd enjoy the boy's company of an evening, just let him start switching over to his favourite programmes when she needed her daily fix of soaps!

So, after the little car, he supposed Cathy would require a little flat, then a little divorce, expecting him to sell up here and split with her whatever he got for the house. What lunatic said an Englishman's home was his castle? Not likely — once he'd carried his fairy princess over the threshold!

He looked at his watch, swore and snatched up his raincoat from the chair he'd thrown it in last night. God, it looked like a flasher's. Maybe its creases would drop out in the car's warmth. He'd be twenty minutes late picking Z up, dammit. And being a woman she'd not let him forget it. Why the hell couldn't Mott have partnered her and left old Ted Silver to him? — someone he could beef at, and feel better afterwards.

In the event, Rosemary didn't remark on anything as he picked her up — except the wind, which had turned to a keen north-easter and was whipping at her skirts. It seemed that her only trousers were uniform ones or some she wore to dig her landlady's allotment, and the smell of those debarred them. "Especially," she added, "as we have to visit the gentry."

It was the lost journey Beaumont had predicted. Although they were both conscious of other people in the house, it was Mrs Lavender who let them in. Before she showed them to the annexe Rosemary asked to see Mrs Sefton. It was clear that the woman had been instructed to prevent them bothering the family.

"There is fresh evidence," Z explained. "Photographs we need identified."

"I'll go and see, miss."

Christopher Sefton came back with her, apparently taking the day off work — probably on account of Kit's troubles.

293

He looked strained and apprehensive. Watching him, wondering how much the girl had told him, Z missed his first words and he had to repeat himself, offering to take the photographs to his mother and sister.

"I'm sorry, sir. I have definite instructions to show them myself."

"I see. In that case, I suppose you must. Come this way, please."

The women were in the conservatory and appeared to have been interrupted in a council of war. Harriet, grim and tense, straightened her back before glancing at the pictures, looked sharply up at the WPC and then down again in evident relief. "No, a complete stranger, I'm afraid. Pretty girl. Has something happened to her too?"

"Not that we know of. We just wish to find her for questioning. She may have been a friend of your son's."

"No, I don't know her either," Josie added. "Do you, Chris?"

He shook his head. "Wrong age group for me. More Kit's generation. D'you think she — ?"

"I don't think we need bother her,"

Rosemary said quickly, beating Harriet to it by a hair's breadth. She put the pictures back in their envelope, thanked them all and rejoined Beaumont outside.

Mrs Lavender was equally unhelpful over the unknown girl, correctly following instructions as she handed over the keys and stood by, watching Beaumont open first the annexe door and then the Chubb safe.

He took out old sketchbooks; two albums of school photographs; a box of new golf balls; a file containing details of Joel's Access dealings; a box of cheque counterfoils, statements and paying-in books for his Classic account at Lloyds; and four typed chapters of what appeared to be a novel. This last might have shed light on the writer except that it had obviously lain untouched for long months, if not years.

From the bank details which Beaumont whizzed through and then passed on to Rosemary, there was evidence only of a minimal sustained balance despite what struck the policewoman as quite considerable outgoings. His allowance from Harriet had been generous and he'd had the sense not to upset the flow of golden eggs by any single outrageous expense.

Beyond those items there were only the normal memorabilia of a frequenter of West End theatres and pubs — folded programmes, one or two publicity pictures of young actresses which showed drawing-pin holes at each corner, and a notable collection of beer mats. The only other photographs, secured with an elastic band, were all of family occasions, presumably taken by the dead young man, since he never figured in them.

"Too good to be true," Beaumont gave as his opinion. "Not so much as an old spoon and a scrap of tin foil with burn marks."

"Oh, he wasn't into drugs, Mr Beaumont," Mrs Lavender said. "Not in this house anyway. If his mother had caught a whiff of anything like that there'd have been the very devil to pay. Like a hawk she is, very much against drug abuse and drunkenness."

"Right. Thank you, Mrs Lavender. We won't bother you any more, then."

They went round the outside of the

house to pick up the car. While Beaumont got in behind the wheel Rosemary turned back to the woman. "Could I drop by your home sometime for a quiet word?"

She received a steady stare in return, then: "Why not, miss? If it's of an evening, after eight would suit us best."

In Burnham Beeches it was the distant pounding of a generator that drew Mott towards the site of the filming. Homing in on it, he turned right off Lord Mayor's Drive and came on three parked vans dappled by sunlight piercing autumn foliage that arched overhead. The white van had a side flap lowered to provide a service counter, and the unromantic smell of fried onions mingled with coffee announced that the film crew were taking a mid-morning break.

Paul Sefton, seated in a canvas director's chair on the edge of the denser woodland, had a can of beer in one hand and a clipboard on his knee. A single camera on a trolley was aimed at a slope ahead shaded by lofty beeches, its bank quilted with a drift of gold-brown leaves. Electricians were busy with cables and lights up a tree to one side, producing artificial sunbeams filtering in a cathedral effect between the silvery trunks, to gild the bronze foliage.

"Right. Final takes. Let's try and get it right first go," Sefton called.

There was a general move away from the vans, and a regrouping behind Paul's chair. Mott motioned to Silver to fall back. A clapper boy appeared, looked towards Paul for his cue and snapped shut his striped boards.

Over the leaf-strewn ridge appeared two heads, then the bodies of a young man and a girl walking hand in hand, their laughing faces turned towards each other. At the top the girl appeared to stumble and they fell together, laughing and rolling to the bottom, over and over in a flurry of dry leaves, like a pair of pretty puppies.

Five times they repeated the brief action, muttering complaints and cleaning themselves off each time between, while scene-shifters fussed over sweeping the leaves back into undisturbed perfection for the next take. And each time the girl and man reappeared they were taken delightfully by surprise as they stumbled, enchantingly spontaneous and unselfconscious, into each other's arms.

At length, "Fine," Paul declared. "That's it, boys and girls. It's as good as it'll ever be." He turned and beckoned to Mott who had thought they were unobserved.

"Visual clichés," Sefton apologized, rising and stretching. "I take it this is an official visitation concerning my brother. My late brother, I should say."

"Yes, sir. Just a few questions."

"I've one or two things to see to for a moment, then I'll be entirely at your disposal, Inspector. My car's the blue one over there. I shan't run off."

They strolled across in the direction of the Saab, appreciating the practised speed with which everything was being dismantled, packed away and stowed. Paul was talking first to one of his camera team, then to the actors, and finally to a verderer standing apart to check that all was accomplished without damage to the Corporation's estate.

"Sorry to keep you waiting," he said when he joined them. "In my car or yours?" He didn't appear in any way disturbed by their unannounced arrival, treating the fact that he must answer their queries as merely the next thing to be tackled and made a good job of.

Equally casual, Angus Mott produced the folder of photographs. "We hoped you might be able to help us with an identification." He watched Sefton's face as he scanned the pictures critically.

"I'm afraid not. Haven't come across the lady."

"Pity. Would you say she was a pro?"

"A pro what, Inspector? I would risk the opinion that she's quite new to modelling in the buff. Nice little face. A bit unsure of herself, wouldn't you say? Who took them? Quite arty effects, but the best pose is spoilt by over-exposure. That one too."

"These were part of a film in the camera your brother Joel used on the afternoon of his death."

"Oh Lord! I guessed it must have some connection with the case, of course. You don't think this girl could have — been responsible in some way? Self-defence perhaps?" He looked concerned now.

"We just wish to find her and ask what Joel went on to after he left her."

"Left her where, Inspector?"

"We ask the questions, sir. Would you tell us when you last saw your brother?"

"A couple of months ago, it must be. I'm sure I've told you this before."

"Perhaps you'd like to alter your statement when you've reconsidered, sir."

"Why should I? Dammit, are you suggesting I'm lying?" At last there showed some ruffling of the calm. The curved, reptilian mouth changed to a straight line.

"You were seen, sir. We have a witness." Mott risked a bluff and for a split second it seemed he might have brought it off. But something flickered in Sefton's eyes and he relaxed almost imperceptibly.

"I'm not invisible. I can be seen here and there at times by anyone with normal eyesight. But not in my brother's company. Not recently, that is."

"Would you mind telling me how you spent last Friday, the day of your brother's death, from midday onwards?"

The light blue eyes looked through Mott. "I do mind, but I suppose privacy on my part would only whet your appetite for imagined evils. On top of the usual bits and bobs it was rehearsal day for a live TV half-hour documentary slot. You can check with the studio if you wish. When I wasn't in full view of the participants I was with my Assistant Director, the continuity girl, or the sound editor."

He sounded convincing, but Mott had to go farther. "Perhaps you would give me the studio's telephone number and your office extension?"

"You can have one of our address stickers. Is there anything else you would like, Inspector?" The voice was over-polite, mocking.

"Yes, sir. If you've finished here, I should like DC Silver to accompany you in your car to Farnham Common and wait while I make the necessary inquiries by telephone." Equally polite, Mott refused to be upstaged.

"No handcuffs?"

"That is not required, sir. We appreciate your cooperation."

A girl answered Mott's call and identified herself as Sefton's secretary. "I'm sorry," she said after a slight pause, "but I can't give any studio information over the phone. You may be police, as you say, but I have no way of checking that."

Evidently not the same girl who had been so helpful to Yeadings the day before. Or perhaps the same one briefed not to make the same mistake twice?

"Hang on. I've got your boss here." Mott handed the receiver to Sefton. "She's being discreet. Tell her to answer our questions, please." His jaw clamped square as he met the amusement in Sefton's eyes.

"Nancy? Good girl, nice try. But they are genuine Old Bill. You can open up."

Paul Sefton appeared to be in the clear, having lunched late off a tray with the girl in their shared office, then spent half an hour in the cutting-room, a little longer with the sound dubber, and then returned to the documentary rehearsal at 4.30. At about 7.20 he and Nancy had "gone home", which was apparently a Battersea flat they shared near the Albert Bridge.

"Satisfied?" Sefton challenged as Mott

came out of the phone-box.

How could he be, while the man retained that wary-eyed look above the smiling mouth?

"That seems to be in order, sir. Thank you." Unimaginative, poker-faced Plod. Detective-Superintendent Mike Yeadings couldn't have done it better himself.

Yeadings was at the home of one of the teenage boys killed joyriding. A sad place and a very sad woman hunched in the pvc armchair opposite. She sat clasping a mug of hot tea as if more to warm her hands than for drinking, and the monotonous flow of complaint went drearily on: her ex-husband, her miseries and frustrations, her boys, their shortcomings and misfortunes.

There was a surviving brother, Leonard, but he'd been in a coach crash in Benidorm, wasn't due back till Sunday.

"Well, you'll have him for company then," Yeadings comforted. "How badly hurt is he?

On crutches, it seemed, and one leg in plaster to the thigh. They'd have flown him back before but something

304

went wrong and they'd had to break the leg again to reset it. Not a lucky family at all.

"Yeah, it'll be nice having him back." She raised a ghost of a smile. "He's a real lively one, Len. Cheers you up. Ever so funny, he is. You ought to hear his imitations. Does Lenny Henry a treat. Of course his dad had a touch, you know."

"Touch?"

"Of the tar brush. Lovely man, he was. Worked on a travelling fair. Six foot two, and Len's the living spit of him. Got killed putting up the Big Wheel in a storm, or else we'd have got married."

Yeadings nodded gravely. He hadn't heard that tar brush expression since he was a very small lad, long before anyone bothered about race relations.

A uniform constable tapped at the open lounge door. "Sir?"

He'd been giving the boy's room the customary going over, noticed the creaky floorboard and prised it up. "A right little Aladdin's Cave," he announced, grinning.

It was a cramped, three-bedroom semi. The mother had spoken of an 'old gent' lodger. He had the back bedroom, she a smaller one at the front next to this big one with the pair of stacked bunk beds.

"As the two sons share," Yeadings observed, "we can't prove this store of goodies belongs to the one who got killed. Cover it up before Mrs P sees it, and we'll come visiting when the older one gets back. Till then keep it under your helmet. I rather think I shall enjoy meeting this character Len."

Then downstairs again to the wretched Mrs Preece, who was sure to be even more wretched within a week.

Yeadings returned to a requested session with the Incident Room Allocation Officer and the usual complaints of resources being thin on the ground, and the case load forever elastic. The M4 had been setting up RTA records due to sections under repair and drivers made witless by impatience. As a result Traffic was under pressure, demanding reinforcement, and at the same time Drugs were setting up a big operation in harness with Customs from Heathrow.

"Mike," CI Atkinson said, stressing

each word, "we — are — scraping — the — barrel."

"Get me the blonde in the photos," Yeadings insisted. "Just that and we could be dismantling the Incident Room next day."

"You think a girl killed young Sefton?"

"Not necessarily. But once we've got her on stage I'm pretty certain the cast's all complete. The one we want is there among them. It just takes sorting out."

"So what about the serial muggings? No connection?"

"That's another matter. And that could be coming up to the boil too. The girl, Acky: that's all I ask."

"And I could be talking to the wall," muttered the CI.

Turning away, Yeadings found a WPC proffering a message slip. Since she seemed uncertain which of them should receive it, he held out his hand.

The two sentences were brief and critical. He ran a hand through his hair. "Just what we needed right now. I'm one more short. WPC Zyczynski urgently called to the Royal Berks Hospital. Her uncle's had a stroke."

"He's my aunt's husband," Rosemary said shortly when he called her in on her return. "No relation."

And no friend either, Yeadings gathered, reading the rebellious face. "And so — ?"

"So poor old Auntie will be in a state," she said, softening. "I'd better go."

"See what you can do. Tuck her up and get back here when you feel she's steadying. They brought you up, didn't they?"

"She was a second mother to me. Maybe I'd better move in with her until it's known how things will turn out. I'll write out the address and phone number for you."

"Good idea. So get away now while you can. I'll see Mott and Beaumont get informed. A pity if you miss the next bit of the action."

She glanced at him quickly.

"Those numbered fivers that Joel Sefton had from his sister's petty cash — two have just turned up. The message came through five minutes back. Paid over the counter at Barclays. By one of three possible depositors."

16

"THE tinker, the tailor and the candlestick-maker," suggested Beaumont.

"Actually it's a ladies' hairdresser's, a gents' outfitter's and a — er, turf accountant." The pro-manager, who had been instructed to give the police 'all necessary assistance but no more', smiled helpfully and reversed the sheet of paper in front of him so that the DS could copy down the addresses.

Beaumont entered them under 'wigs', 'duds' and 'bets', gave grudging thanks and regretted that the counter clerks hadn't been sufficiently alerted to the importance of the bank notes' numbers in time to observe who was handing them in. It wasn't until a bundle of paying-in slips had gone back for entry that a check on notes taken had shown up the wanted numbers. There might even have been more of the numbered notes paid into that till and subsequently handed out to someone making a later withdrawal, but it was quite certain, the bank guaranteed, that those retained had originated from one of the three named sources.

Driving past the Royal Berks, Beaumont wondered how Z was getting on with Auntie. Burning a hole in some chair seat, he guessed. Rotten luck to be pulled off the job at this point. He'd give her a ring tonight at the aunt's number, see what the score was about coming back. Not that he needed her, but it bugged him to keep changing partners.

He took the three addresses in order of nearness, fiddling about with a rack of silk ties till he had the outfitters' salesman on his toes, then showing his warrant card and asking for the boss. In a cramped office next to the two changing-rooms he was shown a ledger with recent bank deposits. These were made twice a week, and since the counterfeit scare of four years back every banknote number was entered beside the cash customer's name.

There hadn't been many fivers because most people now preferred to pay by cheque or credit card. None of the numbers corresponded with the ones Joel Sefton had carried on him the day he was killed. So a clear round for the gents' outfitter.

Next the beauty parlour, stinking of lacquer like a car body plant. "We are not Unisex," said the heavily made-up brunette at the desk, elocuting to a point some six inches above his head.

"It wouldn't worry me what your tastes were, love," he gave back. "I'm police and I want to see the manageress."

Here they weren't so meticulous as at the previous shop, probably because they were ten times busier and the cash flow equally greater. "Dunno. Couldn't say," was all he got about details of the deposit made that morning. All they could show him was the total for each denomination.

"So let's see what you kept back for the float," he demanded.

There were no more of the Sefton notes in that and, more significantly, none in a bundle of notes totalling eighty-five pounds set aside for paying the laundress. Well, it hadn't been likely that Joel Sefton had run up a bill here anyway. Much more likely to do that at the bookie's.

Taddy Bromwich was a translated and naturalized Brit, brought out by his mother from Czechoslovakia as a lad, his father having scraped a living off training horses until he bet on the wrong winner in the Prague Spring. He was small, energetic, totally cynical and hard as a nutmeg. Beaumont, a sporadic gambler, knew him of old and rather liked him.

"I like a good whodunit," Teddy said, neatly seated before the used dishes of a good hostelry lunch. "Tell me the story and where I come in."

"Does the name Sefton ring a bell with you?"

"A distant one. He got topped in a car park, right?"

"Right. And shortly before that maybe four, five hours — he'd had fifty in fivers off his sister. Not on him when found. Two at least of those were paid in by your man at Barclays this morning."

"Mr Beaumont, you are surely not insinuating that any of my punters could possibly be — ever so slightly — *rough?*"

"OK, Taddy. Have a good laugh, and then let's question whoever it was took the money in, shall we?"

And so, because there was plenty of money to look through, and despite the racing calendar offering many diversions that same afternoon, stacks of notes were flicked through like conjuring tricks and five more aces were turned up.

"Fifty in fivers?" one of the flat-eyed tellers repeated. "Could have been the Danish chick. She was owing. Had till two-thirty or we were going to her boss."

And there it was. Astrid Borck, *au pair* to a barrister's family out at Sonning. Only eighteen but already a compulsive gambler. And yes, she was the girl in Joel Sefton's photos.

You can shout 'Geronimo!' to the four winds but it's not like telling someone what you've pulled off. Beaumont couldn't resist stopping off at the hospital to let Z know he'd got a name for the girl.

Rosemary Zyczynski had followed her aunt through the screens as she went to promise the old man she would be back in the morning. He was lying propped up on his pillows, eyes open, the side of his face drawn into a satyr's leer. One

313

clawlike hand was close under his chin.

"D'you hear me, Will? I said I'll be back in the morning." She was trying to shout and yet still not be overheard from the other beds. And she was waiting for him to say it was all right.

But he wouldn't, couldn't. The first thing Rosemary had asked the sister was, "Which side?" and it had been the right. So he had lost his power of speech.

That disgusting old lecher, helpless to forbid his wife to go home and relax. But it didn't mean he couldn't hear. She supposed she'd better say something for her part.

Only, what? She stared at him and it seemed that his eyes grew brighter with anger to see her standing there, able to move away at will. She knew him so well she could see the resentment forming behind the thin skull. God, how she had loathed him, despised him. And now he was so pitiable that if she stayed any longer she would be forced to feel sorry for the garbage he'd become.

"I'll take care of Aunt Grace," she heard herself offer. As if he would care about anyone but himself. And yet there was a link between the two. Something had held them together all those years, if it was only the one's selfishness and the other's sense of duty. When he finally went the woman would be devastated.

His eyes grew meaner. A gurgle in his throat and a thread of saliva ran from his mouth and down his chin. "You'd better go now," the nurse said. "We don't want him getting upset. Doctor will be along again in a minute."

Since she had left their roof and set up on her own he had always been afraid of her getting together with his wife. Suspicious that Rosemary would one day unburden herself and his past wickedness would catch up with him. And now that he had hit rock bottom this was the moment he expected her to do it.

"Don't worry," she said, her hand on the screen. "Just get well."

She tucked her aunt's hand under her arm and squeezed it gently. "He'll get every attention here. We'd only be in the way, love."

Down in the foyer they ran into Beaumont who, not having the man's surname, had been going through the list of admissions for a recent stroke case. "Run you both home?" he offered.

But they had to pick up some things at Rosemary's first, so they settled on ringing for a taxi. While they waited for it outside, the DS explained about Astrid Borck. "DI Mott will want to interview her out at Sonning first," he ended. "Probably this evening."

"With you along. Why not? You found her. I'll not be back tonight. Consider Silver my partner while I'm off the roll."

"Mebbe. I don't know. Anyway, I thought you'd be glad to hear things are moving. I'd better report back now."

"He seems a nice cheerful young man," her aunt said, settling into the taxi.

"Married," Rosemary replied, and that closed the subject. Dear old Auntie; life for her was so simple.

"I don't want her forewarned," DI Mott told Yeadings. "I'd rather have a lost journey and go back tomorrow. If I ring up to make sure she's there, I shall have to explain who I am. Then she'll have time to concoct a tale."

"Or time to start worrying. I've usually found that butterflies under the belt work to our advantage. And she's not likely to do a runner, being a foreigner with a restricted work permit. The family she's with will see to that."

"All right, Boss. Have it your way. Why not make the call yourself? I know you rather fancy your chances."

"Why not, indeed? Give me a small share of your pretty girls, if only an earful. Is that the number?"

The telephone was answered after the fifth ring, and Yeadings asked if Miss Astrid Borck was at home. The woman at the far end seemed dubious, said, "Hang on, please," and went away. Another female voice came on, cool, decidedly English and curious. She regretted that Miss Borck was indisposed and unable to speak; would the caller care to leave a message?

"This is Detective-Superintendent Yeadings, Mrs Burrows," he told her. "It could be that when Miss Borck has spoken to my inspector she may feel a little happier than at present. Would it be convenient for him to call this evening? It's a question of having witnessed something."

"Oh heavens, what else has the wretched girl got herself mixed up in? We've had floods of tears and breast-beating already about some bill she ran up with a *bookie* of all things! Yes, do send your man along. My husband will be here in case she needs any legal advice. She is of age, you know."

She didn't look her eighteen years. Mott gave one glance at her and began to wish he'd waited for Rosemary Z to go with him instead of Beaumont. However, the girl had invited both her employers to sit in on the questioning so she wasn't unprotected.

"I believe you knew Joel Sefton," he suggested. "Did you know he was dead?"

Astrid burst into tears.

Mrs Burrows put a hand out to her. "My dear, *did* you know him? How perfectly awful for you. And we've been talking about it as if — Oh dear, Inspector. No wonder the poor child has been so upset."

"Did you know him?" Mott repeated.

"Yes."

"And were you with him on the afternoon of his death?"

"I — I, yes. He — gives me money to pay Bromwiches."

"Fifty pounds, was it?"

"Fifty, yes."

"In five-pound notes."

"Ten notes, yes."

"Did you sell him something?"

"I *lend* him my ring. One Grandfather gives me. The money is a lend too."

"That's why she told me," Mrs Burrows explained. "Because she wanted some pay in advance, to get it back. But I thought the bookie had it, as security."

"So how did you expect to get the ring back?" Mott asked, "when Joel was dead and nobody else knew anything about it."

Astrid shook her head miserably. "Perhaps I tell Grandfather I lose it. But at first I don't know Joel is dead. I don't read newspapers. My books are hard enough."

"That's right," the woman put in. "She told me about the ring before anyone mentioned the murd — mentioned anything about the Sefton boy. We said we'd help her buy the ring back, taking the money out of her wages, and instead of cheering up she suddenly broke down again. Now I can see why."

"Astrid," said Burrows, intervening for the first time, "why didn't you say he was a friend of yours?"

She didn't answer, staring down at the handkerchief she was winding between her fingers.

"Was he really a friend?" Mott asked quietly.

She looked up, struggling to find the right words. "First I like him. I like him quite a lot. He is polite and he makes me laugh. He has a nice car and I think he likes me to go in it."

"So you went with him that day to visit the properties?"

"He sees houses. Three, he says."

"But you only went to two. Is that right?"

"Because we — dispute ourselves."

"You quarrelled. What time did you leave that second house, the empty one?"

"Time? Oh, perhaps three-twenty, three-thirty. I say take me home now, so we go. But near the town a car comes after us and it makes him stop. He says it is his brother. He was a very angry man, and Joel says I must go. So I get out and I get a bus instead."

"You're sure he said it was his brother, Miss Borck?"

"Quite sure."

"What colour was his car?"

"Blue. Dark blue."

"I don't suppose you would know what make of car?"

She tossed her hair back from her eyes, more sure of herself now that the story had moved away from her own activities. "Of course I know about cars. It was a Saab."

They had gone into a huddle again in Mike Yeadings's office. "So the ball's right back in the family's court, eh?" he said, sounding unsurprised. "All along I've felt the answer was out at Marisbank. Let's try some scenarios."

"Right," Mott accepted. "They're nearly back to town and the blue Saab forces Joel into a lay-by. Astrid Borck is vague about the locality but it was on her bus

321

route. She scarpered, leaving the ring with Joel."

"Which of them had the fifty pounds at that point?"

"Taddy's man. She'd nipped in to pay up before the threatened chop of two-thirty on Friday afternoon. She'd arranged to pledge the ring with Joel at some previous meeting, when he'd taken a fancy to it. They met by appointment after lunch on Friday, her half-day, and did the swap."

"Joel never intending, surely, to let the girl have it back."

"Unless, after due course of time — when she'd saved enough from her wages to repay the loan — Joel could have arranged for his mother to 'lose' the thing. He was ingenious enough."

"So he'd identified the Saab as his brother's," Yeadings said slowly, eyes narrowed. "Do we agree that it was probably his brother Paul in it? Not the other brother? Or someone who knew Joel and was perhaps delivering the car back from a garage, or some such?"

"The Saab's driver had been asking for Joel at Oxford Poly at lunch-time. The description given fits Paul. Christopher is thirty pounds heavier and five inches taller, so that wasn't him. At three-twenty or three-thirty, according to Borck, she left the empty house with Joel after the sexual athletics and camera shots."

"Part payment for the loan facilities," Beaumont put in drily.

"So, driving at normal speed, they'd easily have reached Sonning before four pm."

"We're getting near Dr Littlejohn's early limit for time of death."

"Yes, and the girl said the brother was 'a very angry man'."

"Angry about what?" Yeadings pondered. "Any ideas? The brothers didn't normally meet except on family occasions centred round the mother. Had they previously been in contact by phone, or through a third party? If so, who?"

"The sister Erica? Could she have rung Paul and told him Joel had poked around inside her desk, found out something he shouldn't know?" Beaumont suggested.

"That would imply some association between Erica and Paul. I really don't see it," Yeadings gave as his opinion.

"Erica's very independent, copes with her own problems. Paul's quite cut himself off from the family. They're miles apart."

"If she rang straight after Joel left it wouldn't have given Paul time to get to Oxford from the studio," Mott reckoned.

They all considered this.

"Paul isn't entirely cut off," Beaumont reminded them. "He was called in for yesterday's family conference and appeared on the dot, at cost to his work. And what was that all about anyway? Surely not because the kid was sent home sick from school?"

Yeadings sighed and took two sheets of paper from the drawer at his left elbow. "You'd better both take a look at this. Z talked to the child and the result was disturbing. This is as near verbatim as she could manage. It's not in her official report because Kit's only eleven and there wasn't an adult present. Besides, I wanted to think about it first, decide in my own mind who else might have known the circumstances. Regard this as confidential."

Mott read first, whistled and passed

the papers on. "What decision did you come to?"

"None yet."

"Oh Lord," Beaumont said, catching up. "It's enough to push any of them over the edge."

"Josie didn't know," Yeadings insisted. "Z was sure of that. She hadn't even suspected, wanted to believe Joel had grown out of his prurient habits."

"The little girl wasn't just sick, then?" Beaumont asked. "Has she seen a doctor?"

"A psychiatrist called this morning," Yeadings told them. "I asked Mrs Lavender to let me know at once about all visitors to the house, and I looked his name up. He specializes in anorexic cases. Which makes me think that if anyone in the family does know about the association with Joel, it's not yet been shared. They're still officially trying to treat the symptoms."

"If the girl's father or grandmother knew on Friday, would they have made the child go to school this week?" Mott asked.

"Supposition," Yeadings murmured. "Normally it would be heartless. But if you'd just killed because you knew what her uncle had done to her, wouldn't you want it thought you didn't know? Wouldn't you cling like mad to a calm front and everyday routine? But, as I said, it's all supposition."

"The question we've all wandered off," Beaumont reminded them, "is who was in the blue Saab? Both brothers have alibis for Friday afternoon. Paul or Chris, which? Chris as father would be nearest the child, more likely to find out and more likely to blow his top. Paul, on the other hand, could well have been the one at Oxford during the period his secretary covered for him."

"And they live together," Mott recalled. "Paul and his secretary, Nancy, share a flat. Personal obligations. She was also being very discreet when I first spoke to her on the phone."

"He gets my vote," Beaumont decided. "Let's go and shred Paul's alibi."

17

THE card marked Sefton was opposite the bell for the third floor. A girl's voice came metallically through the grille, demanding, "Who is it?"

"Detective-Inspector Mott with Sergeant Beaumont. We have one or two more points you could help us to clear up."

She hesitated. "I can't imagine why you think that. I thought it was a mugging case you're investigating. Nothing at all to do with me."

"Shall we discuss that indoors, miss? It's a little public where we're standing."

"Why not some other time? It's not convenient now."

"It needn't take long."

In the pause after this a quiet voice came from behind them. "Inspector — er, Mott, isn't it?" Paul Sefton stood there, rain glinting in his pale hair and over his jacket shoulders.

Mott moved aside as Sefton used his

key on the street door. "Do come up, Officers. I always warn Nancy not to let anyone in after dusk when she's alone. Can't be too careful, can we?"

It was an attempt at levity, but under it Mott could detect a note of resignation. He caught Beaumont's eye behind the man's back, and nodded.

The large room they were led into overlooked the Albert Bridge Road, but no sound of London traffic reached them at this level. The furnishings were unfussy and comfortable, a man's room that doubled as lounge and office. Three watercolour landscapes were the only wall decoration, each giving a sense of receding distance. Looking around, Mott felt it would be a good place to get back to after hard work.

"Do sit down," Sefton invited. "What's troubling you, Inspector?"

The girl had appeared in a doorway. She was wearing a dressing-gown and carried a sewing-basket across to a settee where a black cocktail dress was spread out.

"We'll be going out when Nancy's fixed her hem," Sefton explained. "Seven-thirty for eight."

"I'll be brief then, sir. Concerning your alibi for Friday afternoon. Previously when I mentioned a witness you saw no reason to modify your first statement. Would you care to now?"

"Why should I?"

"Because we have a second witness. The first in Oxford, the second in a lay-by in Sonning Lane."

Sefton's grimace implied distaste. "Yes. Well, perhaps it was rather silly of me to cut corners."

"You did a little more than that, sir."

"You're trying to find out who killed my brother. I certainly didn't. It's wasted time checking up on what I might or might not have been doing when it happened."

"Since you're the last known person to speak with him, your account of that meeting could be of vital importance. Quite apart from diverting police effort by issuing a false statement."

Paul lowered himself on the window-seat and ran one hand through his damp hair. "Very well. I stand rebuked. I — I had a bone to pick with my brother and

I was mad enough to chase all the way over to Headington, thinking he'd be at the Oxford Poly. As doubtless you know, he wasn't. I thought he might be having lunch at the Mitre or the Randolph, so I carried on, had the usual trouble trying to park the car in central Oxford, looked for him, had lunch myself and finally gave up. While there I went into the Ashmolean Museum to check on an Egyptian exhibit I need copied for a travel commercial. I returned via Reading and on the A4 thought I saw Joel's TVR turning into Sonning Lane, so I overtook and made him draw up."

"And then, sir?"

"I had it out with him."

"I'm afraid that's not enough, in the circumstances."

"It's all you're getting. Apart from the fact that I knocked him down and left him bloodied. But he was all right. I mean, I saw him get up and get in the car again, with a handkerchief to his face."

Paul Sefton stood languidly up and came across to where Mott was sitting. "Look, Inspector, this time you've got the truth. I'm sorry I lied before. I'm even more sorry I asked Nancy to lie for me. But she will tell you what time it really was when I got back for the rehearsal. My assistant had started without me, and we carried on till after six-thirty. All the rest about lunching in the office, the cutting-room and the dubber — was incorrect."

· "I still need to know the nature of your quarrel with your brother, Mr Sefton."

"Then you must want. I'm bloody well not saying. You'd better go now, Inspector. I have to change, and I'm not yet famous enough to arrive late at this reception."

Mott looked stony. "When you have reconsidered, perhaps you will be more cooperative. We shall, of course, be seeing you again. Good night, sir,"

The girl followed them to the flat door and closed it quietly behind them. For a moment her eyes had met Mott's and he saw some message in them but could not read it. Not hard enough for hostility, not regret exactly, not apprehension, but purposeful in some way. Well, time might tell. He would be back.

"So," he said, when they were again in the car with the wipers rhythmically clearing the windscreen, "what did you make of that?"

"Admits he marked his brother's face."

"Before death. Littlejohn didn't find that under the post-mortem slashings. We'll have to call on the Path Lab again. There'd be a certain amount of swelling from the blow. Was the mutilation meant to cover that up? But why bother when it's consistent with mugging? And how long does it take the bruising to come up on a live person?"

Beaumont grunted. "Did you notice the signet ring on Sefton's left hand? And he unlocked the door with that one. He's a southpaw. No split knuckles but it could be that the ring tore his brother's face. It sounds as if Paul didn't bother to wait and find out the finer details."

"If you believe him. All the same, he had two cars there. His own — to take the body into the Goldbasket supermarket and dump it; the dead man's, to be delivered there later. He's a little taller than Joel, but he could be the 'young man' seen taking the car park ticket."

"We'll need to find out if anyone saw either car left anywhere in the neighbourhood between four and ten-thirty p.m."

"Inquiries to extend from Sonning to Callendar Lane, because if Joel Sefton left that lay-by alive he could have driven somewhere to clean up. The obvious direction would be homewards." Mott sighed. "More leg-work, and CI Atkinson's already reallocating our uniform men. So let's hope Z's back on the job tomorrow."

At 9.30 p.m., having dined off tinned ravioli on burnt and scraped toast while watching the TV news, Beaumont decided that hospital visiting hours were well past. He rang Rosemary at her aunt's number and the girl answered.

"Z," he said, "we have developments, which I'll not give you over the wire. So if you're coming in tomorrow, make it early, will you?"

"I'll be there. Auntie's got a neighbour standing by during the day. Her husband's stable. They think he'll pull through, till the next time."

333

"Good. I'll pick you up at eight sharp. That gives me a chance to put you in the picture."

Tomorrow is Thursday, she thought, putting down the receiver. It would be a feather in everyone's cap if they cleared the case in under a week. But then, once the reports were in, back into uniform. A return to trudge and routine. Not so good.

Mike Yeadings knocked off work soon after Mott had dropped in to report verbally on his meeting with Paul Sefton. He needed space to think in, and too much was going on around his office. He also needed Nan, even Nan up to her elbows in baking or coping with the children. He'd help her clear the decks and then he'd pick her brains, siphon off some of her down-to-earth wisdom.

He found the children were already disposed of for the night, and Nan was curled up on the settee, blow-drying her hair. He kissed her through a puff of scented hot air, went to pour drinks and came back to sit alongside. She shut off the dryer, took her vermouth — soda from him and sighed. "This is bliss."

"Not for long. I have a tale to tell you." And he read aloud to her the private report Rosemary had made for him on her conversation with the Sefton granddaughter. At its end he stole a glance at her thoughtful face. "This is something you must know more about than I do."

"Possibly. Her uncle, it seems. Um."

"And he's dead, murdered."

"Tell me all about the family."

He started in on it, discovered there was more than he realized he knew, so went back to replenish their glasses. "Shall I get us something out of a tin?"

"There's yesterday's goulash. Could you warm it up in a saucepan? And we'll have frozen mixed veg."

He left her to turn the problem in her mind, coming back with two trays laid for supper.

"What you want to know," Nan said slowly, "is which of them, given the knowledge and the opportunity, was likely to have taken the fatal swing at him."

"Well?"

"Any or all of them. If it had happened

to — to my child, I'd have gone for him with my nails, whoever it was and whatever my earlier feelings for him. Is that answer enough? Not that I could really answer for anyone else."

"Yes, I see. When you were nursing, you must have come across cases like this . . . "

"Incest and child abuse? Yes. And always heavily charged with emotion. There could have been violence from any party. There often was. In hospital we patched up what we could and learned to keep a still tongue once the child in question was getting help."

"The trouble here is that we don't know who is aware of what was going on."

"You are pretty sure who knows *nothing*. Josie, the young aunt. So why not approach her? See if she thinks it's feasible, this business between Joel and Kit. Beg her discretion. Either she'll refute it out of hand or she'll start to put indications together and something definite will take shape. Get an outsider's opinion too — Mrs Lavender's, if you can be sure she'll not gossip."

"Josie's pretty inexperienced, I think.

It's a lot to put on young shoulders."

"She'll probably prefer it, if it can take some of the weight off the child's. Does that help?"

In the morning the team met up again in Yeadings's office. "I've made your notes on Kit available to everyone here, he told Rosemary, "and what we now have to decide is first, are your suspicions justified? Second — if so, who also is in the know? And third — is there anyone in whom the knowledge could have provoked sufficient anger to occasion Joel Sefton's death?"

"Z, you've already suggested seeing Mrs Lavender. Is she working today or at home?"

"She was at Marisbank yesterday, so I think she has today free. I'll ring and find out."

"When we've finished here. Then I'll see if PC Lavender can be sent with you to interview his mother. Beaumont has the Danish girl, Borck, coming in to sign her statement. DI Mott wants to go further into the dead man's encounter with Paul. If possible, Angus, get that secretary apart from him and see how much he told her on his return. He's a pretty smooth character, and fisticuffs with your own brother after a considerable pursuit has to have a reason. He wouldn't have been exactly unruffled afterwards, so she's bound to have asked him what was up. With the right handling she may see it's to his advantage in the long run to come clean.

He looked round at them. "For myself, I'm going after Josie Sefton, because I want her opinion on the incest possibility, and she's the only one of the family my nose tells me couldn't have caused her brother's death."

As they left, Yeadings called Rosemary back. "Would you put through the call to Josie for me? On the outside line. If her mother answers she may take you for a London friend."

"Of course, sir." She found the number in her notebook and dialled. Almost immediately the call was answered. "It is Miss Josie Sefton, sir. Miss Sefton, I have Detective-Superintendent Yeadings here. One moment, please."

He nodded to the WPC and she went

out. "Hallo, my dear, could we meet and talk, d'you think? Privately would be best."

Through the open conservatory door Rosemary could see Harriet seated at her little breakfast table. She had stopped reading her letters and now dangled her glasses from one hand, listening.

"It's all right, Mother. It's for me. Just Gaynor." She turned her back and said, "Well, how are things with you?"

"Not alone?" Yeadings inquired.

"That's right. I'm staying on at least for another week." She heard the crackle of the newspaper as Harriet shook out its folds and then the outer door opening as she went out to read it on the garden seat. "OK now," she said. "Sorry about that. I was pretending you were my flatmate."

"It's a long time since I had a clandestine conversation with a young lady. And now I'm trying to set up an assignation. A highly proper one, of course. I have to attend the inquest this morning, but afterwards — "

"I'm going with Mother," Josie said. "Mr Wetherby's representing the family and he said it wasn't necessary, but Mother insisted. And she won't let anyone else go with her. But I'll be free afterwards. She's going back with Wetherby to his chambers. Something about changing her will, I think. Shall I wait around for you?"

"I'll try to get away straight after the adjournment."

"Adjournment? Is that certain?"

"It's usual with this sort of case. The police haven't much to go on. Evidence will be confined to identity, place, time and a brief medical report on the main injury. It will all be very short."

"I see. Perhaps you could drive me home, then? We could talk here. Chris has taken Kit up to see some doctor in London. He wanted a second opinion after the one chosen by Mother came yesterday. For once he's going to make up his own mind about what to do, but he's really as much in the dark about Kit's condition as we all are."

"That would be a good idea. Me driving you home, I mean. Probably the other too. I'll see you later, then, Miss Sefton. Goodbye."

PC Lavender had been on night duty and was still in the canteen. When the duty sergeant's shout came he thought it must be a quibble over his report or a sudden overtime emergency. That he was to accompany WPC Zyczynski to his own home to interview his mother struck him as farcical.

"I suppose you want the lowdown on the Seftons," he assumed as he drove her out there in the Vauxhall banger. "But why take me along? Is this a freebie or am I getting overtime on it?"

"No overtime," Rosemary said firmly. "You are to be there in a family capacity to protect your mother from potential police brutality."

"I like that! Ma could tie you in knots with one arm behind her back. She's no pushover."

However tough she might be, Mrs Lavender was a very good cook and Thursday was her baking day. Rosemary and Nick arrived simultaneously with a tray of hot soda scones from the oven. She seated them on stools in the kitchen and reached for the coffee-grinder.

"Mr Yeadings has sent this — er, us, to get background about the Seftons," Nick explained.

Mrs Lavender looked levelly at Rosemary and said nothing.

"It's a little unusual," the girl admitted, "and we realize you're in a delicate position. But because your son is one of us, and you know we will be utterly discreet about anything you may tell us, Mr Yeadings wanted to know how you personally felt."

"Since when couldn't Mr Yeadings go by his own feelings?" The woman sprinkled flour on a board and threw a lump of pastry on it.

"He has his own ideas, but he knows your opinion is trustworthy — "

"Maybe the Seftons think I'm trustworthy too. How about that? I've been working for them now for six, no, seven years. You might say I've seen young Joel grow up from a little lad to a young man, and now he's been done to death. What would you expect me to feel about it?"

"It is awful, I agree."

"A wasted life."

"Did you like him?"

342

"It wasn't my business to like or dislike anybody there." She floured the rolling-pin and began working the pastry. "But I do find it sad. You would think that young man had everything in the world he could want. But it just wasn't enough. He had to take from others whatever they valued. To sort of build himself up and make nothing of them."

She was turning and rolling the pastry, frowning down at her hands. "I remember one day — he was in the kitchen there, just like you are yourselves now, and I was getting on with my work. He suddenly said, 'Do you know what I'd like more than anything, Lavvy? To go right back and start over again.' And I thought, well he can't be all that bad if he's sad about what he's become."

"Lost innocence. Do you think the idea of innocence attracted him?"

The busy hands stopped. Mrs Lavender looked up and stared squarely at the policewoman. She unbent and brushed her floury palms off on a kitchen towel.

"Nick, just go and dig me a few beets, would you? I want to talk to the young lady on her own."

He protested, but he went, leaving the door ajar. Rosemary went over and closed it firmly.

Mrs Lavender faced up to her, honest face flushed. "I know right enough what Mr Yeadings is after. It's about Miss Kit, isn't it? He wants to know whether Mr Christopher found out about what his brother was up to with his little girl. And if he got in such a rage that he killed him."

18

ANGUS MOTT tried ringing the studio and asking for Nancy. First he got a cool response from the switchboard and cursed himself for not having the girl's surname. "Mr Sefton's secretary," he explained. "And listen, it's her I want, not him."

But he was out of luck. She had the morning off for a dental appointment. Suspecting a euphemism to cover whatever hangover last night's party had left her with, he rang the flat. There was no answer.

Impatient at the enforced inactivity, he went to sit in on Beaumont's signing session with Astrid Borck and her barrister boss. Shortly before the statement was due for re-reading, a message came that a Miss Partridge was asking for him at Reception. He took his time getting there, then found it was Nancy.

"Hullo," she said, almost resentfully. "I thought if Paul's too proud to get himself

345

off the hook, I'm not. Only, does he have to know?"

"Know what, Miss Partridge?"

"That I'm going to tell all. You see, I really am fond of him, and he does expect me to be one hundred per cent his girl."

Mott softened. "We do exercise discretion for a police informer."

She flared immediately at the description, then caught the smile in his eyes and stopped. "I'll trust you, then. Many wouldn't. Can we go somewhere quiet and talk?"

There was no interview room free so he took her to the team's empty office, across the corridor from Yeadings. There was no need to offer refreshments; she was more than ready to unburden herself.

"I met Joel Sefton about a fortnight ago, at a party in Islington," she said. "He was just Joel and I was Nancy. I'd no idea who his family were, but we got talking about our jobs and I said I worked for Paul Sefton. He upgraded himself a bit and claimed he was an architect in Oxford."

So far it sounded true to form. Mott nodded. "Go on."

"At first he seemed to be chatting me up, and then I got the impression he was teasing me. He was very clever about it because I started noticing little things about him — the way he handled his drink, a certain way of talking. When he asked didn't I think Paul Sefton was just gorgeous, I was pretty certain. I started easing off, to go and find someone else to talk to, only he had me in a corner."

"You thought he was a homosexual," Mott prompted her after her next pause became marked.

"Yes. I don't mind them. There are quite a number in our sort of work and often they're easier to get on with than real men. But it was when he talked like that about Paul that it stuck in my throat. And there was worse to come."

"Yes?"

"He boasted that they'd been lovers, that he'd once lived with Paul at the flat. I thought it must be true because he described the place to me, the layout and furniture, even the pictures on the walls, just as if I'd be interested to know more about my boss's background. I felt really sick. I thought about him with Paul, together in our bed. It was awful!"

"So what did you do?"

"I was feeling pretty rotten and I used that as an excuse to get away. I took a taxi home. Paul wasn't there. He'd gone down to Southampton for two days, and when he phoned later that night I couldn't say anything. He thought I had a thick head or something, and for days afterwards we couldn't somehow get through to each other. I kept watching him, looking for signs that he was — unnatural. And I told myself perhaps it had been a phase, that he'd just tried living like that and given it up. I was trying hard to be broadminded and grown-up about it."

"So you never let on."

"In the end Paul made me tell him. He's sensitive to people, and he could see something was very wrong. He assumed that I — that I'd found someone else and was waiting for the right moment to pull out. Eventually it sort of exploded out of me. That was Thursday night, last week."

"I see. It all came out, then Paul explained it had been his brother, not a lover, and you both knew Joel had been setting you up?"

"I didn't know Paul could be so angry. Not loud or raging, but deadly quiet. I was terrified of what he might do."

"To you?"

"Oh no! He was so *comforting* to me. But all the time that terrible look in his eyes."

"As if he could kill?"

She looked away, her mouth held tight as she fought to control herself. "When I heard about the — the murder, that it was a violent mugging, of course I thought ... And the very day afterwards! But then I worked it out; the time he came back, and how I was with him or near him right from late afternoon on. I knew it couldn't have been Paul. I wouldn't have come and told you all this except that I knew he was totally innocent. You heard what he said: he had words, knocked Joel down and then saw him get back in his car. The newspapers said Joel had driven his own car into the Goldbasket yard Friday night about eleven. Paul was with me then, in bed at the flat. That completely exonerates him, doesn't it?"

Mott looked thoughtful. "He certainly

couldn't have killed him that night, it's true." But it had been earlier, as the police now knew. Joel had died between 4.30 and 8.30 p.m. All Paul needed to do after killing him that afternoon was to dispose of the body using his own Saab, then later get someone to drive Joel's car to the same parking area where he'd stashed the body.

"You did the right thing coming to explain," he told her, "but I'm afraid we do have to have it in writing and signed. So shall we do that now?"

Mike Yeadings watched Harriet Sefton emerge and get in the solicitor's car, which was parked behind her own. She nodded coolly to her daughter left standing at the kerbside. He walked slowly across and touched her arm. "That wasn't too bad, was it?"

"It was like waiting about in a modern hospital. Everyone seemed to know exactly what they were doing except me."

"If you felt like that, it didn't show. You looked as cool as your mother." But more human, he thought. "My car's across the road. Shall we go?"

In the town one hardly noticed the drizzle, and by the time they were among the leafy lanes it seemed to have been struck motionless, hanging suspended in fine mist among the tunnels of trees. The smells were all earthy and dank. Hard, Yeadings thought, not to dwell on mortality and decay. They scarcely spoke, and on reaching the house she seemed unwilling to go into it.

"Would you show me the garden?" he asked.

She led him round by a side path to the main lawn which fell away towards the river, merging greyly into the mist. Trees and the nearby gallows shapes of the pergola dripped moisture, all part of the same monochrome theme.

Rounding a bay of evergreens they came on the little potting shed where Harriet had sat the first time Yeadings set eyes on her.

"This is where I found your mother, after she'd heard about Joel," he said. "What a resilient woman she is. I know she grieves inside, but no stranger would ever guess it."

"She believes in discipline. It was the

core of her training. It's very hard, you know, to become a good ballerina. You have to give up a lot, and drive yourself. And it's physically painful."

"But the strength was in her to begin with. She has an uncompromising nature."

"Yes." Josie smiled wryly and went for a lighter tone. "Mother's pretty pushy. Once she'd given up pushing at her career, she started on Daddy and us. Maybe we've inherited it. As a family we're all pushy in our different ways."

"How different?"

"Oh, it's because of the self-regarding thing; and compensation. Erica's big-framed like Daddy was, but she longed to be petite and feminine. So she's dissatisfied with herself always impatient for change. She directs it into her work. She wants to impress everyone with her ability, because she doesn't see herself as beautiful . . .

"Chris — well, basically he's modest. He regards his personal life as a disaster area, and he did get trampled on by that luscious wife of his. It's his jellyfish side. But when he comes to business, organizing people's money, he's as buttoned up as a clam, successful to satisfy himself not appearances.

"Paul's ambitions are less for himself than for the art he's producing: a sort of Pygmalion complex. He's a bit shadowy, but I've hopes that maybe — "

"Maybe — ?"

"Something will come along to make it worth his emerging, as a solid, demanding person. There's a new girl in his life. He's never volunteered as much before. Love, you know." She smiled almost wistfully. "It does things."

"Then, chronologically, we come to you."

"Um, yes. I'm a compulsive interferer. I tidy up other people's things and leave my own in a mess. Pushy in that way."

"A do-gooder perhaps."

"God, I hope not. I mean, that's a terribly arrogant thing to be. Am I arrogant?"

Yeadings cocked an eyebrow at her. "Anything but. Simply kind, I should say."

She eyed him doubtfully, then shrugged and started walking again. "We've reached

Joel now. That's what you've been working towards, isn't it?" She shot him a shrewd glance. "What and who was Joel Sefton? And all you're really sure of is that he's dead. So you ask me, and that makes me responsible for him in a way. I think I'll pass on this one."

They continued for a way in silence, then, "Pity," said Yeadings. "I need to know him. You see, I'm pretty sure he wasn't a random victim like the others. This time it was more than a mugging. No stranger killed him, but someone close. I trust my nose for things like this. A relationship gone wrong, a doubtful deal, a ditched friend, broken faith: something that blew up in his face."

Josie stared fiercely at the ground, hands thrust deep in the pockets of her long cardigan. When she looked up her face was flushed with anger. "Yes. Any of those circumstances. Sooner or later someone would have had enough of being let down. Joel was the most pushy of us all, but with him it was different. He never saw what he was pushing against. Only himself needing to

354

score. He was in love with the charming, handsome, brilliant boy he saw in the mirror. For him no one else existed, except as a factor in getting what he wanted and a subject to exercise his talents on."

She walked on, thinking backwards, remembering. "In all our childhood together I can't recall one generous impulse from him, or a flicker of genuine sympathy. When he cried it wasn't from fear or loneliness, but frustrated anger. He was a clever little horror, and he grew up a manipulator."

"Clever, you say." Yeadings picked on that single quality. "His college records don't bear that out. Did you know that?"

"No." She considered it. "That simply means he hadn't bothered. He could do anything he set his mind to." She didn't follow the point any farther. At the end of the rose walk she turned abruptly to face Yeadings. "There, you've got what you wanted: the portrait, warts and all. I was the nearest to Joel in age and, because of that, often the first he worked on. So you may say that we had to compete for Mother's attention, and it's sour grapes on my part, because I lost out. Perhaps it's better if you do think that. Because I've said too much."

Again the brief fierce, challenging stare and then she turned back towards the house, walking away into the mist between skeletal black stems of roses, scratchy charcoal lines against a grey-washed backcloth.

Yeadings coughed as river damp reached his throat. He dismissed the sour grapes excuse. Josie was too kindly to be burnt up by acid envy. She would have expected much at first of her little brother, been constantly disappointed and then retreated to avoid further hurt. That withdrawal had given her the perspective to observe him with a detachment none of her siblings seemed to possess, observation from within the family, enabling her to make what Harriet called 'Josie's thumbnail sketches'. And now, with Joel dead — and his short life bound to be dissected — she retained the vision, but a slow anger had finally swamped the detachment. Josie felt involved by Joel because of her private knowledge of him, and the fact upset her very much.

Pondering this, Yeadings went circuitously back towards the house. She had left the conservatory door open and he followed her to the kitchen.

Without speaking, she filled and switched on the kettle, set out a teapot, crockery and spoons. Not until he had a filled cup in front of him did he pull out a chair and sit down opposite her. For the first time she could not avoid his eyes.

"Your account of the family was one short. You left out the youngest. Was Kit omitted protectively, because being a child she was as yet unformed, or was it because she presents a special problem?"

Josie continued stirring her tea, refusing to look up. Yeadings went relentlessly on.

"Kit was nearest in age to her uncle Joel after you. It would be interesting to find out the child's opinion of the dead young man. Not perhaps a job for me or Mott, but Rosemary Zyczynski seems to have got quite close to her. Perhaps if she saw her again . . . ?"

"Leave her alone!" Josie said fiercely. "Why can't you leave us all alone?"

"You know why I can't. It's my job,

Josie. Think: not a stranger who killed him, but someone close who knew him well. So where does that lead us? Back to the family. Harriet Sefton, Erica Sefton, Christopher Sefton, Paul Sefton, Josie Sefton, and — why not? — Kit Sefton. All of you with good reason to strike out at him in anger."

Josie raised a white face drained of life. "What did that policewoman tell you? About me, I mean?"

"That your brother played unkind tricks on you and you resented it enough to go away and live on your own."

"Is that all?"

"And then we wondered whether you hadn't been just a little uneasy that five years later Christopher brought his daughter here."

In the silence he was suddenly aware of the soft whirring of the electric clock behind him.

Josie was struggling with herself to be truthful. He could barely hear the low voice when she replied. "Of course I was uneasy, but Joel was no longer an adolescent, and I knew Mother would give Kit a room near her own, on the first floor. She should have been safe there."

"You said, 'should have been', not 'was'."

"Oh God, I don't know. I told myself it was dirty-minded to suspect. But once I caught them looking at each other and — "

"And didn't want to believe what you saw."

"Couldn't!"

"But if it was true — no, I'm only saying *if* — who else would have had that knowledge? And might have acted on it?"

"Nobody! Superintendent, Joel was killed *in Reading*. Right away from the family. How can you possibly twist the facts to make it seem one of us was involved?"

"*Was* he killed in Reading? Certainly his body was found there. But on Friday afternoon he came back. It's only a matter of time before we discover who else was here in the house then. The family *is* involved, Josie."

"How can you prove he was here if no one saw him?"

Yeadings leaned back, his eyes still holding the girl's mesmerized. "I was watching you both this morning, your mother particularly, from close by. I noticed the ring she wore. An antique worked silver one, set with a ruby. I hadn't seen it on her before."

"What has that to do with anything?"

"Your brother bought it as a birthday gift for her. How did it reach your mother?"

"It was with the other presents on the table in the drawing-room on Saturday morning."

"Gift-wrapped?"

"Yes, of course. Wait a moment. It was in the same kind of paper Kit used. Shiny pink with silver spots."

"How was it recognized as being from him?"

"There was a gift tag with his name on, and the usual sort of message. And it's no good being clever about how did it get on the table, because I remember now. Kit went up to see if Joel was in his room, and she brought it down. She probably wrapped it too, thinking he was running late and wouldn't have time. You see, he *hadn't* been here to do it himself."

"Yes, I do see. But he bought the ring as late as Friday afternoon. So I ask again: when he came home with it, who else was here?"

They met in an atmosphere of suppressed tension. Mott gave his opinion that Paul could have been the killer, but would have needed help with the later removal of Joel's car. His immediate motive would have been the way his brother set out to destroy his relationship with Nancy.

"So he didn't need to know what Joel was up to with Kit," Yeadings agreed. "But it's possible the others knew, living in the same house. Z, what did Mrs Lavender give you?"

"She had no doubt about it," Rosemary said slowly. "A fortnight ago the laundry was brought forward a day, so she had to go and collect bed linen and night clothes for the wash. Normally the family all make their own beds before leaving each morning. It's one of Harriet's rules. Mrs Lavender found an empty condom packet in Joel's pyjama pocket. She couldn't understand it because he hadn't slept

361

away and there was no woman in the house but his mother and the child. She kept it to herself but she began to watch, and she found marks in the child's bed. She still hadn't made up her mind who to tell when suddenly Joel was killed."

She caught Mott's eye and he nodded for her to go on before there was general discussion. "After Mrs Lavender, I went on to Kit's school and spoke to the Head. She had already written to the girl's father asking him to take her away as she was a disturbing influence. She spoke of hysterical behaviour, the eating problem we already knew about, and one final thing. On the Friday afternoon Kit was down for a House netball practice. Instead it was reported that she was seen getting into a sports car with a young man. That was about four-thirty. No description of the young man because he kept a handkerchief up to his face and was only there a brief moment before roaring off."

"So Joel met her from school and they went home, thinking the house was empty." Yeadings looked round at them. "You know the alibis given: the father at work in the City, the grandmother at a charity meeting for the Thames Valley Hospice, Paul returned to rehearsal, Erica in conference over the merger, Josie supposedly at the DTI, and Mrs Lavender off the premises because she'd changed Friday to a full day Saturday on account of the special birthday lunch. I think we have to consider Mrs Lavender, since it's now certain she knew about what was going on."

"And Josie knew."

"Well, did she? At most strongly suspected," Yeadings said. "Isn't it reasonable to suppose that sharp-eyed Harriet had also noticed something? And suppose she told Kit's father? It's a valid motive for them all, even for the child herself in view of the pressure she's under. We have to do a little more intensive delving into their whereabouts on Friday afternoon and evening. And I want that completed by tomorrow."

Josie heard the crunch of tyres on gravel as Harriet's Mercedes came round to the rear garage. She had cleared away the tea things after the superintendent left but she still sat on in the kitchen, overcome by a mental block that affected her limbs as well. She listened to her mother's footsteps crossing the tiles of the conservatory floor and wondered how she would ever find the words to talk to her again.

It was as if over the years they had merely made noises at each other and never said anything. Harriet's daughter, and she could not communicate with her. But then, for Harriet there had surely been only one child permitted to come close. And in a few days they would be burying him. Today's piece of officialdom was something much less.

The footsteps halted in the doorway. She could picture Harriet peeling off her gloves, looking around. "I was surprised to see my car still there. You could have taken it. There are always taxis."

"I had a lift. Superintendent Yeadings brought me back. I gave him some tea."

"And what had he to say? Or to ask, more likely."

"Yes, there are still questions. Do you think they will ever find out who — ?"

Harriet appeared to consider this a

moment. "Probably not."

"Don't you *mind*, Mother? Your own son?" Josie hadn't meant to say that. It just came out of itself. And Harriet wasn't slaying her with a look. She came closely round the table and looked down at Josie with something like compassion.

Her voice appeared to come from a distance. "How can you know what having children means unless you have given birth? The only time in life that you're not utterly alone is when your child is inside and a part of you; when you have not one but two heartbeats.

"What they call having a baby is really losing it, becoming alone again. You go on losing it more and more as the years build up between. And then one of you dies, so the cord is finally severed. It doesn't matter which one goes. It is merely more ironic if the older flesh continues and the newer body fails, but it's the same rupture."

As Josie watched her, Harriet seemed somehow outside her own personal sorrow, something more, almost personifying grief itself and despite her inevitable staginess, it moved the girl. It struck her then as

365

almost impossible that, even in anger, she could have killed her son.

"Mother, Joel's death — it was because of Kit, wasn't it?" It came out as a whisper, but Harriet caught it.

"In a way, yes."

There was a longer silence, then Harriet carefully removed her raincoat, folded the two shoulders together and put it over her arm. When she reached the doorway again she turned and said vaguely, "It was an accident."

19

JOSIE sat on a few minutes, transfixed. But there was only one way the turmoil in her mind could be settled. Heavy-limbed, she went after her mother. The bedroom door was open as if she was expected. Harriet was sitting upright on the side of her bed, holding on to one slender post supporting the canopy.

Josie went in and sat beside her, briefly touched one hand to break the torpor. "Mother, what happened on Friday?"

It took a moment for Harriet to connect, then she laid the back of her hand against her brow, unconsciously using the language of dance. "That — *nightmare* — day!" There followed a long silence before slowly, but reasonably, she began to relive it for Josie.

Due to attend a charity meeting to arrange a flag day, she had rung up the secretary and begged off. She was not exactly unwell but horribly apprehensive and,

367

as ever when disturbed, she turned to the garden, set in some polyanths picked up from the nursery the previous day, then began rooting out dandelions from the rear lawn below the terrace.

Unknown to her, Joel had come back with Kit, picking her up from school where she had deliberately cut a House netball practice, and leaving the car at the blind side of the house. When Harriet, kicking off her shoes and coming in to make herself some tea, heard voices she had gone upstairs and caught them together.

The memory of that moment made her tremble even now. "Kit was — sitting on his bed — completely naked, except for an elaborate crown. A glittery paste and rhinestone thing, some theatrical prop Joel must have picked up. With him kneeling by her feet. And her face — covered in make-up. But for her red hair I wouldn't have known her."

"What happened?"

"She'd been — comforting him, with his face in her lap. It was cut, with congealed blood over one cheekbone. He looked up when he heard me come in.

They were — petrified.

"I was scathing, completely and coldly in command of myself. The shock came later. Kit was still in the aftermath of sexual excitement, uncomprehending. Joel was scared out of his — life. I watched the sweat come out on his face. Such a transparent face. I suddenly saw him for what he was, a practised weaver of deceits. On me too, with the same endearing charm he had cruelly employed on the child. But on me for so much longer. All his shallow life.

"And I was terribly afraid, because of the power he had. He knew I couldn't stand withdrawal of all affection, false as it must be — and I was fearful for him too because he was so — unspeakably horrible.

"And while I was feeling this, watching them both, I could hear my voice lashing at them. I was outside myself and trapped inside as well.

"Then there was someone calling from downstairs. I realized that the front doorbell had rung several times without my properly being aware. Now the caller had gone round to the back and come in by the kitchen. I went down to keep whoever it was from coming up and discovering the children."

It had been Mrs Dawes. Why? Josie asked herself. Whatever would bring her here? Everyone knew Mother couldn't stand the woman, because of the way she'd walked out eight years back, when Daddy died.

Harriet stopped short at the question and seemed to be searching about in her mind for the answer. "She had troubles, money troubles. Or rather, her married daughter had. A stupid girl, she'd run up debts through carrying on as agent for two mail order houses. Her husband was unemployed. She wasn't used to having money in her hand and she'd spent what her neighbours paid in for their purchases. She'd ordered all manner of things from the catalogues for herself too and when the reckoning came she had nothing to pay with. She wasn't the first one to get caught that way, but she was desperate, owed almost seven hundred pounds."

"And Mrs Dawes thought you would

help her out, lend her the money. What did you do?"

The pause was longer this time. Harriet put both hands over her face. Josie lost the next few words.

"What was that you said, Mother?"

With a deliberate effort Harriet moved her hands back to the chair on either side of her knees. "Dawes was blackmailing me. For years now, ever since — "

"Oh no! Surely — but go on. Since Daddy died. That's what you meant, wasn't it?"

"How did you — Had you guessed, then?"

"No, but that's when you and Mrs Dawes suddenly split up. We never could understand. Paul said she'd been too fond of Daddy and you were punishing her for it."

"She was punishing me."

"But how could she blackmail you? What did she know?"

Harriet turned a harrowed face towards Josie. "I think it's more than time I told someone. Josie, you are going to find this very hard to accept. You see — Eric, Daddy, I killed him. There! at

371

last someone else knows. I couldn't bear for him to suffer, Josie. I've seen what it does to people. The pain and the indignity. Eric wouldn't have been able to bear it. I couldn't. When he caught that chill and it went to his chest I was so grateful. It seemed the answer, sent from God. I wouldn't let him go to hospital. A nurse came in for the daytime and I sat up with him during the night."

"Yes, I remember. You were worn out looking after him."

"And worrying in case he didn't — die."

"You said you killed him. You mustn't think that. It was pneumonia. You did everything you could. He was too weakened to come through."

"You don't understand. I did it deliberately. You remember how the weather turned very cold, heavy frosts for two nights?"

"I believe it was cold about then, yes."

"The second night. He'd had an easier day. I knew he was going to — pull through and live on to suffer. I couldn't stand it, I couldn't. Josie, I loved that man! Like I never loved anyone in my life, not even — you children."

"What *did* you do?" Josie couldn't escape the pressing horror.

Harriet shook her head, refusing at the last. "When — when Dawes came in in the morning it was all over. She had to wake me in my chair. I said he'd slipped away, but when she pulled the curtains open she guessed. The edges were soaked through and the window-sills were still dripping. Towards dawn it had snowed and blown in. I had been too weary when I shut the windows again and drew the curtains even to notice."

"You lowered the temperature and exposed him — "

"He looked quietly asleep. There can be dignity in death."

"But surely Dr Gayford recognized hypothermia?"

Harriet laughed shortly. "The good old man was far too concerned for the living to take much notice of the dead. He barely glanced at Eric before he made out the certificate. 'A blessing in disguise, my dear Mrs Sefton. You must try to see it in that light,' is what he said. I can hear him now. But Dawes, the wretch, knew how black the blessing's disguise was and she condemned me out of hand."

"But she agreed to hold her tongue."

"I would have denied any story she tried to spread. Who would have taken her word against mine? But you see, she knew. And I knew she knew. She was a passive blackmailer, a silent threat. Every time we encountered each other she would stare hard at me, and I would remember her shut, vindictive face as she discovered the truth. And the way she trampled over me straight after the funeral."

"I remember. She gave notice then, straight away."

"As soon as the guests had gone and we were alone. She has never actually asked for money or anything till now. Her power was in just knowing. And then, on Friday, that nightmare day, as I came down from confronting those two guilty children, there she was, ready to strike at me."

"Oh my God! Does she know about that too?"

"About what? You mean Kit, seduced

by my son? No. Strange, but that hardly seems to matter now. Other things have wiped it out.

"No, Dawes was just astonished at my reaction. It made me so angry that at that — *abysmal* — moment she should come and torture me more. I think I must have been out of my mind. She had barely got out what she wanted — said that now it was time for me to pay for my sins — when I turned on her. She must have seen that I was half out of my mind. She simply ran, and left me standing."

Josie let the silence build up again before she asked, "But where does Joel come into all this?"

"He had stolen downstairs after me and he overheard her threat. He came round the kitchen door. A white-faced demon! So bitter; said he'd better run and get her back so that I could pay her off. Couldn't have a scandal in the family. I could leave it all to him and he'd fix it.

"Oh, if you had seen the look on his face, the gloating because he thought he had something to barter against my knowledge of his spoiling of Kit!"

375

"You went for him instead of for Mrs Dawes. Is that it?"

"No. Oh no! I let him run after her. And I never saw him again alive. I told you, it was an accident.

"She'd hidden from me in the double garage and when she heard him following she thought I was coming to attack her. She picked up the heavy yard broom — you know how strong her arms are — and she waited for my head to come round the door. She didn't know it was Joel until he was laid out on the stone flags. She set up a terrible wailing and when I heard I ran out to see what had happened. Joel must have died instantly. His neck was broken."

"Dead! How appalling."

"I actually said it. After a while I said, 'He's dead. You've killed my son. Do you understand? You are a killer too.' She was like a piece of damp blanket, quite incapable of thought or movement. She could barely stand. I put her in my car and drove her home. I knew that when she got her senses back she would remember what I said and know I was right: that we both had to keep silent, one protecting the other. But it was up to me then to hide what she'd done."

"Mother, I can't believe this."

"No. I couldn't either. I still don't completely. It was like some powerful play that takes you along with it. And not real people you know. Actors taking parts. Half of me still expects Joel to come back and take a bow, pleased with the way he put it over."

"But, Mother, what about Kit?"

Harriet sighed deeply. "When I look at her, that's when I know it's all real. What can I possibly do to make it come out right for her?"

"How much does she know or guess?"

"She believes he went off to Reading in a temper and some time later was mugged."

Josie walked across the room, then turned to face her mother. "She feels guilt about what she was doing with him. She says he was 'struck down'. She expects some equal punishment from God for herself. Mother, do I understand her periods have begun?"

"What has that to do with it? Oh, if you insist, yes. She started, then stopped after two months. Eleven's very young, but modern girls do mature early. I had a little talk to her. She hadn't any idea what it was, which surprised me. Most girls nowadays are so crudely open about such things."

"She doesn't have any real friends, does she? Who would discuss it with her? I think she confided in Joel and that's when he took advantage of her. Probably she thought she'd had a hæmorrhage, and he enjoyed being the knowledgeable adviser. A little biased information about sex, explorative demonstrations, talk about being adult, a gift of exotic make-up: it was all too easy for him. I wouldn't put it past him to have slipped her contraceptive pills to keep 'the curse' at bay."

Harriet faced her daughter with horror. "Where did you get such a debased opinion of your brother?"

"It isn't the opinion that's debased. I speak from experience. He didn't attempt seduction in my case, but he was a nuisance. A Peeping Tom; and nastily suggestive. Why else do you think I was in such a hurry to leave home? Then Chris's marriage had to break up and in walked little Kit to fill the empty space I'd left. I should have foreseen it, that he had grown further into his nasty ways, not out of them. But I never dreamt he'd dare to abuse a child."

"It just goes on, the nightmare. What else am I to discover about my children?"

"What else have we to learn about you, Mother? Joel was killed by accident, you say, right by the doors to the garage. But he wasn't found there."

She watched Harriet's expression slowly change from one of tortured concern to an almost detached recall. "When I arrived back from taking Dawes home I parked right by the garage doors," she said in a low monotone. "I'd used one of the big plastic sheets, bought to protect the cuttings from frost, to wrap him up. Somehow I got him into the car boot. He was heavy, and I lifted him in stages, putting seed boxes underneath."

"But where was Kit?"

"She'd locked herself in the bathroom. I left her there. She would curl up and hide away for hours when anything upset her. Later when I got back from Reading I put her to bed with a hot-water bottle and some aspirins."

"The Goldbasket superstore," Josie reminded her. "Tell me about that."

"I knew the body had to be hidden away somehow if we were to survive. I thought first of the river, but it's too close. Then I remembered the muggings. Whoever did those deserved to be caught and punished. I thought if Joel's death could be laid at their door, the police would do the rest. Either catch up with them eventually or let the case rest as the others have done."

"So you drove down to the centre of town and looked for somewhere to leave him."

"In Reading I saw someone taking a carton of rubbish into the supermarket car park. Then I remembered the great bins they have in there. When no one was about I drove in close and pushed the body out, rolled it round the corner out of sight. It was easier than it had been lifting it in."

"In broad daylight? Anyone could have caught you at it. So you unwrapped him and brought the plastic sheet away?"

"That was later, after I realized his

car had to be there too. I was afraid the plastic sheet could be traced back to me, so I went back after dark, got it off folded it and disposed of it on a nearby building site, spread over fresh concrete and weighted down with loose bricks."

"And in between you had gone home to get the evening meal, as though nothing unusual had happened?"

"Yes. Chris was almost due back. I cooked pizzas straight from the freezer. He accepted that I'd put Kit to bed early, and Joel was as often out as in for supper. Chris said I looked tired, but apart from that noticed nothing.

"Later on I went out again, to take Joel's car down. Days before, I had arranged to watch the Kirov ballet that night on my bedroom television, so I knew I wouldn't be disturbed. Chris was to write down any phone messages. Any noise made by the car leaving was covered by the TV serial he was watching in the drawing-room. I put on dark clothes — trousers, gloves, and Joel's old duffel jacket with the hood — so no one would recognize me. When I'd parked the TVR I took a ticket from the machine and left it inside. By then the car park had practically cleared of people. It was only later I realized how the ticket helped my alibi.

"Nobody saw me get rid of the plastic sheet. Then I caught a bus out to the stop before Callendar Lane. It was blowing up chilly then and I kept my hood up the whole time.

"When I got back the ballet programme was nearly over. I called down to Chris and said I was ready for my nightcap. When he brought it up I was in my dressing-gown, and on the box the credits were rolling. I made a few remarks about the principal dancers and then said I was going to turn in. Chris had no idea that I'd been out."

Josie shook her head in wonder. Not then, perhaps. But by now, seeing the ravaged face, he must realize that she was going through hell. But everyone saw Harriet as the grieving mother: that would be explanation enough.

"It was an accident," Harriet insisted again. "Dawes heard him coming and thought it was me. It was an unlucky blow. She never meant to kill."

"So what next?" Josie asked, confounded. Harriet lifted both hands and dropped them hopelessly. "I have told you. So now somebody knows it all. Perhaps I shall be able to sleep now."

"I'll get you a hot drink, Mother."

"Thank you, Josie, but later perhaps. There's something I have to do first, only I can't remember what it is. I'm so confused, everything going round in circles in my mind but not connecting properly. Eric — Dawes — Joel — me. It's so awful. You can't imagine."

"Don't make any decisions for the moment. Don't even think. Give me a little while to get used to what you've told me. Will you do that? And get some sleep. I'm going for that drink now. To wash down the sleeping pills the doctor prescribed. Tomorrow we'll talk about it again."

That wasn't the whole story, Josie warned herself. Joel killed by a single mistaken blow was one thing. The mutilation was something else. Could it have happened later in the car park? Apparently the police hadn't yet found the drunk who phoned in after finding the body. Suppose he had been so frantic that he'd used a knife on the dead face that frightened him. In her bones she felt certain the true explanation was something quite different.

Mother had done it. To her beloved Joel. In fear and anger and revulsion she had slashed at the face that she had last seen gloating. Kneeling beside his body she had seized on some familiar tool — perhaps the old potato-peeler she used to get up the weeds — and in a paroxysm of grief and loathing had slashed at the memory of that cruelly mocking face. A face so like her own. Perhaps in her tortured mind it had been her own face and she was punishing herself. But that was a secret shame she was never likely to share with anyone.

Three hours later Harriet awoke with the single realization, "They're gone. My husband, my son. Eric and Joel. But Dawes is still alive and so am I."

That was the significance of the four names endlessly chasing each other in her mind. It was the only thing left unblurred. She could do nothing about the dead, but about Dawes she must. Do what, though?

She struggled to come totally awake but the tranquillizers numbed her brain. Get up, dress, she ordered herself. Money; she must give Dawes money for her daughter. Then the dead could sleep.

And then? She found herself at the open conservatory door. The night was dark in patches as low cloud blew like black smoke across the moon's face. Somewhere in Callendar Woods an owl screeched. Harriet sensed the claws crooked to lift the soft, furry limpness of its prey. So cruel. She was sick of cruelty, sick of her own obdurate harshness. Dawes's daughter, that was it. Poor, stupid young woman. The unfinished thing.

Not for Dawes, because Dawes was as bad as Joel in a way; as bad as Harriet herself. But the daughter was pitiable. And all she needed was money. Such a simple solution.

Harriet went out into the garden. Her car stood at the front door where she'd left it. Just as she'd done with the TVR on the night of Joel's death, she let off the handbrake and allowed it to roll, first gently, then with gathering speed, until down near the gates she turned on the ignition.

Raggedly the moon appeared low over shadowy trees and she accelerated into the reflected light on the wet road ahead. Then the tatters of cloud closed over again and it was totally dark. Strange, unfamiliar darkness. She had never driven so blind before.

She must be asleep, dreaming in her bed, dreaming she was in her car racketing along through tunnelled trees without headlights. She knew she should switch them on, knew where she should reach out her hand to do it, but there was this dream paralysis. Her hands stayed locked to the wheel, couldn't be pulled away. Her right foot drove demon pressure on its pedal. She soared through the night like a swooping bird of prey. Into darkness suddenly shattered into a million brilliant lights falling round her like the white slivers of a bursting firework. But quite silent, she thought, surprised.

20

THE phone's insistence cut through her sleep and she put out a hand automatically, knocking the receiver off. Only half awake, she raised herself on one elbow and followed the cord to its end. "Zyczynski." At this time of night it had to be shop.

The call was from DI Mott, but she was to be picked up by Yeadings himself on his way out to Callendar Lane. Mrs Sefton was dead. An RTA. The Superintendent needed a policewoman immediately to help with the family.

Quickly she flung on the clothes she had dropped off less than five hours before, fetched her raincoat, now dry, from the airing cupboard. She was huddled in the doorway as Yeadings's Rover came hissing through the puddles, and ran forward to open the passenger door. "Good girl," he said briefly. "You heard she's dead?"

"A genuine accident or — "

"We'll know soon enough."

"Who's at the house, sir?"

"The eldest son, his sister Josie and the girl Kit."

"Do we send for the child's mother?"

"That's up to her father, but I can't imagine it would do much good. Might just add more hassle." He risked a quick glance sideways at her. "There's something behind that question."

"The grandmother was a deciding factor in custody of Kit. If she's no longer there — "

"And with the mother's arrival, there'd be a helluva lot to have to bring her up to date on. Anorexia and child abuse. God almighty, what a mess!"

His hands tightened on the wheel. "I tried to push things along a little yesterday. And now Harriet's dead. It makes me feel responsible. Josie must have spoken to her after I'd gone, and then it would all have come out."

"You saw them both, then?"

"No. I passed Harriet's car on my way back. She would have come on Josie in an emotional state, exhausted."

"So what was Harriet Sefton doing later, out on the roads at a little after two in the morning?"

Yeadings stared stonily ahead through the metronome sweep of the wipers. "Making sure I didn't get that confession, I guess."

At the house, Josie was dressed in a sweater and cords, her hair unbrushed. She had been crying and hadn't bothered to wash the evidence away. With her brother Christopher she was sitting at the kitchen table while a young PC stood over the coffee percolator, keeping his eyes averted.

"Where's Kit?" Rosemary asked, while Yeadings was waiting silently to be acknowledged.

"Upstairs, asleep, I hope." Christopher Sefton looked to his sister for advice. "You don't think she ought to be down here, do you?"

Yeadings came forward from the doorway. "She's bound to hear all the coming and going. Someone ought to go up and be with her," he suggested.

"Not me," Josie pleaded. "Later I'll see her, but I've something to tell you first. It's all my fault, you see. I should have let Mother go to bed in peace, not that she'd have been likely to sleep. She hasn't done properly since Joel was killed, and she didn't like taking those barbiturate things. But last night — "

"Go on." Yeadings had dropped on to a seat opposite her. His voice was quiet, understanding.

"I followed her up. Because of something she said as she went out of the kitchen. Something I thought she'd said, but I wasn't sure. I couldn't leave it like that."

"What had she said?"

"'It was an accident.' She meant Joel's death. It sounded as if she knew about it, had even been there and seen."

"So naturally you were anxious."

"It was true, Superintendent. An unfortunate accident. Not even of Mother's doing. Someone else was the direct cause, but it all reaches back far into the past, to something Mother did years ago. Because of that, this other person came here last Friday and it happened. So Mother felt guilty, as if she had killed him herself."

"Yes," said Yeadings, and he seemed unsurprised. "We can sort all that out later, but for the moment there is one thing only I want to know. Where was your Mother off to in the early hours when she crashed her car, and why?"

"That's what I meant about it being my fault. After we'd talked I gave her a hot drink and waited while she took her sleeping tablets. I thought she was tucked up safely for the night. But despite that she got up and dressed without, I think, being properly awake. I don't suppose she knew herself where she was going, just an urge to drive off and away. Worried out of her mind and in no state to cope with a powerful car."

"Sir?" DI Mott was at the kitchen's outer door with a flat green object in his hand. Yeadings rose and went across. Their low voices were covered by the constable's clashing of the coffee cups as he maladroitly lined them up on their saucers. Yeadings came back with a leather address book in his hand and something longer overlapping from inside.

"This was on the floor of the car." He showed it to them. "Someone's name beginning with D," he told Josie. "Does that mean anything to you? And your mother's cheque book marking the page?"

"Dawes. Oh yes, yes! Our old house-keeper from years ago. Her daughter had run up debts and she asked Mother to help. That's what we were talking about last night. Mother had that on her mind — "

"Meant to give her money?"

"Mother must have come half-awake, remembering, and just knew she had to go to her, not realizing what time it was, or her own helpless condition — "

"So helpless, it seems, that she hadn't even switched on her lights. Driving through the half-dark, managing gears and steering from sheer habit. But switching on headlights isn't part of the purely automatic sequence. It needs a conscious decision, and she wasn't that far awake."

"So don't you see? — she never meant to crash!"

"That's very much what it looks like to me," Yeadings agreed cautiously.

Christopher stood up. "Thank God," he said fervently. "We had so dreaded — " He stopped and turned towards the door to the hall. It opened slowly and Kit was standing there in her pyjamas, red hair tousled round the thin, haunted face. Her eyes went first to Josie's, then slid away ashamed, briefly passed on to Rosemary and rejected her too. But she needed someone. Hesitantly she came forward. "Daddy? Is something the matter? Is it me?"

"Kit dear, no. I mean, you're right; something very sad has happened but it's nobody's fault. An accident."

She was watching him apprehensively. "Where's Nana?"

He went over and took her hand, knelt beside her so that she stood taller looking down at his worried face. "She's had an accident in the dark with the car. It went into a tree down the lane. I'm sorry, love, but Nana's dead. It was over very quickly. She probably never knew what happened."

The girl's face showed no shock, only puzzlement. "I thought it would be me."

Josie leaned forward. "No, Kit. Not you. It's Nana who's gone after Joel. She was his mother, after all. And she did love him a lot. They were very close, you know. You belong with us."

Kit looked at them both. The police didn't seem to exist for her. "Yes, I see. Is it time to get up yet?"

"Not for quite a while. Shall I tuck you back in?"

Kit shook her head. "I'll manage." She turned towards her father again. "Will you be here tomorrow?"

"Yes. I'll ring and say I can't go in to work. And we'll have a talk, shall we?"

Yeadings watched them part at the door, Sefton holding back from any demonstration that the child wasn't yet quite ready for. Perhaps things would be easier for them now. She was roughly the same age, he reflected, as his own little Sally. Perhaps it was even more hurtful for a child to face tragedy like this than Sally's Downs' Syndrome. Yet here there was some chance of a cure, given time and understanding. He sighed and turned to Josie. "Now, if you feel up to it, Miss Sefton, I'd like you to fill in the blanks."

Harriet was cremated after a quiet family service a week later, following the inquest at which no suggestion of suicide had arisen. The press were kept at bay by a promise from Detective-Superintendent Yeadings of a full statement on the Joel Sefton case the same evening.

He had attended the service, sitting at the rear with Rosemary Z, conscious that for her as for himself the grieving family would linger on in the mind.

He was glad she'd been with him on Sunday when they'd picked up the chief mugger, Len. Even without her identification of his Afro-imitation voice, they had enough proof against him with the goodies under the floorboards. He'd grassed on his partner, so both of them would come up for trial. The first, single mugger had been his fourteen-year-old brother who had been killed on the joyriding spree. A more straightforward crime to crack and it had taken all those weeks! Well, that was police work for you.

Back at Marisbank Erica and Paul stayed on overnight for the reading of the will. Harriet's entire estate, except for a few charitable bequests, was to be shared equally by her four surviving children. Surprisingly, it had been her wish that if the house were sold, first option should be granted to Erica to use it for whatever enterprise she had in mind.

None of the others had raised any objection, Christopher having already agreed with Josie that they should throw in their lot together, for at least a while, and buy a smaller house farther downriver, say Windsor or Henley, wherever they found a good day school for Kit and suitable medical attention.

She, in her turn, seemed relieved at the prospect of distancing herself from all that had happened at Callendar Lane. Harriet's death, which she had blindly accepted as a kind of substitute for her own expected punishment, seemed to have logically completed the circuit which Joel had started. Full understanding of it could only come later. She was beginning half-heartedly to turn up to meals without being cajoled, although she ate little and still had trouble swallowing.

With the others' approval Chris settled the outstanding debts of Mrs Dawes's daughter and recommended a solicitor to stand by to watch the older woman's interests at the resumed inquest on Joel.

Once Erica and Paul had departed, Josie began to plan the disposal of her own expected inheritance. She made out a cheque and tucked it into the edge of her bedroom mirror. Next morning when Christopher came in bringing an early cup of tea he advanced on it suspiciously. "What's that?"

"A sub for the Bangladeshi Flood Appeal."

He peered closer and shook his head. "It won't work. You must know that, Josie. 'The sum of £$x/4 - x/5$.' What does that mean, for heaven's sake?"

"It means that I won't touch blood money. x is whatever Mother's estate comes to in the end. That cheque is for the difference between Joel being alive to share in it and his being dead. And it stays there in the mirror to remind me, until I can make one out for the correct amount."

Christopher sat down heavily on the side of her bed. "Blood money. You want clean hands, don't you?" He made a helpless gesture with both his. "Like poor Mother."

"Where in God's name does Mother come in? After all she did to the family . . . "

"Ah, I've something to tell you. The house option for Erica wasn't her only surprise. She left Kit a letter. It was posted, as instructed, by Wetherby to arrive the day after he read the will. In it Mother explained why she hadn't made any gift to her only grandchild, not even in trust. Kit didn't understand it, and she brought the letter to me. First time she's ever-confided."

"This is weird, Chris. What did Mother say?"

"She said possessions were dangerous. They made you feel too safe. You had to be really mature before you could cope with them. She wanted her to enjoy her childhood as long as she could. She said Kit was right to think that life could be full of dangers, but she should school herself ready for any bad times as they came along. She reminded her that the family was always there to encourage her and help out when needed, but the effort to make it through safely must come first from herself. Without cushioning."

"Does Kit realize what unique faith Mother must have had in her?"

"She does now."

Josie was silent because something in her throat prevented her voice coming out normally.

"Another aspect," Christopher said whimsically at length. "Do you realize that in letting us inherit, Mother implies finally that we are 'really mature' — able to cope with the corrupting influence of wealth?"

"Yes. Amazing, isn't it? I wonder how Erica will take it all."

"I talked to her last night after Wetherby had left. She hadn't wanted to come, as you guessed, because she was sure Mother would have written her out. The will was such a shock that she just stomped out when she heard about the house."

"What did she say?"

"You know Erica. Swore a bit. Then said, 'Oh, what a shit that woman could make one feel. What will the estate add up to?' When I gave her a rough figure, she was quiet for a minute, then she said rather sadly, 'So much? Wish I'd earned it by my own efforts. Still, maybe I'll rethink the merger now, get my own boatyard downriver.'"

Josie smiled. "You'll be hearing from Paul. Don't sound too surprised if it's an invitation to his wedding."

"God, that's rash. But I mustn't say that. I do hope he'll make it work. Probably will. For all his creative imagination, he's not the incurable romantic I was."

He rose and went over to look from the window. Low sunlight slanted across frosted lawns and already one grey corner was turning bright green around the saffron of fallen chestnut leaves. He walked back to the dressing-table and bent towards the mirror. "If I may, I'll add to your memo."

He uncapped the pen she had left on the trinket tray and wrote on the cheque. That done, he gazed a moment or two at her through the mirror, nodded and went out.

Josie drank her tea. Then she went across to look.

He had put a bracket round her

algebraic formula, with a figure 2 before it. And under her signature he had added his own.

THE END

TO FIGHT THE WILD
Rod Ansell and Rachel Percy

Lost in uncharted Australian bush, Rod Ansell survived by hunting and trapping wild animals, improvising shelter and using all the bushman's skills he knew.

COROMANDEL
Pat Barr

India in the 1830s is a hot, uncomfortable place, where the East India Company still rules. Amelia and her new husband find themselves caught up in the animosities which seethe between the old order and the new.

THE SMALL PARTY
Lillian Beckwith

A frightening journey to safety begins for Ruth and her small party as their island is caught up in the dangers of armed insurrection.

CLOUD OVER MALVERTON
Nancy Buckingham

Dulcie soon realises that something is seriously wrong at Malverton, and when violence strikes she is horrified to find herself under suspicion of murder.

AFTER THOUGHTS
Max Bygraves

The Cockney entertainer tells stories of his East End childhood, of his RAF days, and his post-war showbusiness successes and friendships with fellow comedians.

MOONLIGHT AND MARCH ROSES
D. Y. Cameron

Lynn's search to trace a missing girl takes her to Spain, where she meets Clive Hendon. While untangling the situation, she untangles her emotions and decides on her own future.

THE TWILIGHT MAN
Frank Gruber

Jim Rand lives alone in the California desert awaiting death. Into his hermit existence comes a teenage girl who blows both his past and his brief future wide open.

DOG IN THE DARK
Gerald Hammond

Jim Cunningham breeds and trains gun dogs, and his antagonism towards the devotees of show spaniels earns him many enemies. So when one of them is found murdered, the police are on his doorstep within hours.

THE RED KNIGHT
Geoffrey Moxon

When he finds himself a pawn on the chessboard of international espionage with his family in constant danger, Guy Trent becomes embroiled in moves and countermoves which may mean life or death for Western scientists.

THE LISTERDALE MYSTERY
Agatha Christie

Twelve short stories ranging from the light-hearted to the macabre, diverse mysteries ingeniously and plausibly contrived and convincingly unravelled.

TO BE LOVED
Lynne Collins

Andrew married the woman he had always loved despite the knowledge that Sarah married him for reasons of her own. So much heartache could have been avoided if only he had known how vital it was to be loved.

ACCUSED NURSE
Jane Converse

Paula found herself accused of a crime which could cost her her job, her nurse's reputation, and even the man she loved, unless the truth came to light.

MORNING IS BREAKING
Lesley Denny

The growing frenzy of war catapults Diane Clements into a clandestine marriage and separation with a German refugee.

LAST BUS TO WOODSTOCK
Colin Dexter

A girl's body is discovered huddled in the courtyard of a Woodstock pub, and Detective Chief Inspector Morse and Sergeant Lewis are hunting a rapist and a murderer.

THE STUBBORN TIDE
Anne Durham

Everyone advised Carol not to grieve so excessively over her cousin's death. She might have followed their advice if the man she loved thought that way about her, but another girl came first in his affections.

A GREAT DELIVERANCE
Elizabeth George

Into the web of old houses and secrets of Keldale Valley comes Scotland Yard Inspector Thomas Lynley and his assistant to solve a particularly savage murder.

'E' IS FOR EVIDENCE
Sue Grafton

Kinsey Millhone was bogged down on a warehouse fire claim. It came as something of a shock when she was accused of being on the take. She'd been set up. Now she had a new client — herself.

A FAMILY OUTING IN AFRICA
Charles Hampton and Janie Hampton

A tale of a young family's journey through Central Africa by bus, train, river boat, lorry, wooden bicycle and foot.

DEATH TRAIN
Robert Byrne

The tale of a freight train out of control and leaking a paralytic nerve gas that turns America's West into a scene of chemical catastrophe in which whole towns are rendered helpless.

THE ADVENTURE
OF THE
CHRISTMAS PUDDING
Agatha Christie

In the introduction to this short story collection the author wrote "This book of Christmas fare may be described as 'The Chef's Selection'. I am the Chef!"

RETURN TO BALANDRA
Grace Driver

Returning to her Caribbean island home, Suzanne looks forward to being with her parents again, but most of all she longs to see Wim van Branden, a coffee planter she has known all her life.

BALLET GENIUS
Gillian Freeman and Edward Thorpe

Presents twenty pen portraits of great dancers of the twentieth century and gives an insight into their daily lives, their professional careers, the ever present risk of injury and the pressure to stay on top.

TO LIVE IN PEACE
Rosemary Friedman

The final part of the author's Anglo-Jewish trilogy, which began with PROOFS OF AFFECTION and ROSE OF JERICHO, telling the story of Kitty Shelton, widowed after a happy marriage, and her three children.

NORA WAS A NURSE
Peggy Gaddis

Nurse Nora Courtney was hopelessly in love with Doctor Owen Baird and when beautiful Lillian Halstead set her cap for him, Nora realised she must make him see her as a desirable woman as well as an efficient nurse.

IN PALE BATTALIONS
Robert Goddard

Leonora Galloway has waited all her life to learn the truth about her father, slain on the Somme before she was born, the truth about the death of her mother and the mystery of an unsolved wartime murder.

A DREAM FOR TOMORROW
Grace Goodwin

In her new position as resident nurse at Coombe Magna, Karen Stevens has to bear the emnity of the beautiful Lisa, secretary to the doctor-on-call.

AFTER EMMA
Sheila Hocken

Following the author's previous auto-biographies — EMMA & I, and EMMA & Co., she relates more of the hilarious (and sometimes despairing) antics of her guide dogs.